Matthew held her gaze, his ragged breathing loud in the silence of the room. She pushed harder against him and stepped back. Instantly his gaze sharpened and he gripped her shoulders, preventing her from retreating further, wringing a gasp from her.

"I have been searching for you…following you…trying to catch up with you…*worrying* about you…'

'But…why? I thought you were—'

'You need protection. I—'

'Protection?'

Eleanor, now with her wits fully about her, stiffened. For one fleeting, joyful second she had thought maybe he had followed her for her own sake—because he felt something for her. As speedily as the thought arose she quashed it, inwardly berating herself for being a romantic fool, beguiled by a handsome face and rugged charm. She and Mr Thomas were worlds ap

Author Note

Eleanor, Baroness Ashby, is a rarity: a peeress in her own right. The early English baronies were created by a writ of summons to Counsel or Parliament (rather than by letters patent, as later became the norm). The remainders of these baronies by writ devolve upon the 'heirs-general' rather than being limited to male heirs, meaning an only daughter can inherit the barony. It's interesting that if there are two or more daughters the title will fall into abeyance until the co-heirs can come to an honourable agreement as to which of them will claim the title. The claimant must then petition The Crown to have the abeyance terminated.

I really enjoyed writing about Eleanor—she is loyal, courageous and independent, but her outer confidence masks a deep insecurity at her core. She is also impulsive at times, and I knew she needed a resilient hero. Enter Matthew: strong and honourable, but with a secret in his past that might easily damage Eleanor's determination to be fully accepted by Society and to gain admittance to Almack's Assembly Rooms.

I thought it would be fun to see how a proud man like Matthew would cope with falling for a wealthier, higher-ranking woman than him.

If you have read *Mary and the Marquis* you might like to know that Eleanor is the cousin of Lucas, Marquis of Rothley. Lucas's mother, Lucy, is Eleanor's chaperon, and his younger brother, Lord Hugo Alastair, also makes an appearance.

Janice Preston grew up in Wembley, North London, with a love of reading, writing stories and animals. In the past she has worked as a farmer, a police call-handler and a university administrator. She now lives in the West Midlands with her husband and two cats and has a part-time job with a weight management counsellor (vainly trying to control her own weight despite her love of chocolate!).

Books by Janice Preston

Mills & Boon Historical Romance

Men About Town

Return of Scandal's Son

Linked by Character
to *Men About Town* duet

Mary and the Marquis
From Wallflower to Countess

Visit the Author Profile page at millsandboon.co.uk.

For Elizabeth Bailey,
whose encouragement and advice
during my early writing attempts was invaluable.

RETURN OF SCANDAL'S SON

Janice Preston

Published in Great Britain 2015
by Mills & Boon, an imprint of Harlequin (UK) Limited,
Eton House, 18-24 Paradise Road, Richmond, Surrey, TW9 1SR

© 2015 Janice Preston

ISBN: 978-0-263-24809-8

Harlequin (UK) Limited's policy is to use papers that are natural,
renewable and recyclable products and made from wood grown in
sustainable forests. The logging and manufacturing processes conform
to the legal environmental regulations of the country of origin.

Printed and bound in Spain
by CPI, Barcelona

Chapter One

April 1811

Eyes streaming, coughing and choking, she tugged at the window, but it refused to budge. The floorboards scorched her feet and she could hear the ominous roar of the fire below. Dragging the pungent air deep into her lungs, she screamed.

'Ellie. *Ellie.* Wake up!'

'What?'

Eleanor, Baroness Ashby, roused to the gently rocking rhythm of her carriage. She stared groggily into the anxious eyes of Lucy, Dowager Marchioness of Rothley. Eleanor levered herself upright on the squabs, her nightmare still vividly real.

'You screamed. Was it the nightmare again?'

Eleanor drew in a deep breath—fresh, clean, untainted. 'Yes. I'm sorry if I frightened you, Aunt.' Her heart slowed from a gallop to a fast trot. 'Everything seems so real in the dream. And I can never get out.'

'Well, we must be thankful you escaped the real fire, my pet. It doesn't bear thinking about, what might have happened.'

'Milady?' Lucy's maid, sitting on the backward-facing seat, opposite Eleanor, leant forward.

'Yes, Matilda?'

'Is it true someone set fire to the library deliberately?'

'Yes.'

Eleanor did not elaborate. Someone had broken into Ashby Manor—her beloved home—at the dead of night, piled books into the middle of the library floor and set fire to them. The whole east wing had been destroyed. All those beautiful books!

'I *told* you.' Lizzie, Eleanor's maid, also travelling in the carriage to London, nudged Matilda. 'If milady had not woken up when she did, she'd be—'

'Lizzie!'

Lizzie cast an apologetic glance at Eleanor as she subsided into silence. Eleanor needed no reminding of what would have happened had she not woken when she did, two weeks before. She shuddered, recalling that terrifying moment when, climbing from her bedchamber window, her searching toes met empty space where the top rung of the ladder had, only moments before, been placed against the wall by her head groom, Fretwell. If Lizzie had not come looking for her when she did… Fear coiled in Eleanor's belly. Lizzie had arrived just in time to see a shadowy figure knock Fretwell out cold before flinging the ladder to the ground.

Who was he? Was he really trying to kill me?

They had been unable to find any trace of the culprit. Fretwell had not seen him, and Lizzie's description was so vague it was no help at all, but there had been no further incidents and no one could recall seeing any strangers in the vicinity.

'I hope Aunt Phyllis will be comfortable staying with Reverend Harris,' Eleanor said to Aunt Lucy, keen to distract them all from the events of that night. Aunt Phyllis—Eleanor's paternal aunt—had lived at Ashby Manor all her life and had helped raise Eleanor after her mother left when Eleanor was just eleven. She had also been Eleanor's chaperon since her father's death three years before.

'Oh, I make no doubt she will thoroughly enjoy her captive audience,' Aunt Lucy said. There was no love lost between Lucy—the older sister of Eleanor's mother—and Aunt Phyllis. 'It's the Reverend and his wife I feel pity for. Still, it is to my benefit that she refused to accompany you to London, my pet. I shall enjoy the opportunity to get you settled at long last.'

Eleanor shook her head, laughing. 'You know

very well the only reason I am going to London is to escape the building work at home. I have no wish to find a husband.'

Unless I fall in love with someone and he with me. And that is unlikely in the extreme.

'You will feel differently if you meet someone who sets your heart a-flutter,' Aunt Lucy replied, her dark eyes twinkling.

'You take a different view of matrimony to Aunt Phyllis,' Eleanor replied. '*Her* only concern is that any suitor should have the correct breeding and be wealthy enough to add to the estates.'

'Ah, but she does not have to live with your choice. You do. Believe me, you do not want to be trapped in a marriage with a man you cannot respect. Or one who is unkind.'

Aunt Lucy fell silent and Eleanor guessed she was thinking back to her own unhappy marriage. The late Lord Rothley had been a violent and un-predictable man.

'No, indeed,' Eleanor said, heartened by the realisation that her aunt would not spend the Season trying to pressure her into a match she did not want.

'Where did James say our house is?' Aunt Lucy asked.

Eleanor fished Cousin James's letter from her reticule and smoothed it, scanning the lines until she came to the relevant section.

'Upper Brook Street,' she said. 'I hope it will prove suitable.'

James, upon being told of the fire, and Eleanor's desire to visit London for the Season, had taken it upon himself to lease a house on her behalf. *Thereby making certain I do not land on his doorstep*, Eleanor had sniffed to herself upon receipt of his letter. Ruth, his wife, had clearly not mellowed towards her yet.

Relations between Eleanor and Ruth had been strained ever since Ruth had discovered that Eleanor, and not James, would inherit Ashby Manor and the title, becoming Baroness Ashby in her own right after her father's death. The barony was an ancient title—one of the oldest in England, created by King William I—and, as was often the case with such ancient baronies, the title devolved upon the 'heirs general' rather than the nearest male relative.

Marry in haste... Eleanor allowed herself a quiet smile. In her opinion, Ruth only had herself to blame for trapping James into marriage before she had ascertained the truth of his prospects. Eleanor was just relieved she had seen through Ruth's brother, Donald, on the eve of their betrothal, although the scandal when she rejected him had revived the old stories about her mother's disgrace.

Blood will out, Aunt Phyllis's voice echoed— the same refrain having been drummed into

Eleanor ever since her mother created a scandal by running off with a rich merchant fourteen years ago. Eleanor was determined never to give the *ton* any cause for such salacious gossip about *her*. She forced her attention back to Aunt Lucy's contented chatter.

'Upper Brook Street is more than acceptable,' she was saying. 'I've always loved the Season—nothing can quite compare. Let us hope you have a happier time of it than during your come-out. I told your papa and that sourpuss Phyllis you weren't ready for society. You were too young, too shy. And that was hardly surprising, given your poor mama… Well! I shall say no more on the subject. Oh, I can't tell you, my pet, how delighted I am. Between you and me, this is just the remedy I need. I was bored to death at Rothley. I've come to the conclusion I'm far too young to retire to the dower house, despite what that reprehensible son of mine says.'

It was early afternoon on their first day of travel when a deafening crack jolted Eleanor from her daydreams. The carriage lurched violently sideways, slammed to a stop and then, very slowly, tilted until it fell on to its side with a crash. Eleanor flung her arms around Lucy to cushion her as they tumbled over to land on the side of the carriage. Lizzie and Matilda landed beside them in a tangle of arms and legs, shrieking hysterically.

Hip throbbing from the impact, Eleanor pushed herself up, still clutching Lucy.

'Oh, my life! Oh, my head… We're trapped! Milady, milady…oh, how shall we ever get out?'

'Gunshot! Highwaymen! Highwaymen! We'll be robbed and murdered, and no one to save us. Oh, dear Lord…'

'Lizzie! Matilda!' Eleanor raised her voice to be heard over the wailing of the two servants, who were still huddled together, eyes tight shut. 'Do please stop that infernal noise. Is either of you hurt?'

'My head…oh, milady—blood! I shall bleed to death.'

Eleanor twisted to look at Lizzie, who was clutching her head, a look of horror on her face. There was a minor cut on her scalp, which, like all scalp wounds, bled freely.

'Nonsense, Lizzie. Do please calm down. Here, take my handkerchief and press it to your scalp— it's only a tiny cut.'

Aunt Lucy had wriggled free from Eleanor's grasp and was talking to Matilda.

'Aunt? Are you all right?'

'Shaken up, my pet, as are we all. But not hurt, thanks to you. You provided a soft landing, for which I am vastly grateful. And Matilda seems uninjured, just shocked.' She grimaced at Eleanor as, at the sound of her name, Matilda burst into fresh sobs. 'And you, Ellie? Are you hurt?'

'I banged my side, but nothing broken, thankfully.'

'What on earth do you imagine has happened? Oh, do hush, Matilda. Really, there is no lasting harm done. We are all still alive.'

'I cannot imagine, although Lizzie is right—it did sound like a gunshot.' Eleanor strove to speak calmly, to conceal her fear and the panic lurking below the surface. Were they being held up?

She looked up at the window above their heads. The carriage, despite being on its side, was still jerking and she could hear the men outside trying to calm the horses. She manoeuvred herself upright, her legs still shaky from the shock of the accident, and braced one foot on each side of the door frame that now formed the floor. There were some advantages in being tall, she thought wryly, as she shoved at the door above their heads. It crashed open, provoking another series of jerks from the horses, accompanied by a frenzied whinnying. She stuck her head through the opening, but was unable to see much. She shouted and the grizzled head of Joey, Eleanor's coachman, appeared over the side of the upturned carriage.

'Joey, thank goodness. What happened? Help me out, will you?'

Eleanor reached up and grasped Joey's hands and, with much heaving and kicking, she was hauled out of the carriage and helped down to the ground. She took in the scene, gasping at the mayhem.

The lead pair plunged and scrabbled to regain their footing against the weight of the wheelers, both of which were off their feet. The offside of the wheelers was lying prone, blood pumping from its side, and the nearside of the pair, lying half beneath its teammate, eyes rolling wildly, was making intermittent half-hearted attempts to struggle free. Fretwell was trying desperately to free the lead horses, sawing at the leather harness with his knife, whilst the footman, Timothy, who had also accompanied them on their journey, was at the leaders' heads, trying, not very successfully, to keep them calm, whilst dodging their flailing hooves.

Eleanor was about to go to his aid when Joey clutched her arm.

'We just come round a sharp bend, milady. Get back there, lass, make sure nowt's coming. Last thing we need—another pile up.' Stress made the old coachman revert to speaking to her as the child he once knew.

Eleanor looked back, past the carriage, and only then did she appreciate the peril they were in. They had come around a sharp bend just before the carriage had overturned and the vehicle now blocked most of the road, which was enclosed by dense woodland. She shuddered at the thought of what that woodland might conceal, but there was no time to worry about that now. Surely any vehicle coming around that blind bend at even a modest speed would be upon them before they knew it. Picking up her skirts, Eleanor sprinted back along the road, suddenly aware of the approaching thunder of horses' hooves.

Her heart leapt with fear. The horses sounded almost upon her, but were not yet in sight. Pain stabbed in her side. She could run no faster. The driver was unlikely to see her in time to react, he was travelling so fast. She did the only thing she could to avert disaster. She ran into the middle of the road, arms waving, just as a curricle drawn by two black horses raced into view.

Curses filled the air as the driver hauled desperately at the reins, slewing the curricle across the road as they came to a plunging stop, missing Eleanor by mere inches. Lungs burning, legs trembling, she could only watch, mute, as a groom jumped from his perch and raced to the horses' heads. The driver speared her with one fulminating glare, then tied off the reins and leapt to the ground. Eleanor hauled in a shaky breath, flinching at his livid expression as he strode towards her.

Chapter Two

Eleanor stumbled back as the irate driver, frowning brows beetled over penetrating ice-blue eyes, loomed over her.

'What in God's name were you trying to do?' he bit out. 'Get yourself kill—' He stopped abruptly as his gaze slid past Eleanor to the scene beyond. He grasped her upper arms, steadying her as he searched her face.

'Are you hurt?'

Eleanor shook her head.

'Good. Now, I need you to stay calm and be strong. Go over to Henry—' he indicated his groom '—and tell him to come and help me, whilst you hold my team. Can you do that?' She nodded. 'Good girl.'

He stepped around her and strode over to the stricken carriage. Eleanor, still in shock, stared after him for a few seconds, then, shaking out of her stupor, she did as instructed and went to hold his horses as the stranger took charge with an ease that spoke of a natural leader.

Good girl? Who does he think he is? He cannot be much older than I am.

The minute those uncharitable thoughts slipped into her mind, she batted them away. Never mind that he had relegated her to the role of helpless female, she must remember he was only trying to help. Like a knight in shining armour. She bit back a smile at such an absurd thought. In her experience, men rarely felt chivalrous towards tall, independent and managing females such as herself.

The stranger's presence focused the servants and the leaders' traces were soon cut, allowing the horses to stand and be calmed. Whilst they were occupied, Eleanor gathered her courage and forced herself to study the surrounding woodlands for anyone who might be lurking. She saw no one…no movement.

Timothy was dispatched to a nearby farm, just visible through the trees, to summon assistance, and the injured horse was examined. A heated discussion appeared to take place between the men before the stranger placed his hand on Joey's shoulder, bending down to speak in his ear. He pushed him gently in Eleanor's direction whilst nodding to Fretwell, who extracted a pistol from behind the box of the carriage.

Joey stumbled over to Eleanor, tears in his

eyes. 'They're going to shoot her, lass. My Bonny. She's been shot and her leg's broke. There's nowt we can do to save her.'

'Oh, Joey, I'm so sorry. I know how you feel about the horses.' Eleanor's vision blurred. 'Don't look.' She clasped his arm and turned him away from the grisly scene. A few seconds later a shot rang out and they both stiffened. Then Joey sighed.

'That's that, then, lass…beg pardon, I mean, milady.' He straightened. 'There's still three horses there needing me. I must get back.' He began to walk away, then stopped, looking back at Eleanor with troubled eyes. 'Oh, milady, who d'ye think could do such a wicked, wicked thing? Shooting at an innocent animal is bad enough, but that shot could've killed any one of us.'

His words echoed as Eleanor watched him return to the other men, who were now heaving Bonny's carcass from on top of her teammate, Joker. A chill ran down her spine as she saw Fretwell reload the pistol and pace slowly back along the road, gazing intently into the dense woodland along its edge. Eleanor pulled her travelling cloak closer around her, as if it could render her invisible.

Joker scrambled to his feet as soon as he could and stood, shaking, allowing Joey to clasp his drooping head to his chest whilst he murmured into his ear. Henry returned to take charge of

the curricle and pair and Eleanor made her way
slowly towards the men and the carriage.

She was self-consciously aware of the stranger's scrutiny, which she returned unobtrusively.
His curricle and pair were top quality, but his
clothing—a greatcoat hanging open over a loose-
fitting dark blue coat, buckskin breeches and an
indifferently tied neckcloth—was not of the first
stare. No gentleman of her acquaintance would
settle for comfort over elegance. His build was
athletic, his face—sporting a slightly crooked
nose that had surely been broken and badly set
in the past—was unfashionably tanned and the
square set of his jaw somehow proclaimed a
man who would be ill at ease in society's drawing rooms.

He would make a formidable opponent. The
words crept unbidden into her head. Opponent?
Mentally, she shook herself, irritated that she
imagined menace all around her since the fire.

She braced her shoulders, lifted her chin and
met the stranger's stare. Cool blue eyes appraised
her, sending another shiver whispering down her
spine, this time of awareness. His features spoke
of strength and decisiveness and, yes, even a hint
of that menace she had imagined earlier. His eyes
narrowed momentarily before he smiled. It transformed his face—still rugged, but softened as his
eyes warmed.

'I thank you for your assistance, sir.'

He bowed. 'It was my pleasure, ma'am.' His smile widened. 'I have long dreamed of rescuing a damsel in distress and now—' his arm swept the scene '—my dream becomes reality.'

Eleanor glanced at his face, suspecting him of mockery, but the candour of his expression and teasing light in his eyes appeared to hide no malice.

'Nevertheless,' she said, 'I do thank you and I am sorry to have so nearly caused another upset.'

'You did the right thing. There could have been serious consequences had you not been so decisive. Or brave.' He studied her anew and she recognised the devilish glint in his eye as he added, *sotto voce*, 'Or foolhardy.'

Eleanor stiffened and opened her mouth to retaliate, but he was already spinning round, his attention caught by a faint shout from within the overturned carriage.

'Good heavens!' Eleanor put her irritation aside as she remembered Aunt Lucy and the two maids, still trapped inside. 'Sir, might I impose on you once more?'

'Who is in there?'

'My aunt and our two maids.'

The stranger leapt on to the carriage, knelt and reached down through the open doorway to help out Aunt Lucy, Lizzie and Matilda before lowering them safely to the ground.

He was certainly accustomed to taking charge,

Eleanor thought, watching him work, wondering who he was and where he came from as Aunt Lucy joined her, pale and shaken.

'How are—?' Eleanor got no further.

'Who is our rescuer, I wonder?' were the first words Aunt Lucy uttered, in a sibilant whisper. 'I wonder where he is from. He is very attractive, in a *manly* sort of way, is he not, Ellie?'

'Hush, Aunt Lucy. He'll hear you,' Eleanor hissed as he strode towards them, his greatcoat swinging open to reveal muscular, buckskin-clad legs. He was hatless, and his dark blond, sun-streaked hair fell over his forehead at times, only to be shoved back with an impatient hand.

'It seems I am in your debt again, sir,' she said.

'I repeat, no thanks are necessary. It was…is… my pleasure. If I might introduce myself? Matthew Thomas, at your service, ladies.'

Aunt Lucy, her small dark eyes alight with curiosity, replied, 'Lady Rothley.'

Mr Thomas bowed. 'I am honoured to make your acquaintance, Lady Rothley. And…?'

'Allow me to present my niece, Eleanor, the Baroness Ashby.'

Mr Thomas bowed once more. 'Enchanted, Lady Ashby.'

As he straightened, his bright eyes locked with Eleanor's, appreciation swirling in their depths. Eleanor's insides performed a somersault. Oh, yes, she agreed silently with her aunt, he was certainly attractive. She switched her gaze from Mr Thomas to Fretwell, who had returned and now joined them, a frown creasing his brow.

'Fretwell, I do hope this hasn't aggravated your head wound. It has only just healed.'

'I'm all right, milady, barring a few bruises. Lucky nothing was broken; leastwise, nothing human,' he added gloomily.

'Indeed, it could have been much worse. What—'

'Milady—' Fretwell shot a suspicious glance at Mr Thomas before lowering his voice '—if I might have a word?' With a jerk of his head he indicated the far side of the road.

Mystified, Eleanor excused herself and followed him. 'What is it?'

'We must get away from here as soon as we can, milady,' he said. 'It's not safe. You're too exposed and we don't know who *he* might be, either. He appeared very timely after that shot, don't you—?'

'Fretwell! Surely you're not suggesting the horse was shot deliberately?' Eleanor denied Fretwell's suspicions despite her own doubts. 'Why would anyone—?'

'After the fire, milady, it seems a mite coincidental.'

The fire... The by-now-familiar coil of unease snaked through Eleanor. Irritated, she suppressed it. It was her duty to maintain her composure in front of her servants. If they began to view her as a feeble woman, their respect for her, and her authority, would soon diminish.

'Nonsense!' she said. 'There is nobody there—it was surely a stray shot and, as for your suggestion that Mr Thomas might have had any part in it, I'm surprised at you. You are not normally given to such flights of fancy.'

Fretwell reddened, but stubbornly held her gaze. 'Be that as it may, milady, I know what happened to me the night of the fire. That was no accident. It was deliberate.'

'Very well, I shall take care, but please keep your conjectures to yourself. I don't want Lady Rothley upset and there is no reason for Mr Thomas to become further embroiled in our problems.'

Movement further along the road caught her attention. Her footman was on his way back, accompanied by another man leading a pair of draught horses.

'Come, Timothy is here now with help. Let us go and sort the carriage out, then we can all get away from here and put your mind at rest.'

Although how she was to contrive that, with a damaged carriage, she could not imagine. Aunt Lucy, Lizzie and Matilda, the latter still sobbing into her handkerchief, were sitting on a grass bank a short way along the road. Eleanor, more shaken by the accident than she would admit, wished for nothing more than to join them, leaving the men to cope.

But this was her carriage, her horses and her servants.

Ergo, her responsibility.

She joined the men, ignoring the curious looks of both Mr Thomas and the farmer, a wiry, weatherbeaten individual of few words, but surprising strength. Her own men knew better than to question her desire to be involved.

It soon became clear that Mr Thomas still considered himself in charge and Eleanor, at first bemused at being relegated to a mere onlooker, grew increasingly indignant at being totally ignored.

She stepped forward, preparing to assert her authority.

Chapter Three

Matthew Thomas studied the overturned carriage.

'Tie the chain there,' he said to Timothy, pointing to a position on the spring iron at the rear of the carriage and trying to ignore the baroness, who was clearly itching to get involved.

'Timothy,' she said in an imperious tone, after the footman had attached the chain, 'you ought to attach that chain further forward—it is too near the back there.'

Matthew straightened from checking that the chain was secure and turned to face Eleanor, lifting a brow.

She raised her chin, holding his gaze in typical aristocratic haughtiness.

'If you pull from there it will surely pull the carriage around, rather than upright,' she said.

He felt his temper stir and clamped down on it hard. He was not the wild youth he had once been and the intervening years had taught him to control his emotions, particularly in fraught situations like the present.

'When the other chain is attached—as it will be shortly—towards the *front* of the carriage, it will counteract the pull on *this* chain. And pull the carriage upright.'

He deliberately blanked his expression, hiding his amusement at her indignation as she drew herself up to her full height—which was considerable, for a woman. She was barely four inches shorter than his own six feet. Her bright blue cloak had swung open to reveal a curvaceous figure, which Matthew perused appreciatively before returning his gaze to clash with her stormy, tawny-brown eyes. Her dark brows snapped together in a frown.

His interest had been aroused the minute he had leapt from his curricle and stared down into her face, pale with shock. She was strikingly attractive, although not a conventional beauty—courageous, too, leaping in front of his horses that way. His heart had almost seized with terror as he had fought to avoid her. Admittedly, he *had* been springing the horses—keen to test their paces—but that fact had not mitigated his fury, which was fuelled as much by the fear of what might have happened as by anger.

Now his interest was still there, but tempered with reality. He could admire her beauty, as one might admire, and even covet, a beautiful painting or a statue. But he would admire from a distance. He was no longer part of her deceitful world. He turned his attention once more to the stricken carriage.

'We will need some poles to lever the carriage as the horses pull,' Eleanor declared some minutes later.

Matthew once more stopped what he was doing. He took a pace towards Eleanor, catching a glimpse of—was that fear?—in her expression as she retreated. Then her lips tightened, and she stepped forward, bringing them almost nose to nose. Pluck? Or was that merely her innate feeling of superiority?

'If—' he kept his voice low, in order that the others shouldn't overhear '—you are so keen to help, might I suggest you go and hold the horses so Henry can come and assist? Unless, that is, you really *are* capable of putting your shoulder to the carriage as the horses pull? I would suggest, with the utmost respect, that you are neither built, nor dressed, for such an activity.'

'Hmmph!' Her gaze lowered.

'Good point about the poles, though, my lady.' He waved an arm to the rear of the carriage, where two stout poles lay on the ground. 'The farmer, as you can see, has thought of everything.'

She followed the direction of his gesture. A flush coloured her cheeks.

'Oh.' There was a pause. Then, 'I hadn't noticed them.'

Shame pricked Matthew's conscience. He had not meant to make her feel foolish. He should not have risen to her arrogance—it was not her fault she was a part of that world he so despised. He reminded himself she must still be in shock after the accident.

They were still standing very close, her perfume tantalising his senses—floral notes interwoven with the undeniable scent of woman. A wave of desire caught him off guard and he spun away, forcing his attention back to the problem at hand.

The carriage was pulled upright with much heaving and straining, and they examined the extent of the damage. One wheel would need replacing, but the rest of the damage could be repaired. Try as he might to ignore her, Matthew was constantly aware of Eleanor's presence. He could *feel* the frustration radiating from her as she peered over his shoulder at the carriage.

'There's a wheelwright in the village over yonder,' the farmer, who had introduced himself as Alfred Clegg, said. 'I'll send word. The horses can go in the home paddock for the time. Where're you folk heading?'

'We have rooms bespoke at the White Lion in Stockport,' Eleanor replied.

The farmer scratched his head, peering at the sky. 'That's a tidy way, mum. And it looks like rain.'

'Do you have a carriage or some such that you could loan or hire to us?'

''Fraid not, mum. The missus is to market today in the gig. Hay wagon is all I got.' He looked at her dubiously. 'It might do for your luggage, and mebbe the maids there wouldn't object, but…' He paused, shaking his head. 'Anyways, my horses couldn't get all the way to Stockport and back—they'm built for power, not speed.'

'It so happens that I have a room reserved at the Green Man in Ashton tonight,' Matthew said. 'It is much nearer than Stockport and it is clean and comfortable—I'm sure there will be enough accommodation for us all. The hay wagon is an excellent suggestion for the luggage and the servants and I can take the ladies in my curricle, if they have no objection to squeezing in.'

He looked around the group as he spoke. Approval shone on the faces of the majority, the exceptions being the baroness, who looked mutinous, and Fretwell, who was eyeing him with deep suspicion. Lady Rothley had joined them in time to hear Matthew's proposal.

'That sounds an excellent suggestion, Mr Thomas. Do you not agree, Ellie?'

Matthew returned Lady Rothley's smile, praying she would not recognise him. He had known her sons, of course—wild rakes, the pair of them—but he was certain he had never met the marchioness. It was many years since he had been cast out from the world these ladies inhabited and, although in his youth he had borne a striking resemblance to his mother, he had lived a full and eventful life since then. He suspected the similarities were no longer so apparent. At the thought of his mother, his heart contracted painfully before he dismissed his weakness with a silent oath. His family had not believed his innocence; they had banished him from their lives and forgotten his very existence. Bitterly, he forced his black memories into the box where he confined them and slammed the lid.

'I should prefer to continue as planned to Stockport, Aunt,' Eleanor was saying. 'Fretwell, you may as well stay here—if Clegg does not object—and then take the remaining horses home tomorrow, as planned, as long as they are all fit.'

The farmer nodded his consent.

Fretwell scowled, shooting a suspicious glance at Matthew. 'I think I should stay with you, milady. For protection,' he muttered.

Matthew felt his brows shoot up. What was he missing here?

'No, Fretwell, I will not alter my plans. I shall hire another carriage to convey us to London. Joey, you can also stay on here and oversee the repairs. I shall arrange for a team to be sent out so you can follow us down to London with the carriage.'

She was certainly a lady used to having her own way, Matthew thought, listening as she set out her expectations. Fretwell was clearly unhappy with her decision, but he raised no further objections.

'I shall hire a chaise at Ashton to take us on to Stockport,' Eleanor continued, 'as Mr Thomas has offered to transport us as far as there.'

Her clear reluctance to spend the evening in his company irritated Matthew. Who the hell was Lady Ashby to dismiss him as a nobody? She appeared to believe that he was not worthy of her time or attention. Tempted to just forget her and be on his way, he paused. Lady Ashby needed dislodging from that high perch of hers. Besides, some female company that evening would be a welcome change to his planned solitary dinner. And she was without doubt prettier than the locals in the taproom of the Green Man, where he would most likely end up after his meal.

His devil got the better of him. He lifted one brow in deliberate provocation before directing his words at Lady Rothley.

'With everyone so shaken, you will be far better advised to remain at Ashton tonight, my lady. I'm sure you will find the Green Man to your liking, and, forgive me, but you look as though you would welcome a fireside to sit beside and a warm drink.'

'That is an enticing prospect, Mr Thomas,' Lady Rothley said, with a warm smile.

Eleanor's lips tightened.

'Excellent,' Matthew said. 'That's settled, then. I shall convey you and your niece in my curricle, and the servants and luggage can follow on in Clegg's wagon.

'Of course—' he switched his attention to Eleanor, grinning at her poorly concealed pique '—once we arrive at the Green Man, should you *still* insist on continuing your journey then you must do so.

'Shall we go?'

Chapter Four

The journey to the Green Man was both uncomfortable and, for Eleanor, disconcerting. The vehicle, designed to seat two comfortably, was a squeeze for three and, to her vexation, Matthew handed her into the curricle before Aunt Lucy, leaving her squashed in the middle when he leapt aboard the other side. Her objection that her aunt would feel safer sitting between them was summarily dismissed, both by Matthew and by Aunt Lucy herself, who appeared to thoroughly approve of their rescuer.

The heat of his touch through the fine kid of her gloves as he handed her into the curricle sent an unsettling quiver through her, despite her irritation. Quite simply, Matthew Thomas rattled her, with his knowing smile and the tease in his voice and his undeniable masculinity.

During the drive, Aunt Lucy was uncharacteristically quiet.

'Are you sure you were not injured, Aunt?' Eleanor asked, concerned.

'Yes, I am sure. Do not mind me, my pet. I am a little tired, that is all.'

Her lids drooped even as she spoke. Eleanor squeezed her hand. They had all had such a shock. She, too, felt drained, but Matthew's rock-hard thigh pressing against hers and the heat radiating from him ensured she remained on edge. Try as she might to focus on the road ahead, her attention kept wandering to his hands, gloved in scuffed leather, as he handled the ribbons with dexterity, controlling his highly strung pair with total confidence.

'How long have you had them?' she asked, indicating the jet-black horses trotting in front, their powerful haunches gleaming in the late afternoon sunshine. 'They look…' She hesitated, appalled by what she had almost said. 'That is, they are a splendid match.'

'They look…?'

What a careless slip of the tongue. Eleanor firmed her lips, conscious of his head turning and those blue eyes boring into her.

'They look too good for the likes of me? Is that what you were about to say?'

She had struck a nerve there. She risked a sidelong glance. 'I meant no offence.'

'It is as well I took none, then, isn't it?'

She did not quite believe that. For several minutes there was no sound save the horses' hoof-beats. Eleanor bit her lip.

'You are quite right, nevertheless,' Matthew said, eventually. 'They are far superior animals to anything I usually aspire to and, in answer to your question, I have owned them since last night.'

Eleanor bit back her exclamation of surprise. For an unfamiliar team they were going very sweetly indeed. Matthew Thomas was clearly a skilled whip…but he had no need of her praise to boost his already puffed-up opinion of himself. She kept her gaze fixed firmly on the road ahead.

'Take care, my lady,' Matthew said, after a couple of beats of silence, amusement threading through his voice. '*You* are determined not to admit your surprise, but I must inform you that *I* interpret your very silence as a compliment and a welcome salve to my bruised pride.'

'They have obviously been extremely well schooled,' Eleanor replied tartly, exasperated by his ability to read her thoughts.

Matthew shouted with laughter. '*Touché*. An impressive put-down.'

Eleanor arched one brow, but could not prevent a corner of her mouth from twitching. 'When you warrant a compliment, Mr Thomas—whether for your driving skills or for any other purpose—please be advised that I shall not stint in offering one. Until then…'

Silence reigned for a moment, then Matthew laughed again.

'You are a hard lady to please,' he said. 'Let me see…' from the corner of her eye Eleanor saw him lean forward and glance across at Aunt Lucy, who appeared to be dozing '…you almost cause an accident by running in front of my curricle—an accident that was only prevented by my superior driving skills. I cut your injured horses free, rescue your aunt and maidservants, help pull your carriage upright, and now I am transporting you to an inn to recuperate, and *still* I do not warrant any praise for my actions. Tell me, Lady Ashby…' his voice lowered to a husky whisper as he put his lips close to her ear '…what, precisely, can I do for you that *will* earn your approval?'

Eleanor suppressed a quiver as his breath tickled across her sensitive lobe and caressed her neck. Risking a quick glance, she could see he was fully aware of the effect he was having on her. She stiffened, her earlier amusement vanquished. She ignored his question.

'Do you travel far, sir? I do not believe you said where you are heading?'

'No, I do not believe I did.'

He did not elaborate, and Eleanor gritted her teeth against the extended silence, raising her chin and keeping her eyes riveted to the road ahead.

Eventually, he sighed in an exaggerated fashion and continued, 'I stay at Ashton for two nights.

After that, I plan to visit Worcestershire before I return to London.'

She itched to question him further, but held her silence.

'Do you travel to London for the Season, my lady?'

'We do.'

'And do you go every Season?'

'We do not.' Two could play at being evasive.

'Have you travelled far today?' His voice quivered.

'From Lancashire.'

'North of the county or south?'

She slanted a suspicious look at him.

'Is that where you call home?'

His voice was now definitely unsteady. Eleanor stifled her *hmmph* of irritation.

'You, sir, are being deliberately provoking.'

His laugh burst free. 'Pax. I could continue this game of question and answer all day, but I suspect you do not share my enjoyment of the ridiculous. I shall not bore you with further impertinent questions.'

Unreasonably, Eleanor was stung by his assumption that she lacked a sense of humour. She was unused to this kind of byplay between a man and a woman and she was aware her embarrassment caused her to appear stiff and unfriendly. Although why she should care about his opinion of her, she did not know. However well he spoke, he was not of her class. She wondered what he was—a prosperous farmer, perhaps, or a merchant or a military man?

She felt his eyes on her and risked another sideways glance. He captured her gaze—his eyes warm, his expression open. His easy smile transformed his face, giving him a charm that Eleanor found instantly appealing. To her confusion, she read admiration in his regard and her blood heated instantly at the notion. She felt a telltale blush creeping up her neck and cheeks and, uncertain, she tore her gaze from his.

She was her own woman—rare in this day and age—in control of her own life and finances, answerable to no one, not even her trustees since she had reached her twenty-fifth birthday. She was strong and decisive when running her estates, responsible for not only her own comfort and lifestyle, but also the livelihoods and wellbeing of everyone who worked for her, plus their families—a responsibility she discharged with assurance. However, for all her outward confidence, she found herself regressing to the awkward, tongue-tied girl of her past in the presence of Matthew Thomas, simply because he was passing time with a light flirtation. Her experience with Donald had caused her to doubt her judgement of men and their true intentions. And had Aunt Phyllis not warned her time after time of the danger of showing too much encouragement to any gentleman?

'If you truly wish to earn my approval, sir, might I suggest that you keep your eyes upon the road? We have already suffered one upset today.'

She fixed her eyes once more on the road ahead and it was with relief that she saw the Green Man come into view.

As they pulled up in the courtyard of the inn, Aunt Lucy came to with a start.

'Of course,' she said, 'it could have been another attempt on your life, Ellie.'

Chapter Five

Matthew, on the verge of springing from the curricle, paused, his interest roused.

'Aunt Lucy! That is preposterous. Bonny's death was an accident.'

'You cannot be certain of that, Ellie. What about the fire at the Manor? Someone set that fire and lurked around to see what happened. He brained Fretwell to stop him rescuing you, in case you had forgotten.'

'Brained…! Aunt! What a thing to say.' Eleanor's voice lowered, holding a clear warning. 'Mr Thomas does not want to hear those wild conjectures. I'll warrant it was as I said—a burglar, and Fretwell was simply in the wrong place at the wrong time.'

'A burglar? In the library? Why would a burglar deliberately set fire to a pile of books? You must not dismiss this as coincidence.'

Eleanor glared daggers at her aunt, who took

no notice, continuing, 'Your bedchamber is directly over the library and now a shot is fired at our carriage. Who knows what their intention was, but you are a common factor to both, you cannot deny it.'

'I think you have been indulging in too many Gothic novels,' Eleanor said. She laughed in a dismissive fashion, but Matthew caught the haunted look that flashed across her face. 'That sort of thing simply doesn't happen in this day and age. Do you not agree, Mr Thomas?'

Matthew completed his descent from the curricle. Eleanor was regarding him with her brows raised, clearly awaiting his agreement, but he was by now intrigued. He would not be pressed to give his opinion before he knew the facts. He did not doubt that, beneath her dismissal of her aunt's words, Eleanor was more troubled than she would admit.

'I should prefer to hear the full circumstances before passing comment, my lady.'

He assisted Eleanor from the curricle, biting back a grin when she snatched her hand from his as soon as she was on solid ground, her cheeks now glowing pink. She was certainly a woman of contrasts: one moment acting the *grande dame*, the next blushing like a schoolgirl. Not the response he expected from a married woman. Most likely her husband was one of those aristocrats— plentiful enough in the *ton*—who did not inconvenience himself with romancing his wife. A sad waste, in Matthew's opinion.

'In the meantime, ladies,' he continued, with a pointed look at the innkeeper, who had emerged to welcome his guests, 'I think we should continue this discussion inside, in private.'

Eleanor turned to the innkeeper, but Matthew stepped forward to forestall her. He might not dress the gentleman, but his upbringing—slowly stretching and awakening after what seemed like a long sleep—dictated that he, as the man of the party, should deal with innkeepers and their ilk.

'Good afternoon, Fairfax. We shall require two additional bedchambers for the ladies, plus accommodation for their servants, who will be arriving shortly. I trust there is room to accommodate the whole party?'

Fairfax's face fell. 'I'm sorry, sir; would that I could accommodate you, but the place is full to the rafters.' His voice dropped discreetly as he shot a sideways glance at the two ladies. 'What with the prize fight tomorrow, sir, I doubt you'll find a spare room anywhere in Ashton tonight.'

Matthew swore beneath his breath; the fight had slipped his mind after dealing with the aftermath of the accident. The illicit match was the reason he had returned to Ashton after the successful conclusion of his business in Rochdale.

Eleanor stepped forward, interrupting his reflections.

'It appears we have no choice but to continue our journey after all, Mr Thomas,' she said, with barely concealed satisfaction, a distinct challenge in her tawny eyes.

Matthew clenched his jaw. The provocative *grande dame* had materialised once more.

Eleanor turned to the innkeeper. 'I shall require a carriage to convey my party to Stockport, where we have rooms bespoken for tonight, if you please.'

Before Fairfax could respond, Lady Rothley swayed, groaning quietly, her hand to her head. Eleanor was instantly at her side, her arm around her aunt's waist.

'Aunt Lucy! Are you all right?'

'A little shaken still, my pet—I feel utterly overcome of a sudden.'

'Come, let us go inside. You need to sit down and rest. Oh, what was I thinking? How could I even *consider* making you travel any further after what you have been through? Only…what are we to do now, with no rooms available?'

Matthew could not resist the hint of desperation in Eleanor's voice.

'Might I suggest you ladies take my room here? It is not ideal, with so many strangers in town, but I am sure you will be safe enough. And I am in no doubt Fairfax will be able to provide a cot somewhere for your maids.' It would mean a longer drive to view the fight tomorrow, but that would be a trivial inconvenience. 'The ladies' carriage was involved in an accident,' he continued, by way of explanation to the innkeeper.

'Of course, sir. If the ladies don't object to sharing, I'm sure we can find a corner for their maids, and any men can bed down above the stables. I dare say they're used to making do.'

'I shall continue on to Stockport today and stay at…the White Lion, was it not?' Matthew said.

Lady Rothley perked up, reminding Matthew of a bird that had spied a juicy worm, with her tiny, delicate frame and her bright, beady eyes. 'That is a splendid notion, Mr Thomas, is it not, my pet? I must confess that the thought of travelling further today quite overset me.'

Eleanor ushered her aunt into the inn. 'I am sorry, Aunt. I hadn't given a thought to how you must feel. You've had such a shock. Well,' she added, 'so have we all. I make no doubt the servants will also welcome the chance to rest here.' She paused on the threshold, turned to Matthew and held out her hand. 'Mr Thomas, we greatly appreciate your assistance today but, please, do not let us detain you any longer. I am sure you have many demands upon your time.'

Anger rumbled through Matthew at her arrogance. What was wrong with the woman? First, she resented him helping out at the roadside and now she was dismissing him—after having sacrificed his bedchamber, no less—when at the very least she could invite him to stay and take some refreshment.

'Thank you so much for your concern,' he replied, ignoring her outstretched hand, 'but, if you care to recall, we have a discussion to continue, and I have every intention of staying until I am satisfied you and your aunt are not in danger.'

Lady Rothley had stopped to listen. She frowned at her niece. 'Really, Eleanor, how can you be so ungracious after all Mr Thomas has done for us?' She smiled at Matthew. 'I am most grateful for your assistance, sir, and I assure you that we shall *both* be delighted to take a dish of tea with you, if you would care to join us?'

Eleanor had reddened at her aunt's rebuke. 'I apologise, Mr Thomas. I was concerned for the time, considering you still have to drive to Stockport. Of course, you must stay and take tea with us, if you have the time.'

Matthew studied her expression. There was contrition there, but she could disguise neither the strain she was under nor the distrust that haunted her eyes. Perhaps, in view of the dark picture painted by her aunt, he should not blame her.

'You have no need to be concerned on my account,' he said, understanding full well the mendacity of her words. 'I have plenty of time to get to Stockport before dark.'

'Very well. Fairfax, we should appreciate some

refreshments served, if you would be so kind,' Eleanor ordered.

Fairfax bowed. 'Of course, my lady. Please, follow me.'

They were shown into a small but clean parlour. Matthew waited until Eleanor and her aunt were seated before settling on a small sofa on the opposite side of the fireplace and, before long, two maidservants served them tea with thinly cut bread and butter and rich pound cake.

Eleanor had removed her bonnet, cloak and gloves on entering the parlour and Matthew studied her with appreciation. She was even more attractive than he had first thought: her smooth ivory skin—enhanced by the rosy hue of her cheeks as she was warmed by the flames—invited his touch, and her wide mouth and soft pink lips were ripe for kissing. Her hair was a glossy dark brown, the curls that framed her face glinting as they caught the light from the flames. How would her hair look—and feel—loosened from the restricting hairpins, cascading over her shoulders and down her back? It was a long time since he had been so attracted to a woman. Were it not for her air of superiority, he might say she was his idea of the perfect woman.

It's a shame she is married.

The thought caught him unaware and he tore his gaze from her.

It is not a shame. Even were she not wed, she

moves in a very different world to you. You know she would never give you a second glance had circumstances not thrown you together.

Matthew's modest fortune had been built from his own hard work, a touch of luck at the tables—he had won his curricle and pair in a game just the night before—and from trade, that term that was despised by the idle aristocracy. No, the likes of Lady Ashby would never look at the likes of him.

He waited until the servants withdrew before raising the subject on his mind. 'Will you tell me about the fire your aunt spoke of, my lady?'

After some initial reluctance, Eleanor recounted the night of the fire—the smell of the smoke that woke her; the terror of her escape through her window; the mystery of Fretwell's injury and his shadowy assailant. Through it all, her anguish at the damage to her beloved home shone through.

Matthew's fascination with Eleanor marched in step with his mounting concern. Her eyes, framed by thick lashes and strong, dark brows, revealed her every emotion as she warmed to the telling of her tale. They sparkled with impish amusement as Lady Rothley sprinkled the story with a selection of servants' lurid tales, learned through Matilda. They lit up in laughter at some of the more ghoulish speculations that Eleanor had clearly not heard before, her generous mouth widening into a stunning smile that transformed her already attractive face into one of mesmerising loveliness. Glimpses of the real woman were revealed when she forgot to stand on her dignity and Matthew had to keep reminding himself of her earlier arrogance and also that she was married and, therefore, out of bounds.

Her uninhibited and infectious laugh triggered an unexpected surge of loneliness that he swiftly thrust aside. Apart from his business partner, Benedict Poole, he was dependent on no one and no one was dependent on him, and that was exactly how he liked it. His burgeoning desire for Eleanor was as unwelcome as it was unexpected and he forced his thoughts from the direction they were taking to concentrate on her words.

'As for this afternoon,' she was saying, 'you have already heard what happened. A stray shot—surely an accident—hit one of the team, causing the carriage to overturn. It was no more a deliberate attack on me than the fire was, despite my aunt's vivid imaginings. Mark my words—it was a burglar, or someone with a grudge. It must have been.'

He recognised the faint hint of desperation in her final words. Eleanor was nowhere near as confident as she pretended to be. Still, it was none of Matthew's concern. He would go on his way very soon—and, judging by his increasingly salacious thoughts, the sooner, the better—and he would likely never see either of the ladies again.

'I must agree with your aunt that a burglar would be unlikely to set fire to a library,' he said, 'but I also think you may be right that a grudge was the cause. If someone was intent on killing you, surely they would pick less haphazard methods? After all, both the fire and the carriage accident had the potential of injuring, or even killing, many more individuals than you and with no guarantee that you would be amongst the casualties.

'It would appear that, for once, you and I are in agreement,' he added, unable to resist a final teasing comment, biting back his smile at her disgruntled expression.

Chapter Six

Eleanor had begun to relax despite her suspicions about Matthew, initially roused by Fretwell, and her earlier irritation at his relegation of her to the role of helpless female in a crisis. After all, had she not pictured him in the role of a white knight before lamenting she was not the sort of female to arouse protective instincts in a man? And he had proved an easy man to converse with, when he was not deliberately goading her, or flirting, that was. When his blue gaze settled on her in that particular, assessing way he had, her blood heated and her insides fluttered in a way they never had with Donald.

'It would seem that, *for once*, you are right, Mr Thomas,' she retorted. How *did* he manage to ruffle her feathers quite so effortlessly?

He laughed. Their eyes met and Eleanor felt a jolt of pure energy shoot through her. Her cheeks flamed. Flustered—and irritated by her reaction—Eleanor jerked her gaze from his and stared at the flames, saying, 'Goodness, this fire is hot.'

She searched in her reticule for her fan and plied it, grateful for an occupation as she fought to control her inner turmoil. Thankfully, Aunt Lucy appeared not to notice anything amiss, and launched a determined crusade to discover as much information as possible about their rescuer. Matthew proved adept at evading her questions, clearly relishing their verbal swordplay, and Eleanor viewed her aunt's increasing frustration with quiet enjoyment.

She relaxed back in her chair, allowing her nerves to settle. Without volition, her gaze wandered over Matthew, admiring the breadth of his shoulders and the solid muscle of his legs. She watched as he picked up his cup with a broad hand—no gentleman's soft, well-manicured hand this, but strong and masculine and capable. He drained the contents, his penetrating eyes flicking to her face as he leaned forward to set his cup on the table, his lips still moist from the tea. Desire coiled deep within her as the rumble of his voice enveloped her. She could listen to him for ever. How wonderful would it be to be able to lean on such a man, to share the burden of her life?

Even as that thought flitted into her brain, she suppressed it. She needed no man to lean on. She had spent the three years since her father's death striving to prove that point. Besides, he would end up the same as all the men who had ever shown her any attention—interested only in her fortune.

She dreamt of being swept off her feet, of being wooed by a man who was besotted with her and declared his undying passion for her, but could she ever trust her own judgement?

Donald had fooled her with his eager courtship after they met at James and Ruth's wedding. He was an army officer and had returned to Ashby, shortly afterwards, when he was on leave. Eleanor had believed he was in love with her and, even though his kisses had left her strangely unmoved, she had persuaded herself her love for him would blossom given time.

She studied Matthew and desire flickered deep within her...surely a kiss from a man like Matthew Thomas would not leave her unmoved? She tore her attention from his sensual lips, vaguely scandalised by her outrageous thoughts.

Would she ever know the feel of a real man in her arms?

She blessed the day she had discovered Donald's true intent. She had overheard him discussing her with his sister, Ruth, and their contempt for Eleanor was clear. Donald was interested only in her position and the wealth she would inherit from her ailing father. The following day, to her father's distress, she had refused Donald's offer of marriage and he had returned to his regiment. Sadly, she had heard, he had not survived the war.

Eleanor's father had died the following spring and Eleanor still regretted that he had died worrying over both her future and that of the estate.

The room had fallen silent. Eleanor came back to the present with a guilty start.

'You appear lost in your thoughts,' Matthew said. 'It would seem they are not all pleasant?'

Blushing, Eleanor realised that she had been staring directly at Matthew whilst her mind wandered. Aunt Lucy was dozing by the fire and they were effectively alone together.

'I am sure they would be of no interest to you, Mr Thomas.'

'I think you would be surprised at my interests, my lady,' he replied softly, his blue eyes aglow.

There was admiration in his gaze. Awkwardly, Eleanor gazed down at her hands, entwined in her lap, uncertain how to respond. Her come-out, as well as her experience with Donald, had taught her to be cautious of reading too much into a man's supposed admiration for it seemed, more often than not, that it was disingenuous.

Matthew continued to regard her steadily, waiting for her reply. Irritation at his persistence clambered over her discomfort.

'Indeed, you are mistaken, sir.' She injected a bright, vacuous note into her voice. 'My thoughts were exceedingly pleasant. I was thinking of all the gowns and hats and shoes and other fripperies I shall buy in London and of all the wonderful parties and balls I shall be invited to. Why—' she fixed him with an arch look '—I dare say I shall never be at home, what with all the shopping and the amusements London has to offer.'

His lips twitched and his eyes crinkled at the corners.

'In other words, your thoughts are none of my business. I shall pry no further. We are all entitled to our secrets, after all. Now, let us return to the innocuous subjects you seem to prefer; do you go to London for the Season every year?'

Eleanor laughed, unaccountably pleased that he had not been fooled by her performance. He was clearly intelligent and she did have some pride. She had no wish for this man to believe she was a brainless ninny, despite her subterfuge.

'I believe I answered that query the first time, sir. But I shall expand upon my previous effort, which was, I admit, a little brusque. This will be the first time I have been to London in seven years.' She faltered momentarily, memories of her first Season all too raw even after all this time, before continuing, 'I am looking forward to it. I have become quite dull at home, you know, and I am more than ready for all the excitement and diversion London can offer.'

She saw his eyes narrow as she stumbled over her words. She cautioned herself to take care. *Intelligent? Oh, yes. And disconcertingly perceptive, to boot.*

'I am most fortunate that Aunt Lucy is accompanying me,' she continued. 'To lend me countenance, she would have me believe. She has not been to town for several years, but she was a notable hostess in her day. I suspect,' she added, smiling, keen to eliminate her slip from his mind, 'she is eager to see if she can still wield the same influence.'

'She appears to be a most redoubtable lady— I have no doubt she will be setting the standards with ease. Will you be joining other family members in town?'

'My cousin James and his wife, Ruth, live in London. James has kindly leased a house on my behalf, however, so we shall not be obliged to reside with them. My family is small in number, I fear. Other than James, there are only my cousins on my mother's side—Lucas and Hugo, Aunt Lucy's sons. Lucas is at Rothley, but I hope Hugo might be in town, for Aunt Lucy's sake.'

'Rothley,' he said. 'I know the name, but I cannot quite place where it is.'

'It's in the county of Northumberland.'

'And a colder, more desolate place you could never imagine,' Aunt Lucy interjected, 'although it's very wildness is extraordinarily beautiful, too, in its way. Exactly what part of the country do *you* hail from, Mr Thomas?'

Chapter Seven

Aunt Lucy—wily lady that she was—had out-manoeuvred Matthew. Eleanor could see his frustrated struggle to avoid answering such a direct question without telling an outright lie. Somehow, she did not think him so dishonourable. Evasive, yes. Secretive, yes. But not out-and-out dishonest.

'Worcestershire, my lady.'

'Ah.' There was a wealth of satisfaction in that one word. 'I believe you said earlier that you are headed there before you return to London. Do you visit family?'

Matthew's eyes widened and he shot a stunned glance at Eleanor. She could not help but smile. He had just realised that Aunt Lucy must have heard their every word during the journey to the inn. Eleanor was unsurprised, knowing from experience just how far her aunt would go to hear a juicy morsel of gossip, even if it did involve deceiving her only niece by pretending to doze.

'No. I merely plan to visit a few of my youthful haunts, for old times' sake.'

'A beautiful county, Worcestershire. What part of the county did you say?'

'Near the town of Bromsgrove.' Matthew's brows were now low enough to almost conceal his eyes. 'It is many years since I have lived there, however.'

Eleanor intervened before her aunt could continue, afraid she would poke and pry until Matthew became annoyed. Better to cut straight to the point. 'Forgive my direct speaking, Mr Thomas, but what my aunt is trying to ascertain is whether she might know your family.'

The crease between Matthew's brows deepened as their gazes fused. Eleanor waited for his answer, brows raised. She recognised his irritation with her persistence, but stood her ground.

'I am a merchant,' he said to Aunt Lucy, after a long pause. 'Can you think of any reason why a lady such as yourself should know my family?'

Oh, clever! He blocked that thrust with ease.

'You are clearly well educated,' Eleanor said.

'Indeed. My family were…are…not poor. I went to Harrow.'

A knock at the door announced Fairfax. 'Your luggage and servants have arrived, miladies.'

He disappeared, and Lizzie and Matilda soon appeared at the parlour door. Aunt Lucy rose from her chair, extending her hand to Matthew.

'Mr Thomas, I beg you will excuse me, for I am very tired. I am afraid the events of the day have caught up with me. I have the headache and am exceedingly stiff and sore. I shall go to our bedchamber for a rest now that Matilda is here to assist me. I do hope we shall meet again. Perhaps you will call upon us in Upper Brook Street, once you have returned to town.'

Matthew bowed over her hand. 'I shall be pleased to, my lady, if only to ascertain you have reached your destination without further mishap.'

Then Aunt Lucy turned to Eleanor.

'Eleanor, would you speak to Fairfax and request a light supper be sent up later for the two of us? As the inn is so full, I do not think it would be wise for us to dine downstairs. We should not wish to attract unwarranted attention.

'Mr Thomas, allow me to thank you once again for all your assistance today. I do not know what we should have done without you.'

Looking pale and drawn, Aunt Lucy clung to Matilda's arm as they left the room. Lizzie hovered in the doorway, clearly awaiting Eleanor, who waved her away.

'You go on upstairs, Lizzie, whilst I speak to Fairfax. I promise I shall be up in a trice.'

'You make sure and come upstairs as soon as you have spoken to him, milady,' Lizzie hissed over her shoulder as she turned to go, having cast a suspicious glare at Matthew. 'There are some most undesirable characters a-wandering around this inn.'

She stalked off down the passageway, muttering. Fretwell's suspicions must be contagious.

Eleanor smiled at Matthew, ready to take her leave.

'I regret we appear to have started on the wrong foot, my lady,' Matthew said. 'May we call a truce? I have accepted your aunt's invitation to Upper Brook Street, but I should like to feel that you, too, are happy for me to call.'

Eleanor was aware she had been both snappish and arrogant in many of her responses to Matthew, but she could not help but be flustered by him. He was by turns aggravating and flirtatious and she didn't quite know how to respond to him, other than with a sharp retort or by pokering up. She forced a smile and extended her hand.

'I, for my part, owe you an apology, Mr Thomas, for I did not mean to appear ungrateful for your help this afternoon. I am not always so quarrelsome—I dare say I am too used to ruling the roost and it is increasingly difficult to allow another to make decisions on my behalf.'

'No apology is necessary, I assure you.'

'I should also like to start anew. I shall be delighted to welcome you to our house in Upper Brook Street when you return to town.'

He took her hand in his, but instead of a shake, as she had intended, he carried it to his mouth.

Her stomach fluttered as his lips pressed against her bare flesh. He captured her gaze with piercing eyes, setting her pulse skittering.

Heat washed through her and her legs trembled as her body seemed to sway towards him of its own volition. Disconcerted, she took a step back, and then another. She gasped as he followed her, his blue eyes intent.

'Sir… Mr Thomas…?'

Matthew halted and Eleanor saw his jaw tighten before he executed a brief bow. 'I fear I was in danger of forgetting my manners, my lady. I can only beg your forgiveness and hope you won't hold it against me when we meet again.'

What had she done? Although she had scant experience of men, Eleanor was aware, on some deep, primeval level, that when they had locked eyes she had *wanted* him to…what? Touch her? Follow her? *Blood will out.* She had, somehow, enticed him without words and honesty compelled her to admit it, if only to herself. She couldn't censure him when she was equally at fault. She was simply grateful that he was too much the gentleman to accuse her of leading him on.

'As we have only just agreed upon a truce, Mr Thomas, it would be a little poor spirited of me to resume hostilities so soon. It has been a long, trying day, so perhaps we may blame it upon that?'

'You are all generosity. Now, I must be on my way but, with your leave, I shall convey your aunt's request to Fairfax before I depart. And might I suggest you return to your aunt forthwith, before that fierce maid of yours comes in search of you?' He made an exaggerated pretence of looking behind him, a comical expression of fear on his face.

Eleanor tried, and failed, to swallow a giggle. 'Goodness, I never took you for a coward, Mr Thomas. Lizzie was only doing her duty as she saw it, with Aunt Lucy too exhausted to look out for my reputation.'

As she laughed up at Matthew his eyes darkened and Eleanor saw a powerful emotion swirling in their depths before he blinked, and it was gone. When he spoke, however, his voice was steady. Had she imagined his response?

'I trust you will spend a comfortable night, my lady, and I will see you upon my return to town.'

'I shall not say goodbye, then, but *au revoir,* Mr Thomas, and thank you again for your assistance today.'

'It was my pleasure. Until we meet again.'

He bowed and was gone.

Chapter Eight

Just before dawn the following morning, Matthew was jerked awake from a fitful sleep by a piercing scream. It took a couple of moments for him to register his whereabouts—he was in one of the two rooms bespoken for Eleanor and her aunt at the White Lion in Stockport. He catapulted from his bed as a series of thuds sounded from the next bedchamber. It was dark in his room and he groped his way to the door.

In the passage, the next door but one to Matthew's room had opened and the occupant peered out, holding aloft a candlestick. The wavering flame illuminated the scowling features of an elderly gentleman, clad in his nightcap and gown.

'What's to do?' he grumbled.

Matthew didn't waste time answering, but ran to the door between them and flung it open, vaguely aware of the man hurrying along the passage, quavering, 'That's my Jenny's room!'

The bedchamber was as dark as his and all Matthew could make out was a shapeless, struggling mass on the bed. He darted forward, yelling, 'Bring the light.'

As the elderly man reached the open door, the scene was suddenly revealed: a figure in black, turning in Matthew's direction, eyes glinting through holes in a mask; the flash of a blade; blood, streaking the bed linen in vivid splashes of red; a girl's terrified face, mouth suddenly slackening as her eyes closed.

Matthew grabbed the man, hauling him from the bed. He staggered backwards as the assailant swiftly changed from resistance to flinging himself at Matthew. Stiff fingers jabbed at Matthew's windpipe as a blade burned his arm and the man wriggled free, barging past the man with the candle as he fled the room. Matthew dragged in a painful breath and rushed to the door, but the assailant was already out of sight. The elderly man—presumably Jenny's father—stood frozen, his mouth gaping in horror.

On the verge of giving chase, a moan from the bed stayed Matthew. The victim needed help. He found a candle on the mantelshelf and lit it. He went to Jenny's father, gripping his shoulder, then shaking him hard.

'Sir, you must be strong.' He could hear the sound of people stirring, voices getting louder. 'Find the innkeeper. Tell him there has been an accident and to send for a doctor immediately. And send his wife here, to me.' He pushed the man out into the passage. 'Hurry!'

He crossed to the bed, shrinking inside with the dread of what he might find. Jenny lay motionless. Her face, shoulders and arms were the only parts of her visible. Her arms and hands bore the signs of struggle. Blood seeped from her wounds, but it wasn't pumping out. That was a good sign. Matthew put a finger to her neck, feeling for a pulse. It was there, not as weak as he feared. He lifted the candle, to examine the bedclothes that covered Jenny. The slashes he had feared to see were not there. The blood appeared to have come from Jenny's arms and hands and one long diagonal slash from her left collarbone that had ripped through her nightgown. Matthew grabbed a towel from the washstand to try and stanch the bleeding. Jenny did not stir.

As he worked, Matthew's mind travelled back to India and to his great-uncle, Percy, who had been so kind to a bewildered and resentful youth, unjustly banished from his family and his homeland. Poor Uncle Percy, who had died after being attacked and stabbed during the course of a robbery. Matthew's throat squeezed tight as he relived his futile efforts to save his great-uncle. He prayed Jenny had suffered no injuries other than those he could see.

His thoughts returned to the present as the innkeeper's wife, Mrs Goody, bustled into the room, followed by Jenny's father.

'Lord have mercy, sir,' Mrs Goody gasped, hands clasped at her ample bosom as she halted by the bed. 'Whatever happened?'

'She was attacked. Her hands, arms and upper chest are bleeding, but I do not think she has been stabbed elsewhere.'

'Stabbed? My Jenny? Oh, Jenny, Jenny, my love…' The elderly man cast himself on to his knees by the bed, clutching at Jenny's hand. Her eyelids fluttered.

'Goody's sent for the doctor,' Mrs Goody said. She glanced at Jenny's father, then leaned towards Matthew, lowering her voice. 'Did you examine the girl for more injuries, sir, or…?'

Matthew felt heat flood his cheeks, understanding both her question and her discretion. Her father had enough to worry about.

'No,' he said.

Poor girl. Depending on her position in society, if news of this got out there would always be gossip and innuendo about her innocence. The thought made his blood simmer. *'No,'* he repeated. 'I merely examined the bedcovers and, as they do not appear torn, I took that to mean she was only injured in those areas we can see.'

'Thank you, sir. We will do all we can to protect her. Can I ask you to find Goody and ask him to boil water and send up some clean linen? If you

close the door on the way out, I'll check the lass
for any further injuries. Oh, to think such an evil
thing could happen here.'

On his way to find the innkeeper, Matthew
came to a dead stop, his knees suddenly weak.
Dear God! The realisation robbed him of his
breath. Had he not swapped accommodation with
Eleanor and her aunt, it could have been one of
them in that room tonight. He quelled the wave
of nausea that invaded him—there would be time
enough for that horror later.

After speaking to Goody, Matthew sped back
to the bedchamber, with a bundle of clean cloths,
to find Jenny awake. As he entered, her eyes widened and she clutched at her father. Mrs Goody
shooed him from the room.

'She's had a terrible fright, sir. It'll take her
time to get over it. You go on back to bed. You've
done all you can.' Her eyes skimmed him and
then she touched his arm. 'You're bleeding. I'll
fetch a cloth to bind it.'

Matthew remembered that burning sensation
as he had grappled with the attacker. He pulled
up the sleeve of his nightshirt. It did not look
deep. Mrs Goody soon returned with a strip of
linen. She wrung a cloth out in cold water from
the washstand.

As she bathed and bound his arm, she said,
'The lass has no other injuries, sir, thank the good

Lord. None at all, if you get my meaning. It was a lucky thing for her that you were there.'

Matthew nodded, relieved for poor Jenny. At least she did not have that nightmare to deal with on top of everything else. He pulled on his clothes and sought out the innkeeper again. Goody had already roused some of his ostlers to search for Jenny's attacker and Matthew joined them. How he regretted not chasing the villain immediately but, with Jenny's father in a state of shock and without knowing how severe Jenny's injuries were, he knew he had been right to tend to her first.

A lengthy and thorough search of the area around the White Lion—joined by other local men—proved fruitless. Whoever the culprit was, it seemed he was long gone, or holed up somewhere. Matthew returned to the inn and ate a hearty breakfast, after which Goody beckoned him into a room at the back of the inn. Jenny's father levered himself to his feet as Matthew entered.

'George Tremayne,' he said, in a gruff voice, holding out a trembling hand.

Matthew shook it. 'Matthew Thomas.'

'I must thank you for what you did for my daughter. I don't know what I should do if…' His voice cracked, and he harrumphed noisily, taking a large handkerchief from his pocket and blowing his nose.

'How is Jenny?'

'As well as she can be. Physically, at least. She is still very shaken. The doctor advised her to stay here for a few days' rest, but she doesn't want to spend another night under this roof.'

'Understandable,' Matthew said.

'The magistrate and the constable were here, asking questions,' Mr Tremayne said. 'They want to speak with you.'

Matthew grimaced. 'I don't think I can tell them much to help. The rogue was masked. Do they know how he got in?'

'A window at the back was open. There's a lean-to roof just below. They think he was a thief and Jenny woke up at the wrong time. She doesn't remember much. That's probably for the best.'

'Indeed. Is the magistrate still here?'

'No, but he said he will come back later and asked that you remain here until then.'

Matthew quashed his frustration. The sooner he left, the sooner he could catch up with Eleanor and her party on the road and assure himself of her safety. Had she been the real target? If the attacker had meant to kill, he would know he had failed. And, if he was still in the town, he would soon discover he'd attacked the wrong girl anyway. Eleanor was still very much in danger.

It was mid-morning before the magistrate returned and Matthew could recount his version of events and answer his questions. At first, he seemed disposed to believe Matthew the culprit, until Matthew pointed out—with some vigour— that Mr Tremayne had also seen Jenny's masked attacker. Finally, satisfied Matthew had given all the information he could, the magistrate gave Matthew leave to continue his journey. The interview had seemed to Matthew to last a lifetime and he had fretted throughout. All thought of returning to Ashton to attend the boxing match was forgotten. He was convinced Eleanor was in grave danger and his one thought was to protect her.

The minute he was free to leave, he leapt aboard his curricle—with Henry perched on the rumble seat behind—and whipped up the horses. It was almost noon already. Even though he doubted Eleanor would have set off early—bearing in mind she must arrange a suitable replacement for the damaged carriage first—her party must surely have passed through Stockport already, on their way to the capital.

Matthew drove south, worry gnawing at him as he wondered what further dangers Eleanor might face. He varied the pace, mindful of the need not to overtire his horses, but also needing enough speed to give him some chance of catching up with Eleanor's party. He was conscious of Henry muttering behind his back and, upon hearing his man's sharp intake of breath as they flew past a lumbering farm wagon with mere inches to spare, Matthew shot a quick glance over his shoulder.

'You do know, I s'pose, that this is the wrong road for Ashton?' Henry said, leaning forward to speak into Matthew's ear.

'Indeed.'

'Can I ask where we're headed?'

'That,' Matthew replied, setting his teeth as he narrowly avoided a stagecoach coming in the opposite direction, 'is a very good question. I don't precisely know. But we are following Lady Ashby and her party. They are heading for London. I need to find out where they will stop for the night.'

'You think that attack was connected to them?'

Matthew tamped down the surge of fear as the image of Jenny, lying bloodied in her bed, rose in his mind. Her features rearranged themselves in his imagination until it was Eleanor's face he saw and he knew, deep in his gut, that she might now be dead, had they not swapped accommodation.

'I am certain of it,' he replied. 'We must enquire at the posting inns we pass, to find out if they have changed horses. We can ask if anyone knows where they plan to stop for the night. Whoever was responsible for the accident and the attack clearly knows the route she is taking and could try again.'

'Last night brought it all back, didn't it?' Henry said. 'You aren't responsible. You *weren't* responsible. You can't protect the whole world and everyone in it.'

Matthew clenched his jaw. Henry had been with him since the early days in India, and was a trusted employee, taking on the roles of both servant and groom as required. He knew Henry referred to Uncle Percy's death, but Matthew was still haunted by his insistence on going out that night. If only he had been at home... The guilt had near overwhelmed him at the time. His uncle's death had spurred Matthew's decision to return home. There was no one to anchor him to India now and he and Benedict could run their business equally well from England.

He was driven by the need to protect. It was in his nature, a part of him, but that did not fully explain why the thought of Eleanor being hurt made his stomach clench with such fear. Frustration flooded him as their progress was slowed by the need to enquire for the travellers at every likely-looking inn they passed, and the need to rest his own horses.

'Where on earth can they be?' he bit out, as they drew yet another blank. 'They must have stopped for the night by now.'

'Maybe they just had too much of a head start on us, sir. Now, don't bite my head off, but them cattle are getting weary and you'll be risking their tendons if we carry on much further.'

Matthew knew Henry was right. He cast a worried look at the sun, sinking to the horizon, then straightened in his seat as a milestone proclaimed they were one mile from Leek.

'This must be it,' he muttered. 'They surely can't have gone any further today. They have to be here.'

Shortly afterwards, they drew up in the yard of the George, situated right in the middle of the small market town, where the first person they saw was Timothy. Leaving Henry to see to the horses, Matthew strode into the inn, breathing easily—it seemed—for the first time that day.

'William Brooke at your service, sir—landlord of this fine hostelry. How may I be of assistance?'

'Good evening, Brooke. I understand Lady Ashby is a guest here tonight? I wish to see her.'

The innkeeper lowered his gaze. 'Lady Ashby, sir? I'm sure I couldn't say. Might I ask who is enquiring?'

Matthew resisted the urge to grab the fool by his neck. Drawing himself up to his full height, he looked down his nose at Brooke. 'My good man,' he announced haughtily, 'I am *Lord* Ashby. Now, please be so good as to conduct me to my wife.'

The innkeeper bowed low, almost wringing his hands in his obsequiousness. 'My humblest apologies, my lord, I wasn't expecting you. Your lady is in the private parlour, if you would please follow me?'

Matthew followed Brooke along a passageway to the rear of the inn. The innkeeper paused outside a closed door and Matthew stayed him before he could announce Matthew's presence.

'Thank you, Brooke, that will be all. If you could see that we are not disturbed, I should be grateful.'

'Very good, my lord.' Brooke backed away, bowing as he retreated.

The fear that had plagued Matthew since before dawn that morning receded only to be replaced by a rush of anger, stoked by Brooke's meek acceptance of his identity.

I could be anybody.

He hauled the door open and stepped inside the room.

There, sitting at her ease on a comfortable sofa, glass of wine in hand, was the object of all his fretting and fears throughout the long day. Relief exploded through him and all his pent-up emotions surged to the fore as he slammed the door shut and crossed the room in three swift strides.

Chapter Nine

Eleanor's eyes flew open, fear seizing her throat as the door crashed shut, startling her from her drowsy thoughts. She barely had time to register his identity before Matthew Thomas was looming over her, taking her glass from her hand and hauling her to her feet. Before she could utter a word, she found herself clasped in a pair of strong arms, her head pressed hard against a broad chest, the sound of his heart thundering in her ear.

'Thank God you are safe.'

As soon as his hold relaxed, she pushed her hands between them, against his chest, leaning back to look into his face.

'Mr Thomas…whatever is wrong? Why are you here?'

He met her gaze with eyes that swirled with anger and fear. What had happened? Why was he so anxious? How had he found her? She gradually became aware of their surroundings. They were entirely alone, in the private parlour she had reserved for use by herself and Aunt Lucy, who was resting in her room. How did he get in? Where was Brooke?

Matthew held her gaze, his ragged breathing loud in the silence of the room. She pushed harder against him and stepped back. Instantly, his gaze sharpened and he gripped her shoulders, preventing her from retreating further, wringing a gasp from her.

'I have been searching for you…following you…trying to catch up with you…*worrying* about you…'

'But…why? I thought you were—'

'You need protection. I—'

'Protection?'

Eleanor, now with her wits fully about her, stiffened. This was about Aunt Lucy's ludicrous idea that the fire and the shooting were somehow connected. For one fleeting, joyful second she had thought maybe he had followed her for her own sake—because he felt something for her. As speedily as the thought arose, she quashed it, inwardly berating herself for being a romantic fool, beguiled by a handsome face and rugged charm. She and Mr Thomas were worlds apart.

'It seems to me the only protection I am in need of is from you.'

Her heart quailed as his eyes flared and he stepped closer. The heat emanating from him surrounded her as his breath fanned her hair, but she was determined not to reveal her rising alarm and stood her ground, glaring up at him as his eyes pierced hers.

'A young girl was attacked—' He stopped abruptly, his voice cracking with emotion, his expression haunted.

'What…? Attacked? But…what has that to do with me?'

'I've been frantic. If anything had happened to you, I—'

'Mr Thomas! You're making no sense. You said someone had been attacked?'

Matthew swiped one hand through his disordered locks and took a hasty turn about the room, returning to stand in front of an increasingly concerned Eleanor.

He hauled in a deep breath, then let it out slowly. 'She was asleep in the room that had been reserved for you. At the inn in Stockport. Luckily, she screamed and fought him off for long enough for help to arrive. Her attacker ran away, but she ended up with several knife wounds.'

'Oh, the poor, poor thing.' Eleanor's stomach churned as the full significance of Matthew's words finally sank in. 'But…you said…in my room? That poor girl was attacked in the bed I would have slept in?'

Her hand rose to her mouth and she felt herself sway. Matthew was by her side instantly, arms around her as she leant gratefully into his solid strength. He helped her to the sofa and sat by her side, holding her hand, rubbing his thumb gently across her knuckles.

'I'm sorry,' she said faintly. 'I am not normally...that is, it was such a shock.'

She raised her gaze to his, only to find his face much closer than she had anticipated.

'For me, too,' he murmured, his blue eyes darkening. 'I can't bear to think...' His voice tailed away as he cradled her cheek and slowly lowered his head.

Eleanor stilled as warm breath feathered her skin. Lips—surprisingly soft and tender—brushed hers...once, twice...then settled, moving enticingly. She leaned into him, feeling his hand in her hair. Pleasure and anticipation spiralled through her as her lips relaxed and she pressed closer. As his tongue probed her mouth, she raised her restless hand to caress his cheek, but her action seemed to return him to his senses. He wrenched his lips from hers and jumped up from the sofa.

'I'm sorry.' Harsh lines bracketed his mouth.

Eleanor tried to gather her wits, to understand what had just happened.

'I shouldn't have done that...I had no intention... It was a mistake,' he said, and then muttered, as if to himself, 'I do not need complications.'

'Complications?'

The word jarred, rousing Eleanor from her dreamlike stupor.

He looked distant and reserved and didn't quite meet her eyes as he said, 'Please forget that ever happened.'

'You regret kissing me?'

Humiliation flooded Eleanor. She had allowed a virtual stranger to kiss her, and had kissed him back, without a murmur of protest. She was her mother's daughter all right. *Blood will out.* Aunt Phyllis's voice—accusatory, censorious—echoed in her head.

'Yes. No!' He turned abruptly from her, raking his hand through his hair once more before facing her again. His eyes met hers, and softened. 'No, I cannot regret it. But I forgot myself. I was frantic with worry, but that is no excuse for my behaviour. You are a lady and I like to suppose myself a gentleman, despite my station in life, yet at the first opportunity I have behaved like the lowest of rogues.'

Complications. The word rankled. He obviously regretted his impulsive embrace. For that is what it had been—an impulse. He had found her alone and taken advantage, stealing a kiss simply because he could. Now, he was shouldering the blame in order to make her feel better and to excuse her shameful conduct in returning his embrace. Furious with herself, Eleanor turned and would have left the room without a further word had Aunt Lucy not chosen that very moment to come in, her bright gaze darting from one to the other before lingering for some time on Eleanor's hot cheeks, triggering another surge of shame.

'Why, Mr Thomas,' Aunt Lucy said at length, her voice icy, 'how very nice to see you again so soon. I had understood you to be heading in a quite different direction from ourselves. Had I been informed of your presence, I should have made sure I came down to greet you immediately. I am, after all, Eleanor's chaperon. I can see I shall have to keep a wary eye on you, sir—it is so very easy for a woman to lose her reputation, as I am sure you are aware.'

Eleanor cringed inside. Not only did Mr Thomas now have a complete disgust of her wanton response to his advances, but Aunt Lucy's suspicions had also been aroused. She could wonder at neither of them, for she had no less disgust for herself. Gathering her pride, she walked to the door and opened it, standing to one side.

'Mr Thomas is just leaving, Aunt Lucy. He has said all he needs to say.'

She raised her chin, boldly meeting his gaze. He might have crushed her feelings, but she would rather die than reveal her humiliation.

'Oh, no, I'm not,' Matthew retorted, holding her gaze for what seemed an eternity before switching his attention to Aunt Lucy. 'I have brought grave news, Lady Rothley, news that has serious implications for the safety of your niece.'

Eleanor clamped her teeth shut on the remark she longed to fling at his head. How had the mere touch of his lips managed to block the news of the attack from her mind?

'What news do you bring? What implications?' Aunt Lucy sank on to the sofa and beckoned Eleanor to sit by her side. 'Please, Mr Thomas, be seated—' she waved her hand at the chair opposite '—and explain yourself.'

'Last night, a young woman was attacked in the White Lion in Stockport,' he said. 'She was attacked by an intruder wielding a knife as she slept in one of the bedchambers reserved for your party. I occupied the other.'

Aunt Lucy gasped, turning stricken eyes to Eleanor, who took her hand, her fear giving way to annoyance at Matthew's brutal telling of the story.

'It does not mean,' she said, 'that the attack was intended for me. Surely...' she faltered as Matthew focused his hard gaze on her once more '...surely, it must be a—'

'Coincidence?' Matthew interrupted roughly. 'One coincidence I can believe, but two? So close together? It would now seem beyond doubt there is a pattern. There have been three attempts on your life in the past few weeks. It is time to take this threat seriously. Tell me, can you think of anyone who would wish you ill?'

'Why, no, of course not. I've barely left Ashby Manor in the past seven years.'

The very idea was absurd.

'Forgive me, but…your husband? Could he wish you harm?'

'Husb— But I'm not married, Mr Thomas. Why would you believe that I am?'

'Not married? But, how…? You're a baroness. You must be wed, or…perhaps you're a widow?'

Aunt Lucy put him straight. 'My niece is a peeress in her own right. Unusual, to be sure, but not unheard of.'

Eleanor watched as Matthew digested this information. He looked, at best, not pleased. The implication of his belief she was married dealt a further blow to her already fragile self-esteem.

Was that why he kissed me, because I was a safe target? A married woman who might enjoy a flirtation in her husband's absence? And how much more disgust must he feel now, knowing I'm single and yet returned his kiss?

'Hmm, that puts a very different complexion on it.'

'What possible difference does my being unmarried make?' Shame made her sharp with him.

'It makes every difference. There are many reasons to kill or harm another. Were you married, the reasons someone might wish to kill you might be hatred, or possibly jealousy or passion.

But now, with greed as part of the equation, it begins to make more sense. May I ask—who is your heir?'

'My cousin, James Weare.'

'Then he must be our prime suspect.'

'James? Never!'

'Greed has driven more than one to kill, my lady. The lure of a peerage, and the power and privilege it bestows, is more than enough, quite apart from any wealth that accompanies it.'

Eleanor was silent, weighing Matthew's words against her knowledge of her cousin and his character. The fear that had plagued her at odd moments over the past few weeks returned to gnaw at her insides and she shuddered, thinking of that poor girl who had been hurt.

That could have been me. But...no! Not James. He couldn't...not the James I know. It's just too horrible. This is nonsense. It must be nonsense.

Eleanor looked at Aunt Lucy and Matthew, both wearing the same troubled expression, and bitter resentment bubbled up inside. How dare he come here and scare her like this, accusing her much-loved cousin of trying to kill her?

She sprang from the sofa to pace the room. 'No, I will not believe it. James and I grew up together at Ashby—we were like brother and sister. It makes no sense. If he had wanted to kill me he could have done so with ease many times. I am convinced the fire and the accident were unrelated.' She rounded on Matthew. 'I will thank you, sir, to keep such wild accusations to yourself.'

Chapter Ten

Eleanor's agitated pacing prompted Matthew to abandon the topic of her cousin's likely guilt rather than antagonise her further.

The news she was unmarried was an unwelcome shock. He was not the kind of man to dally with innocents—although, eyeing her determined stance as the baroness challenged him, innocent hardly seemed an apt description. But also, to his surprise—and equally unwelcome—was a spurt of pleasure that she was unattached. All nonsense, of course. What on earth could he, a lowly merchant without even the backing of his family name, offer a wealthy baroness? His plans for the future were set. He would work hard to build up a successful business and then he would take the greatest satisfaction in repaying his father every last shilling of his debts. He would prove that the son so easily disowned had made a success of his life without his family's backing.

That kiss, though... He clamped down his desire to taste Eleanor's sweet lips again. *Concentrate on the matter in hand, man...surely it's serious enough to warrant your full attention without being waylaid by such thoughts.*

'You are in danger, my lady,' he said. 'That is a fact and, regardless of who might wish you ill, you must take all possible measures to ensure your safety until the culprit is found.'

'Mr Thomas is right.' Lady Rothley went to Eleanor, taking her hands. 'Oh! It doesn't bear thinking about. That could have been *you* attacked in your bed. You could have been murdered.' Her voice quavered. '*Please*, Ellie, do not be stubborn. Surely you must see these happenings cannot all be coincidence? What do you suggest we do, Mr Thomas? Should we return to Ashby? Will that be safer than London?'

'It might be the wisest move.'

Eleanor directed a scathing look at Matthew. 'I'm sorry you are so troubled, Aunt, but I have no intention of returning to Ashby. Besides, Batley, if you remember, was concerned that the house cannot be made secure during the renovations, so we would be no safer there.'

'Who is Batley?'

Eleanor scorched Matthew with an impatient glance. 'He is my bailiff. No, we will not return to the Manor. We shall continue our journey to

London. And that,' she added, jabbing her finger in Matthew's direction, 'is not up for negotiation.'

Matthew bit back his instinctive retort. There was no point in quarrelling with Eleanor in the mood she was in. Never had he come across such an opinionated female.

'I can see you are determined to have your way, Eleanor,' Lady Rothley said, 'so I shall not try to dissuade you. But I give you warning— unless you treat this seriously, we shall return to Ashby, whether you like it or not.' At Eleanor's mutinous look, she continued, 'If I leave London, you will have no option other than to accompany me. You could not remain there unchaperoned. Think of the *scandal*.'

Eleanor visibly subsided. Her aunt's emphasis on the word 'scandal' must have some particular meaning for her. Matthew wondered if she had been embroiled in some sort of scandal in the past. Was that why she was still unmarried?

Lady Rothley returned to the sofa. 'What precautions would *you* advise us to take, Mr Thomas?'

'The servants accompanying you must be put on the alert immediately, as must the whole of your household in town as soon as you arrive,' Matthew said. 'I will escort you for the remainder of your journey and your niece must take care never to go out unaccompanied. And by that—

forgive me, Lady Rothley—I mean that she must take someone other than yourself for protection.'

He watched the conflicting emotions chase each other across Eleanor's expressive countenance. He knew she was still mortified by their kiss, but that could not be the only reason she was so determined to hide her fears over the murder. Was it her reluctance to accept her cousin's involvement?

'There is no need for you to inconvenience yourself, Mr Thomas. I am certain you are reading far more into this than you need to. I am grateful for your concern, but I have no desire to cause further delays for you. You should forget all about this little matter and continue with your—'

'Little matter?' Matthew exploded to his feet, itching to take hold of Eleanor and give her a good shake. Infuriating woman! 'Have you not taken in a word I've said? You have more need of protection than I supposed, if that is your belief. I will *not* allow you to continue to put yourself in jeopardy—I must and I will escort you tomorrow. What if your cousin should try again?'

Eleanor stared at him incredulously.

'Ellie.' There was a wealth of warning in Lady Rothley's voice. 'Please remember your—'

'Will...not...allow? How dare you? You have absolutely no jurisdiction over me, sir. I have known you precisely one day. I have known James *all my life*. I will *never* believe him to be

capable of something like this.' She drew herself up to her full height, standing almost nose to nose with him. 'I know him. You don't.'

She held his gaze, her large eyes defiant. If he continued to pursue the matter, might she stubbornly show her defiance by taking needless risks? Short of throwing her over his shoulder and carrying her off to safety—which, he thought with a silent oath, he would be more than happy to do at this moment—he was not sure how else to persuade her.

But…there was one angle they had not yet considered. 'Who else knew the details of your journey? Maybe that will help us to identify the culprit.'

Eleanor stilled, staring at him, her eyes stricken, her rebelliousness dissipating as swiftly as it had arisen. 'James.' Her voice caught and the word came out as a croak. She cleared her throat. 'James knew.'

She slumped on to the sofa, next to her aunt, who clasped her hand.

'He wrote and reserved the rooms for us in order that we would not be stranded for the night.' She looked at her aunt, her tawny eyes huge in her suddenly ashen countenance. 'I still cannot believe it. Not James. Oh, Aunt Lucy. How shall I ever face him?'

'There, there,' Aunt Lucy patted Eleanor's hand, raising worried eyes to Matthew. 'It seems we are indebted to you once again, Mr Thomas. Your offer to escort us tomorrow is gratefully accepted. Although,' she added acerbically, 'do not for a moment imagine that I have forgotten your earlier behaviour, for I have not.'

Matthew merely bowed his head. He could not deny he was at fault there and could think of nothing to say that would not make an awkward situation even worse. When he raised his head, he found Aunt Lucy eyeing him with suspicion.

'I am curious,' she said. 'How did you find us? And how did you come to be in here, alone, with Eleanor? I am certain Brooke would not have conducted you to our private parlour and left you here with Eleanor without so much as a maidservant in attendance.'

Matthew cursed silently as the enormity of the lie he had told Brooke hit him. The innkeeper was certain to let slip his belief that his guest was a distinguished lord and married to Eleanor to boot.

'I was late leaving Stockport because I had to speak to the magistrate before I could leave—'

'Why should the magistrate wish to speak with *you*?' Eleanor asked.

'I told you—I was in the next bedchamber to the girl who was attacked. When she screamed, I went in. I saw him…but he gave me the slip.'

'Then you know what he looks like. Describe him. I shall soon know if it was James.'

'He wore a mask. All I know is that he was

shorter than me and of a medium build. There are any number of men who would match that description. By the time I left I was sure you would be well on your way. We—that is, Henry and I—enquired at all the posting inns we passed until we found where you had stopped for the night. Mr Brooke was indeed reluctant to admit you were in residence. I'm afraid I had to resort to a little subterfuge.'

Two pairs of eyes watched him expectantly. He drew a deep breath, bracing himself.

'I told him I was Lord Ashby. Your husband.'

There was a moment of stunned silence, then Eleanor let forth a peal of laughter that made Matthew stare in bewilderment. *What on earth...?* She should be furious...ringing a peal of anger, not laughter, over his head.

'What is so funny?' He sounded so stiff and pompous he almost cringed.

Eleanor gasped for breath, hand flat to her chest, as giggles continued to spill from her lips. Was that a note of hysteria? Matthew glanced at Aunt Lucy, who looked as stunned as he felt.

'Oh... I am so sorry...the look of dread on your face...if only you could have seen it...'

'I shall, of course, ensure that you do not suffer by my hasty and ill-considered actions, Lady Ashby—'

Eleanor sobered at his words. 'Oh, no,' she said. 'Please do not. Really, Mr Thomas, I had begun to think you a man of sense, then you come up with *the* most ridiculous ruse to confound poor Brooke, and then find yourself forced to make amends by making an offer you clearly have no wish to make. Oh, this is just the spur I needed to jolt me out of that horrid fear that was near paralysing me. No doubt it will soon overwhelm me again but, for now, I am happy just to enjoy the joke.'

'Joke?' Indignation stirred. 'You believe an offer from me would be a *joke*?'

She rose to her feet. 'Not in the way you are clearly taking it,' she said, in a placatory tone. 'I promise. I only meant it is a joke in as much as we barely know each other, our stations in life are so different and we have done little but squabble since we met.'

A sudden flush stained her cheeks and she turned from him abruptly. Was she, like him, remembering that kiss? But, other than that omission from her list, she was right.

'Well! My niece might think this a laughing matter, but I can assure you I do not, young man,' Lady Rothley said, as she also stood. 'What were you thinking? Brooke and, most likely, all his staff, believe you to be Lord Ashby and are aware that you have spent time alone in this parlour with my niece. You cannot sustain this masquerade—our servants will surely let slip that there *is* no Lord Ashby. And as soon as your trickery is known, Eleanor's reputation will be in tatters. What a tangle.'

She was right. He had acted without thought, driven by his frantic belief that Eleanor was in danger. Now he had succeeded in embroiling her in a possible scandal. That thought brought to mind Eleanor's reaction to Aunt Lucy's earlier threat of scandal. An odd reaction, almost as though she feared for her reputation more than most. And yet she could laugh at this situation. She was certainly a puzzling woman.

'You can say you were with me the whole time, Aunt Lucy,' Eleanor said. 'And Mr Thomas must find another inn to stay in tonight.' She met his gaze. She was deadly serious now, no hint of amusement on her countenance. 'It will not do for you to remain, for you cannot continue the deception of being my husband. Brooke will say nothing. After all, he cannot claim to be blameless. He failed to even announce you, which is inexcusable. After all, you could have been anybody.'

'Precisely,' Matthew growled. 'And if you believe I'm going to leave you unprotected in this place tonight, you are way off course. In fact, I believe it is too dangerous for *you* to remain the night. Knowing he failed last night, I would not put it past the attacker to strike again. And as he's clearly familiar with your itinerary, he will know you are here tonight.'

His words brought a flash of fear to Eleanor's

expression. It was regrettable, he thought, as he pictured her laughing only a few moments ago, but it was surely better for her to be frightened than to dismiss the very real risks.

'When Brooke allowed me to enter your private parlour, simply on my word that I was your husband, he confirmed my belief that you are completely vulnerable. We must all leave.' He paused, pondering. He had caused this problem. He must find the solution.

'Wait here a minute,' he said. 'I have an idea.'

He went in search of Brooke. 'Please attend us in the parlour as soon as convenient, Brooke,' he said. 'I should like to discuss the security of your establishment and the safety of your guests.'

'Yes, my lord. Immediately, my lord.' Brooke followed Matthew back to the parlour.

As Matthew entered, Eleanor said, 'What do you…?' Her question tailed away as Matthew shook his head, hoping she would interpret his warning and follow his lead. He winked, then rounded on Brooke.

'To begin with, I must tell you that I am *not* Lord Ashby. My name is Matthew Thomas.'

'Not…? But, sir, you gave me to believe…I allowed you…'

'Quite. You believed my claim and you showed me into what was *supposed* to be a private parlour for the use of these ladies. I must inform you—and this is not to be spoken of outside this room—that we already had grave concerns over Lady Ashby's safety.

'Now then, I told that lie in order to see how easy it might be for an intruder to gain access to Lady Ashby whilst she is staying here. I not only tricked you into revealing her whereabouts, but also persuaded you—with little difficulty, I might add—to allow me to enter her private parlour unannounced.

'I must inform you, Brooke, that you have failed my test miserably. Had I harboured evil intentions towards Lady Ashby, there would have been nothing to prevent me carrying out my worst. I am extremely disappointed.

'Lady Rothley happened to be with her niece at the time, but you were not to know that. Anything could have happened and, as a result of your failures, I am afraid we have no alternative but to move to another establishment for the night.'

'No, I beg of you, sir, ladies, please do not leave. A thousand apologies, milady—' Brooke bowed to Eleanor, wringing his hands in his anguish '—for my failures. I can promise you it will not happen again. I shall place guards on each door. You are our only guests tonight and I swear to turn any latecomers away. I shall have a man patrolling all night long. The George will be more secure than the Tower itself, of that you have my word.

'Do please reconsider. My wife has prepared a

feast for tonight—it is ready to be served, and it is dark outside and beginning to rain. Surely you would prefer to stay here in the warm than go out in search of other accommodation?

'Besides,' he added, 'if there is someone out there who means you harm, he could attack you more easily outside than if you remain safe and snug in here, especially now I am aware of the danger.'

He looked eagerly from one to the other.

Matthew heaved a sigh, concealing his relief that Brooke had fallen for his ploy. 'Well, if you promise you will put guards on the outer doors— and for the whole night, mind, not just until we retire—we will stay. Although, make no mistake, my man, you are still on trial. If I discover any lapse in attention, it will be the worse for you.'

'Yes, my…sir.' Brooke bowed his way out of the door.

Matthew looked at Eleanor and Lady Rothley. 'Well? Have we come through unscathed?'

Chapter Eleven

'I believe so. Well done,' Eleanor said and smiled at Matthew. 'The poor man didn't know if he was coming or going. I don't think it even crossed his mind to question that Aunt Lucy was in here the whole time.'

Aunt Lucy was not so quick to forgive. 'Let us hope this doesn't get back to Lizzie and Matilda,' she warned, 'for I doubt they will be so easy to deceive.'

Dinner was served at a table set for three in the private parlour. Brooke had not lied when he promised them a feast and they were served with dishes of succulent roast meats, pigeon pie, vegetables and rich sauces, followed by stewed apples, blancmanges, dried fruits and nuts, all accompanied by some very palatable wines.

Conversation at the dinner table was necessarily stilted, with the serving maid and Brooke himself in and out of the room. As the last dishes were cleared away, Eleanor heard Brooke murmur in Matthew's ear, 'Brandy, sir?'

They had eaten in the parlour, so it was impossible for Eleanor and her aunt to leave Matthew to his brandy, as was customary. As he pushed his chair back and stood, presumably to go through to the taproom, Eleanor said, 'If you would care for some brandy, Mr Thomas, please do not feel obliged to leave.'

'No, indeed,' Aunt Lucy said. 'In fact… Brooke, my good man, would you bring two glasses, please? A little tot will help me sleep, I make no doubt. My niece and I shall retire very soon, Mr Thomas, and leave you to enjoy your brandy in peace.'

'Thank you.' Matthew said. 'I doubt I shall be long in following you to bed. It's been a long, eventful day.'

Brooke soon returned with a full decanter and two glasses. After drinking her tot, Aunt Lucy rose to her feet. 'Come, Ellie, it is time for us to retire. Mr Thomas, may we leave you with the task of checking Brooke's security arrangements? We shall see you in the morning. Goodnight.'

'My pleasure,' Matthew said. 'Goodnight, ladies.'

As soon as the door closed behind them, Aunt Lucy said, 'I wonder who our Mr Thomas really is?'

Eleanor paused, her foot on the bottom stair. 'What do you mean: who he really is?'

Aunt Lucy looked back at the parlour door. 'I'm not sure,' she said. 'But there is something… oh, I don't know…something almost *familiar* about him. And, just as I think I'm on the brink of grasping it, it slips away again. Never mind. I am sure it will come to me in time.'

They continued up the stairs to the first landing and Eleanor wished her aunt goodnight at her bedchamber door. Lizzie helped her to undress before leaving and Eleanor climbed into bed, exhausted, ready for a good night's sleep. As soon as her head hit the pillow, however, her mind sprang to life, reliving the fire and the accident, fretting at the attack on that young girl— could it truly be connected to her? Was James responsible? No, she could never believe it of him. Not attempted murder. But the very thought that someone might wish to kill her was too much to bear and she tossed and turned until finally, still wide awake, she decided to go downstairs to see if she could sneak a tot of brandy for herself. If it helped Aunt Lucy to sleep, mayhap it would do the same for her?

Relighting her candle, she found her slippers and wrapped her large woollen shawl around her. Taking up the candlestick, she stepped softly on to the dark landing and crept to the head of the stairs. Stomach churning uneasily, despite

Brooke's promise to post two guards at every external door, she tiptoed down the stairs to the parlour. Surely everyone must have retired by now? She could hear nothing but the distant rumble of snores—a comforting sound, confirming there were people within reach should she need them.

She hesitated a moment at the parlour door, listening, before lifting the latch and pushing the door open.

Her heart leapt into her throat.

Matthew stood before the fire, one booted foot on the fender. He had removed his jacket, leaving him clad in shirt, waistcoat and pantaloons, which clung to his buttocks and muscular thighs. His left hand was propped against the mantelshelf as he stared down into the glowing embers and his right cradled a goblet of amber liquid. Eleanor had not thought for one minute he would still be up, for had he not said he would be retiring soon after them? Thank goodness he had not heard the door open. Her fingers tightened, clutching her shawl closer around her. She must leave. Now. She would be foolish to remain.

Still she hesitated. Something about the way he was standing and staring into the fire tugged at her heartstrings. He looked a little...lost, somehow, and the urge to offer comfort was strong. The memory of his kiss set her lips tingling, despite her confusion over his subsequent reaction when he had said he did not want complications. Eleanor bit her lip, considering.

No. She must go. They had tempted fate once already today. She must not do so again. She stepped back but, before she could close the door, something—a slight noise perhaps, or just the movement—betrayed her. Matthew looked up. She caught a glimpse of loneliness and sorrow before his mask slipped back into place.

She swallowed hard, her nerves in shreds. Why, oh, why, had she lingered? Why did she not retreat the *second* she saw him? It was too late now. She stepped inside the room and closed the door.

'I am sorry to disturb you, Mr Thomas,' she whispered. 'I was unable to sleep and I thought to come down for some brandy, in the hope it might help.'

His voice was low, but she could hear the steel behind his words. 'And so you decided to wander around the inn at the dead of night? Even after everything that's happened?'

'I was careful! Besides, I knew you had inspected the doors and windows, so nobody can get in.'

His jaw firmed. 'You place far too much faith in my abilities.' He lifted his glass to his lips and tipped his head back.

'Why should I not?' Eleanor said. 'I trust you.' She hesitated. What had she said? That sounded... Matthew was appraising her, brows raised, a knowing smile lurking at the corners of his mouth.

'I mean,' she added quickly, 'I trust your *capabilities*.'

'Oh, no,' he said, 'don't spoil it now. I could get very used to basking in your approval.'

Eleanor felt the blood suffuse her face, her insides squirming at his teasing smile. 'I must go. I bid you goodnight.' She turned to the door.

'Don't go.'

She paused, her hand already on the latch.

Are you going to flee every time a man shows a smidgeon of interest in you? Irritably, she tried to shrug away that insidious voice in her head.

'Stay a moment, please. I'd welcome the company.' There was a hint of a plea in those words.

Her awkwardness receded. He *had* looked desolate. Mayhap she could help. She had come downstairs for brandy... She would not scuttle away as though she had done something wrong. There could be no harm in staying for a minute or two, as long as they weren't seen.

She slowly faced him, then gestured to the decanter that remained where Brooke had left it on the sideboard. 'Would you pour me some brandy, please?'

She crossed the room, hugging her shawl even more tightly around her, as he poured out a mea-

sure of the spirit. Her doubts reared up again...
why did I not go when I had the chance?

Because you want to know, the treacherous
voice in her head whispered. *You want to know
how it feels when a man desires you.*

Matthew's blue gaze captured hers as he
handed her the goblet, their fingers brushing.
Eleanor all but snatched the glass from his hand.

'Thank you,' she said, moving swiftly to stand
next to the fireplace.

'You are *most* welcome, my lady.'

His deep voice resonated, sending a quiver
of excitement darting through her core. *Oh, my.*
Warning bells rang loud and clear but she chose
to ignore them. Yes, it was scandalous to be here,
alone, with Matthew, but she was in control.
Nothing would happen. Mayhap she could view
this as practice—to help her conquer the hideous
embarrassment that had plagued her during her
come-out. If she could learn to converse unself-
consciously with the attractive, but undoubtedly
unsuitable, Matthew Thomas, might that not
stand her in good stead in London, where there
would be attractive, *suitable* gentlemen to talk to
and dance with?

Eleanor fixed her gaze on the goblet cupped in
her hands. She swirled the glowing liquid round
the bowl, warming it before lifting it to her lips.
She sipped, then coughed at its fiery strength.
She was aware, without looking, that Matthew

had resumed his stance on the opposite side of the hearth, setting the decanter on the mantelshelf.

Feeling emboldened, she said, 'You know a great deal about me, but I know next to nothing of you. Other than you have a good eye for horseflesh.'

He stared into the dying fire. 'There is nothing much to know and the details are unlikely to interest you.'

'Nevertheless…' She allowed the silence to hang between them. While she waited, she drank again, relishing the warmth as the brandy slid down her throat.

'Since the age of eighteen I have lived and worked overseas. I am a merchant—my world is far removed from the world you inhabit.'

Eleanor raised her brows. He had been more forthcoming in that one sentence than he had since they first met. 'Where did you live?'

'India. I only returned to England a few weeks ago.'

'Do you miss it? Will you go back there?'

He frowned, still gazing into the embers. 'I miss some aspects of it and I may return in the future, who knows? But not to live. England is my home from now on.'

'Why did you go out there in the first place?'

He shrugged. 'I needed to make a living. My great-uncle was an East India merchant, and I went to work with him. When he died, I decided to come home.'

'What about work? How will you make your living now?'

He laughed, softly. 'You ask a lot of questions, my lady,' he said. 'More brandy?' He proffered the decanter and waited, brows raised.

'Thank you.' Eleanor held her glass out and he poured her another measure of the amber spirit. 'It is very nice. I can understand why Aunt Lucy thought it would help her sleep.'

Matthew watched her sip again at the brandy, eyes crinkling. 'Is this the first time you've tasted brandy?'

'Oh, yes. Now, what was it I said?'

'You asked how I will make my living now I am back in England. I warn you, this is the last question and then it is your turn to be interrogated. I shall make my living the same way I always have—in trade. We import tea, rugs, cloth, porcelain, anything really, from India and, sometimes, China. If there's a market for it, we import it.'

'We?'

'My business partner, Benedict Poole, and I. He is, as we speak, sailing back to England with two more cargoes.

'And that is more than enough about me... You told me you have you not been to London for seven years. Was that your come-out? Why have you never been back?'

The swift change of subject had Eleanor replying before she could consider her words. 'It was my come-out, yes, but I *hated* it.'

'*Hated?* That is a strong reaction to something that is meant to be pleasurable.'

'What do *you* know about come-outs and Seasons?'

'Oh, I hear talk,' he replied. 'I thought it was compulsory for *every* young lady to *adore* their come-out.'

She couldn't help giggling. 'Not me. I was shy and, looking back, too immature.'

'That doesn't explain why you have not been back since. You are far from shy now.'

Heat rose to burn her cheeks as their kiss loomed large in her thoughts. Matthew's suddenly intense expression suggested he, too, was thinking of it. She gulped her remaining drink, then held out her glass for more, ignoring Matthew's raised brows as he poured a little...a *very* little...brandy into her goblet.

As she opened her mouth to ask for more, Matthew said, 'Why are you so wary of scandal?'

The breath whooshed from Eleanor's lungs. 'What...what do you mean? I am not—'

'Uh-uh.' Matthew shook his head at her, eyes brimming with amusement. 'I answered all your questions...no avoiding the awkward ones.'

'Yes, but—'

'Your aunt gave me the clue. You were full of indignation and she stopped you with that one phrase—"Think of the *scandal*."'

Eleanor forced a light laugh even as she registered—somewhere deep down—that her mind was a touch fuddled. She concentrated fiercely on her words. 'You show me anyone who relishes their own scandal, Mr Thomas. It seems quite reasonable to me that I should not wish to be tainted.'

'Entirely reasonable, yes. But her words and your reaction suggest something more than the normal desire to avoid scandal. As if, maybe, there is something in your past? Come now, how bad can it be? A few stolen kisses?'

Eleanor stiffened. She could hardly blame him for believing such a possibility.

His lips twitched. 'I promise I will not hold your scandal against you.'

'It is not *my* scandal. It was my mother's. And I do not wish to talk about it.' She put her glass on the mantelshelf. 'I am going to bed.'

Matthew caught her hand. 'No, don't go. I didn't mean to offend your sensibilities.' He smiled, ruefully. 'I fear I am out of practice in how to treat a lady. I promise to pry no further.'

His touch sent a tremor racing through her and she snatched her hand from his. For some reason, his assumption that she needed protection from the truth—that her female sensibilities somehow precluded her from facing up to the harsh realities of life—irritated her. She was an independent woman. She flattered herself she was strong. She was capable of facing up to reality. She did not need a man's protection from that.

'My mother left my father and me when I was eleven,' she said. 'She lived openly in London with another man. *That* was the scandal. I never saw her after she left and she died in childbirth a few years later. You asked why I hated my come-out and *that* was why—the whispers, everywhere I went. The eyes that followed my every move. The *gentlemen* who seemed to believe "like mother, like daughter".' The memory of that horrible time choked her voice. She paused; shook her head; huffed a short, bitter laugh. '*This* time I vow I shall be the perfect lady. My behaviour will be beyond reproach and I *will* have vouchers for Almack's. You *see* if I don't.'

She stared belligerently at Matthew.

'I have no doubt you will be a complete success,' he said, soothingly, as he grasped her arm and turned her towards the door. 'Now, however, it is time you went to bed. Come.'

He guided her to the door, his hand at the small of her back. Warm. Comforting. His scent was in her nostrils—musky, male, a hint of citrus. She spun to face him and had to steady herself with a hand on his chest.

'Whoops. That brandy was stronger than I

thought.' *And it's loosened your tongue, Eleanor. Take care.* She focused her gaze on Matthew's neckcloth.

Matthew removed her hand from his chest and reached for the door latch.

'Thank you,' she said. 'I must be quiet, mustn't I? Can you imagine what Aunt Lucy would say were she to see us here like this? She would, quite rightly, wash her hands of me.'

She lifted her gaze to his face as she spoke. Swayed towards him. His eyes caressed her, warming her as the brandy had done. He lifted one hand, trailing a long finger down her cheek, before tracing the outline of her lips, which parted as she drew in a shaky breath. She closed her eyes, revelling in the swirl of need burgeoning inside her.

'You are very beautiful, Eleanor,' he murmured. 'So hard to resist.'

Her soul blossomed at his words. She was standing so close she could feel his coat brush the tips of her breasts. Her nipples tingled and tightened and her bones felt like they were melting.

Matthew brushed her lips—hardly even touching them—with his own. 'Goodnight.'

Her hands lifted of their own volition and clutched his lapels. She rose on tiptoe. Her kiss was no fleeting flirtation of the lips, but a warm, moist pressure as she angled her mouth to his. Matthew responded with a groan, his arms enfolding her, pulling her against the full length of his hard body. One splayed hand supported her back and the other cradled her head as he returned the pressure of her lips and increased the intensity of the kiss. Warm, brandy-flavoured lips parted and she opened in response. He captured her breath as his tongue caressed and explored. She followed his lead, surrendering to a deeper, darker, more wanton kiss than she had ever imagined possible. She never wanted that kiss to end.

She threaded her fingers through his hair as he gathered her closer, his hand tracing the curve of her spine to her bottom. She lost track of time. The only reality was in their kiss—a wicked, glorious promise of greater delights to come. She clung ever closer, her hands exploring the width of his shoulders and the long line of his back until she reached his taut buttocks, so very different to the soft roundness of her own.

He gasped into her mouth and, with another groan, tore his lips from hers, taking her by the shoulders and holding her away from him, steadying her as her knees threatened to buckle. Bemused, she studied his features, reading his regret and his resolve.

'I think,' he said, his voice husky with desire, 'you should go. This is not wise. It can never be.'

His words brought her back to reality. Heavens! What was she doing? She searched his eyes, deep blue, swirling with so many complex emotions.

'I should not have stayed,' she whispered. 'It was reckless. You are right. This can never be. We should not be alone together.'

He gave a shaky laugh. 'No, we should not and, as you said, heaven help us if your aunt should discover us. Go on, now. Go. We will forget this ever happened.' His deep tones resonated through her. 'I'll see you in the morning.'

Eleanor returned to her bedchamber as if in a dream, her emotions in turmoil. Thoughts and memories tumbled through her mind. What had she done? Dismay at her disgraceful behaviour clashed with desire; regret with joy; mortification with a guilty longing for more. Confused, she slipped into her dreams.

Chapter Twelve

The following morning Eleanor breakfasted in her bedchamber.

'She has the headache,' Lady Rothley announced when she joined Matthew at the breakfast table. 'I'm sure it is not to be wondered at, with all these goings-on.'

No, indeed it is not, Matthew thought, with a wry inner smile.

'I am sorry to hear that,' he said. 'I hope she will feel well enough to travel today.'

'Oh, I am sure she will bounce back. My niece is a strong woman. She will not allow a headache to overset her, or her plans.'

That I can well believe.

'I will send a message to the stables to delay our departure for an hour,' Matthew said. 'Hopefully by then she will feel better.'

'That is most thoughtful, Mr Thomas,' Lady Rothley said, beaming as she beckoned to a serving girl, who had just entered the parlour with a plate of freshly cooked eggs.

The maid curtsied. 'Yes, milady?'

'Please ensure a message is taken to Lady Ashby to tell her our departure is delayed until half past ten.'

'And ask Mr Brooke to relay the same message to one of our men, will you?' Matthew added.

'Yes, milady. Yes, sir.' The maid hurried away.

'I very much appreciate your sacrifice, Mr Thomas,' Lady Rothley said, as she nibbled at a slice of toast. 'This will, I am afraid, delay you even further. I cannot tell you how much better I slept for knowing you are to accompany us on the rest of the journey.'

'I am delighted to be of service, my lady.'

If only Lady Rothley knew how close he had come to leaving the inn at first light, urgent with the need to put Eleanor, and the conflicting emotions she aroused in him, out of his mind for good. He had a plan for his life. And that plan most definitely did not include a beautiful, strong-willed baroness who—having blithely informed him how determined she was to prove to society that she was *not* her mother's daughter—had then kissed him. Very thoroughly. And most enjoyably. His blood thrummed at the memory.

'She is not a *bad* girl, Mr Thomas.'

Lady Rothley's attention was on her plate, so she did not notice Matthew's start at her words.

Was she a mind-reader? He blanked his expression, lifting his coffee cup to his lips.

'She is so determined to prove that she can succeed without a man to lean on,' she continued, 'she becomes a touch...*overbearing*...at times. You may have noticed.'

Matthew almost choked on his coffee. 'No,' he gasped, battling to contain a near-overwhelming urge to laugh. 'No, I cannot say I have noticed. Not overbearing. A little...*managing*, perhaps.'

'Ah, yes.' Her ladyship's dark eyes twinkled. 'That is much more diplomatic. You have a nice turn of phrase, Mr Thomas. Eleanor works so hard, you see, and has been too isolated since her father died. He wished her to wed before he died, but...well, it did not work out. And her aunt— not me, her Aunt Phyllis, the one who lives with her—well, she has no more sense than a noddy-cock, filling poor Ellie's head with dire warnings about bankruptcy and how women don't have the brains for business. Well, what would you expect from a spirited girl like Ellie? She's bound to want to prove everyone wrong.'

'Yes. Of course,' Matthew replied, his head reeling.

'Oh, dear. Now I have put you to the blush, Mr Thomas. I should not let my mouth run on so, but all this business...the attacks...and the responsibility of taking Eleanor to London after last time—' She stopped abruptly. 'There I go again. You are too easy to talk to, Mr Thomas, that is the trouble, and I must confess it is a relief to have someone to confide in. One cannot talk to the servants about such matters and, of course, I could never speak so frankly of my worries to Ellie. It helps, too, that you are not part of our world, so I forget to be discreet.'

Matthew stood, his chair scraping across the floor. He did not want to hear any more of Lady Rothley's confidences…he was intrigued enough by Eleanor already, without learning more about her, or having his sympathy stirred.

Although the temptation to abandon Eleanor and her aunt this morning had been powerful, in the end his conscience had won. He could not forget they were in danger. He had given his word that he would escort them to London and he would do so. But he had vowed to avoid being alone with Eleanor for the rest of their journey. He need only be strong for another few days, and then he need never see her again.

'You may rely on my discretion, my lady. Now, if you will excuse me, I must settle my account with Brooke, and speak to my man about the arrangements for the journey.'

Eleanor, meanwhile, was battling not only her pounding head, but also the lowering memory of her scandalous conduct. She had appeared in the parlour, in the dead of night, clad only in her nightgown and a shawl. Would any red-blooded male not have taken advantage of the opportunity she so naively presented? Although…and she had cringed as the full version of events from the night before unfolded in her mind's eye…*she* had kissed *Matthew*. Not the other way around. And the *things* she had told him. She winced at the memory. She did not doubt that the brandy had lowered her inhibitions, but her decision to stay had been before a drop had even touched her lips. What on earth had come over her? All the tenets of her upbringing, all of her innate sense of self-preservation and good old-fashioned common sense, had simply disappeared.

And what must Matthew Thomas think of her? She must take care in her future dealings with him—she must guard both her reputation and her heart, for he was clearly a danger to both. She conjured up a picture of those rugged good looks and the memory of that kiss, and she quivered. Oh, yes, he was a danger to her all right. A danger she would find hard to resist. But resist she must. Aunt Phyllis had only been half-right about the dangers of men and their seductive ways. She had never warned Eleanor of the treachery of a woman's own body, when she was attracted by a man. Why had none of the gentlemen of her acquaintance ever enticed her like this?

Hmmph. It was no good brooding over it. What had happened had happened. She must ensure she was never again alone with Matthew. It would only be for a couple of days and then their paths would never cross again.

In the yard of the George two chaise-and-fours were standing ready for their journey. Aunt Lucy and Eleanor would travel in the first—as yesterday—and Lizzie, Matilda and Timothy would ride in the second. Eleanor looked around. There was no sign of Matthew, or of his curricle and pair. Perhaps, she thought with a swell of relief, ignoring the sting of disappointment that followed close on its heels, he had decided against accompanying them after all.

A footstep behind her, and the waft of tangy citrus, alerted her to his presence.

'Good morning, my lady. I trust your headache is better?'

Eleanor inclined her head. 'Very much so, Mr Thomas. Thank you for enquiring.'

So formal. She risked a glance. He held out his hand.

'Allow me to assist you into the chaise.'

She placed her gloved hand in his. Strong fingers closed over hers and anticipation whispered deep in her belly. She lifted her chin and climbed the steps into the vehicle, taking her seat next to Aunt Lucy, who was already inside. She looked to the door, to thank Matthew, and bit back a gasp as he climbed in behind her.

'Are you not driving yourself?'

She felt her colour rise as Matthew regarded her, one brow raised. She had not meant to sound so brusque.

'I drove the horses hard yesterday,' he said. 'They will benefit from a day or two's rest and then Henry will drive them to London in easy stages. I am afraid, therefore, that you must endure my presence for the remainder of the journey to London.'

'How pleasant it will be to have your company, Mr Thomas.' Aunt Lucy beamed as she nudged Eleanor. 'Will it not, my pet?'

We will forget this ever happened.

Matthew Thomas had been true to his word, Eleanor granted him that. Not by a single look, or word, or deed did he even hint at what had passed between them at the George. Far from being relieved, Eleanor found herself growing more and more irritated as time passed. When she had vowed never to be alone with Matthew again, she had imagined him contriving circumstances in which they would meet and she would be the strong one, denying him despite his protestations. Instead, he made no effort whatsoever to manoeuvre her into being alone with him. They had not even had the opportunity to exchange a private word.

Not that I want *to be alone with him.*

She simply longed for the chance to spurn him. To prove that kissing him was something she regretted. Deeply.

The following morning, Eleanor paid the reckoning at the White Hart in Loughborough and was about to climb into the post-chaise, when Matthew strode from the inn, a thunderous frown on his face.

'I pay my own way.'

'And a very good morning to you, too, Mr Thomas,' Eleanor said, lifting her chin. Both she and Aunt Lucy had broken their fast in their rooms, so this was their first meeting of the day. His manner did not bode well for a pleasant journey. 'There is no call for you to turn top-lofty. This is my party, my journey. I pay.'

It was the only way she could retain her dignity. The tug of attraction was still strong. The memory of his kiss still set her senses aflame. His assumption of command throughout their first day of travel—overseeing the changes of the horses, arranging refreshments and private parlours to rest in, and checking and organising the security of the inn they stayed in overnight—had lifted the burden of responsibility from Eleanor. And she was both relieved and affronted by it. An inner tussle with her conscience had resulted in her admitting—but only privately—

that, on balance, it was pleasant to have a man to take charge for a change.

She was no longer shy and uncomfortable with him. Mayhap that was because he no longer looked at her in that particular way, his blue eyes penetrating until her innermost thoughts felt exposed to his inspection. And, since that night at the George, he had neither teased her nor flirted with her. His manner had been that of a polite, casual acquaintance. Eleanor had been able to move past the fluster and the blushes, and treat him—on the surface, at least—as the simple travelling companion he was. But the desire to assert her authority was powerful and paying their way was how she chose to salvage her self-esteem. Ultimately, she who pays the piper calls the tune, she thought with satisfaction.

She had known he might object. She had not anticipated such fury. It was rigidly controlled, but fury none the less.

'You may pay for your own accommodation and that of the servants,' he said in a tight, low voice, 'but I will not have you paying for *my* room and board. Here.' He thrust out his hand, opening it to reveal a clutch of coins on his palm. 'Take them.'

'No. You are supplying a service. I will be responsible for your expenses.' Eleanor turned and climbed into the post-chaise.

'By God, you are the most infuriating woman

I have ever met.' Matthew leant in the open door, blue eyes blazing. 'I have no need of your charity, *Lady* Ashby.'

Eleanor swallowed hard. 'I do not view it as charity, but as my obligation.'

'I may not have your wealth, but I am not poor. I can pay my way.'

'I did not think for one moment that you couldn't. Tell me—' she locked gazes with him '—if I were a man, could you honestly say we would be having this same discussion?'

Matthew opened his mouth, then closed it again. Inhaled, nostrils flaring. He climbed into the chaise and sat down, leaning back into the corner, eyes narrowed as he regarded her.

'I don't know,' he finally said. A smile tugged at the corners of his mouth. 'I cannot imagine another man accepting he might need my protection. But do not think that means I will accept you paying for my accommodation or my meals on the rest of the journey, for I will not.'

'And if I pay anyway?'

'Then there will be some very lucky innkeepers between here and London, for they will be paid twice over for the one service.'

Hmmph. 'It appears I must concede the point this time.'

'What point might that be, Ellie?' Aunt Lucy asked as Timothy handed her into the post-chaise.

'Mr Thomas is offended that I have settled his account at the inn.'

'I see,' Aunt Lucy said, as she settled on to the seat between them.

She said no more, but it was clear from the sidelong look she bent on Eleanor that she considered her niece to be in the wrong. The journey passed with very little conversation other than passing comments on the scenery or the weather.

At the first stop to change the horses, however, Aunt Lucy returned to the subject as soon as Matthew left the post-chaise.

'I am surprised at you, Ellie. Have you no consideration for a young man's pride?'

'Of course I have.' Eleanor was stung by her aunt's criticism. What about her own pride? Being kissed by a man—no, *kissing* a man—and then being roundly ignored? 'I meant no slight.' Had she really bruised his pride? Guilt stirred deep inside as she reviewed her actions and their conversation. Although she was determined to prove her capabilities in running her estates, she had always taken care not to flaunt her wealth or her privilege in front of others. Particularly men. She had realised, as she matured, that many men resented her title and her wealth simply because they afforded her that elusive advantage—for a female—of independence.

'The best solution is for you to hand over the

travelling purse to Mr Thomas,' Aunt Lucy said, 'and then *he* can settle the accounts and his pride will not suffer.'

'No. Why should I hand over my money to a near stranger? What if—?'

'What if I were to abscond with your funds?' Matthew had appeared at the open door. His eyes glittered. 'Trust me, Lady Ashby, I have no need of your few paltry coins. I have my own business and my own property. It may not match yours, but it is more than sufficient for my needs.'

He climbed in and slammed the door. The vehicle jerked as the horses took the strain and they were on the road again.

'You have property, Mr Thomas? In London?' Aunt Lucy asked.

Eleanor was, for once, grateful for her aunt's insatiable curiosity. She would never have lowered herself to ask the question, but she was dying to know the answer.

'Yes, in Bloomsbury. My great-uncle bequeathed me a small house in his will. As I said, it is enough for me.'

'What was his name?' Aunt Lucy asked. 'Mayhap I knew him.'

'You would not have known him, Lady Rothley. He spent all of his adult life in India. He was my grandmother's brother—their father was a cloth merchant. They did not move in your circles.'

The conversation was at a close and Eleanor

settled down for the remainder of the journey. *Just two more nights, then we shall be in London.* And then…she closed her eyes and concentrated on planning her campaign for full acceptance in society and those all-important vouchers for Almack's, burying deep the ache in her heart at the thought she would never see Matthew Thomas again.

Chapter Thirteen

Matthew gazed broodingly at Eleanor across the dining table on the evening of the following day. It was the last night of their journey. Tomorrow they would be in London. He would deliver Eleanor and her aunt safely to their door, say goodbye and never have to set eyes on the top-lofty, arrogant, beautiful, stubborn woman again. His brain and his body were in complete conflict. He wanted her. Badly. He was not even sure he liked her. But he definitely wanted her. The tension in his muscles whenever she was close could not be denied.

He'd had to steel himself against the hurt in those beautiful, tawny-brown eyes as he had treated her with cool civility during the first day of travel, when he barely trusted himself to even look at her. After that, it had become easier as Eleanor withdrew behind her *grande dame* persona. Matthew had busied himself as much as possible at every stop they made, lest he reveal the desire that burned deep within him every time he came within touching distance of her.

'You still won't be safe.' The words were out there before he could consider them, or where they might lead.

Eleanor lowered her knife and fork and fixed those luminous eyes on him, candlelight high-lighting gold flecks he had not noticed before. They drew him in, charging his blood, making him wish the impossible.

A man could drown in such limpid beauty.

Pfftt. Next thing, I'll be reciting poetry. That's what happens when a man spends too long in the company of females. He gets soft.

'Would you care to expand upon that remark, Mr Thomas?'

'I meant to say, how will you keep safe in London? There have been no further incidents, but the closer we get to London, the more traffic there will be, the more people on the streets. How will you distinguish friend from foe?'

Eleanor's eyes narrowed before she returned her attention to her plate and resumed eating. Time suspended as he held his breath. Was she ever going to reply?

'I was thinking the same thing myself,' she said, finally, surprising him. He had expected vehement denial of the risk.

'I shall have to employ extra footmen as

guards,' she continued. 'I have Timothy, and there is William, who travelled ahead with the others to prepare the house, but I do not think I can rely on just those two. Not when they have other duties to fulfil as well.'

'Do you truly believe a couple of extra footmen will suffice to protect you?'

She regarded him steadily. 'What action would *you* suggest I take, Mr Thomas?'

Her tone was sweet, at odds with the challenge in her eyes. All day he had been telling himself they would reach London tomorrow and he could walk away. He *should* walk away. It was not his problem, no matter how attracted he was to her. But, deep down, he struggled against the notion of leaving her to her fate. She was still in danger; he would be leaving her unprotected. Yes, she was wealthy enough to hire a small army to guard her, but they would still be hired men, motivated by money. What if her cousin were to bribe one, or more, of them? No, he could never trust hired men to protect her as well as he would.

It is not your problem. There is nothing you can do.

It was true…and yet he could not abandon her.

His dilemma had pounded incessantly at his brain. If he were to stay, how could he protect her? It would mean entering her world. He could not allow Eleanor and Lady Rothley to introduce him as Matthew Thomas, only to have his true identity revealed by someone who happened to remember him and what had happened.

He was the black sheep of his family. He had never felt as though he belonged—the third son, his two older brothers providing the requisite 'heir and spare.' Then Sarah, two years his junior, fêted and spoiled as the only girl until, seven years later, the last of the five siblings—another girl, favoured as the baby of the family, leaving him, smack bang in the middle, with no place to belong.

Yes, he had been a wild youth, up to all and every caper: expelled from Harrow; sent down from Oxford; drinking; gambling deep; huge losses; and affairs, not always discreet, with married women. He understood, looking back, his father's fury. But, no matter how wild and impetuous he had been, Matthew could never forgive his father for believing his own son capable of not only cheating at cards, but also cold-bloodedly attacking and robbing his accuser, Henson, and leaving him for dead.

Neither his father nor Claverley, Matthew's eldest brother, would listen to Matthew's protestations of innocence. *Dishonourable conduct.* Their easy acceptance of his guilt had deeply wounded Matthew. Their sole concern had been to get him out of the country in case Henson died. They had hauled him off to the docks and bought him passage on the first ship to India and to his great-uncle.

He had long ago been cleared of the charge of attacking and robbing Henson—thanks to Uncle Percy's efforts—but the accusation of cheating still hung over him and the knowledge that his father had discharged so many of Matthew's debts still rankled. On his return to England he had vowed to repay those debts come what may. Other than that, he wanted nothing to do with his family…none of them had ever replied to the letters he had written in those early years of exile and he had given up writing after a while. They had disowned him. He would forget them in return— put them out of his mind.

'Mr Thomas?'

He came back to the present with a start.

'I beg your pardon. I was thinking of my commitments. It so happens that I have some free time at my disposal at the moment. I believe I told you I have two cargoes *en route* from India—'

'No, did you?' Lady Rothley interjected. 'I do not recall that, Mr Thomas. When was it you told us?'

Matthew cursed beneath his breath. He had told Eleanor, that night in the parlour of the George. The night they kissed. He should be more cautious. Her ladyship was much too sharp to fool. 'I apologise,' he said, smoothly, 'I thought I did mention it. Obviously not.'

'No. I cannot remember *anything* about that at all,' Eleanor said, nose in the air as her lips tightened.

Ha! She says the words, but her eyes tell the truth. She remembers that night as clearly as I do.

'To continue, I have a few weeks' respite until the ships are due in dock. I can be available to escort you wherever you wish whilst you are in London—only until we can unmask the culprit, of course.'

'Thank you for your kind offer, Mr Thomas.' Eleanor's words were so sweetly reasonable, with just the right hint of apology, they made Matthew's teeth grind. 'I must decline, however. I have no doubt you will still have some business to attend to and I have no wish to further *complicate* your life.'

She was still flinging that ill-considered remark in his face. Resentment bubbled in his gut.

So bloody superior. Leave her to her fate, man, and get on with your own life.

Being back in London had been hard enough, with the memories it evoked, despite his care in avoiding the fashionable haunts where he might be recognised. His pride dictated he remain incognito until he was in a position to pay back his father—which he would be just as soon as Benedict arrived in port. If he reverted to his family name any earlier, it would be bound to rake up the past.

'Very well, my lady. I shall say no more on the subject.'

The idea was preposterous. Did Matthew really believe he could pass himself off as a gentleman? Guilt nibbled at Eleanor at that ungenerous thought. She was being unfair. He was intelligent, educated; he had presence. Of course he could pass as a gentleman. She had long since stopped viewing him as anything but. He might be a merchant, but no one else would know, only herself and Aunt Lucy.

That presence of his: he exuded raw masculinity—it enticed her, enthralled her, terrified her. Honesty compelled her to admit that her real objection to his protecting her in London was the way her heart leapt every time she saw him.

The way her lips tingled every time she relived their kisses.

The way her blood boiled every time she recalled those words: *I do not need complications.*

How ironic that the only man who had ever made her heart beat faster was the one man she could never have. He might have the wherewithal to fool society for a short time, but she knew the truth. He was a merchant. He might be successful. He might even be wealthy. But she could never, ever, ally herself with a man of his class. *Like mother, like daughter*. It would bring all the old scandal tumbling out of the past, piling on to her head. It would bury her. She could never hold up her head in society again and she would *never* be accepted for Almack's.

Nevertheless, she could see by his scowl that her words had touched a nerve.

She drew breath. 'I meant no offence, Mr Thomas. I am persuaded you would loathe kicking your heels at those interminable society parties. You have had a fortunate escape. Members of the *ton* can be very narrow-minded and are not welcoming to outsiders.'

Matthew's eyes narrowed. 'I quite see that you are doing me a favour.'

Was that bitterness? The urge to soothe his ruffled feelings was strong, but Eleanor forced herself to continue eating. Their mutual attraction was undeniable. But that was all it was. There were no tender feelings there.

Not on his part.

Nor on mine!

They had been thrown into one another's company during the journey, and she had come to rely on him. Too much. Once she made new acquaintances in London, she would lose this dependence on him. It was all false. Not real. She rubbed at her temples and then pushed back her chair.

'It has been a long day. If you will excuse me, I shall retire.'

Chapter Fourteen

Matthew came awake instantly, his eyes wide as he strained to see. He leapt from his bed as he heard the click of the door latch and, as his eyes grew accustomed to the darkness of his bedchamber, he could make out the slowly widening crack as the door inched open. One stride and he hauled it wide. A tall figure stumbled against him. Soft curves, a feminine gasp and the scent of jasmine identified the intruder as Eleanor. Every fibre of every muscle tensed as his arms came around her in reflex.

'What—?'

'Mr Thomas!'

Even in the extremes of arousal, he identified the panic in her whisper.

'What is it?' He gripped her upper arms, moving her away from his rampant body, giving thanks he had chosen to sleep in his nightshirt.

'I thought I heard a noise downstairs. And I saw someone outside, from the landing window.'

'What were you doing on the landing? No, never mind.' Matthew grabbed his jacket from the chair and bundled it into her arms, pushing her towards the bed. 'Stay here, wrap up and don't, whatever you do, make a sound.'

He slipped out on to the landing. At the top of the stairs he paused, straining his ears. Nothing. The window was along the landing, a few feet beyond the door of Eleanor's bedchamber. Silent in his bare feet, he ran along and peered out. Nothing. Then a movement caught his attention. A bulky figure, in the shadows of the outbuildings. The figure moved, split in two, came together again. A flash of pale flesh as skirts were bundled up…and Matthew retreated from the window. That was the last thing he needed…to watch some lovelorn fool of a stable boy tupping his lady love when his own body was crying out for the same relief.

He gritted his teeth, willing his desires back under control. He would check Eleanor's room, then go downstairs to make sure there was no one there, even though it appeared likely one of the maids had slipped outside to meet her lover. Which was all very well, but it had left the inn insecure, despite his impressing on the innkeeper the importance of barring the doors and posting a guard.

Where the hell was that guard? How had the maid got out without alerting him? The quicker he checked Eleanor's room, the sooner he could go downstairs and find out what these fools were about. Galvanised into action, he entered her bed-chamber. A quick glance around showed nothing amiss. He crossed to the window and flipped the curtain aside. It faced a different direction to the landing window. All was peaceful. He returned to the door and stepped out on to the landing.

And collided with a soft, familiar body.

'What the…?' For the second time that night, he steeled himself as he forced Eleanor away from him. 'I told you to stay put.'

'You were gone an age. I needed to know what was happening. Have you seen anyone?'

'Yes…no…look, wait in there…' he pushed her through the door into her room '…and I will come to tell you as soon as I've searched down-stairs.' He grasped her chin, forced her to look up at him. Her eyes glittered in defiance. *'Stay here.'*

Eleanor huffed a sigh but, thankfully, made no attempt to follow him on to the landing.

Ten minutes later, Matthew knocked softly on Eleanor's door and went in. A solitary candle flickered, illuminating Eleanor, sitting on the bed, his jacket hugged around her shoulders, her hair… her glorious hair…framing her face, flowing over her shoulders…a river of silk. He itched to plunge his hands into those fragrant tresses.

Eleanor bounced to her feet, his jacket gaping. After one glance at the thin nightgown beneath, Matthew riveted his gaze to her face.

'Well? Was there anyone down there?'

'Just one of the maidservants.'

She had breezed in through the back door, bright-eyed and pink of cheek, as he had reached the kitchen. She had halted, momentarily disconcerted, then, with a calculating eye had swayed provocative hips as she approached him. He had declined what she offered, bolted the door, and searched the rest of the ground floor of the inn. The guard was sprawled on one of the settles in the taproom, snoring. Tempted as he had been to wake the fellow, solely in order to knock him senseless again, Matthew resisted. It was two in the morning. The inn was safely locked up again and, in a few hours, they would be gone.

At that moment, it had seemed more important to return to Eleanor…before she decided to follow him again to find out what was happening.

'What was a maid doing up at this time?'

'She said she had forgotten to do something.'

'What?'

'I don't know. I didn't ask.' He wasn't about to tell Eleanor the truth about the maid's night-time wanderings. 'She's back inside now and the doors are all bolted. It is safe.'

Eleanor visibly relaxed. She took a step towards him, into a shaft of moonshine that slid through a gap in the curtains. 'I am sorry I disturbed you,' she said. 'I…I was scared.'

'And yet you came out of your room.' His gaze returned again and again to her bare toes, washed by moonlight, as they peeped from the hem of her nightgown. Blood thrummed through his veins. The after-effects of danger, nothing more, he told himself. 'You could have bolted the door—'

'The door was already bolted.'

'And you considered the wisest course of action was to *unbolt* the door and venture out on to the landing? Have you no…?' He bit his tongue against the diatribe he longed to heap on her head. He did not want an argument now. Not here. Not with her standing there like that. Passion simmered dangerously close to the surface as it was. Anger would fuel an already tense situation. 'Why did you not just shout for help?'

She cast him a scathing look. 'I had no wish to cause a fuss by waking everyone. Aunt Lucy would be petrified and, as for Lizzie and Matilda, they would be in hysterics. Can you imagine?'

He could…but still…

'You have no concept of your own safety, do you?' he growled, closing the gap between them.

Her eyes were large and watchful, glinting as they held his gaze. Her lips firmed. She did not retreat.

'I was completely aware of the risk,' she said. 'The noise I heard was downstairs. I merely peeked out of my door. There was no one there, or I would have screamed. Loudly. I am not a fool. But neither will I cower in my bed until trouble finds me.'

Her stubborn courage infuriated him; it terrified him; it made his heart swell with an emotion akin to pride. Her breath had quickened, her chest rising and falling. Without volition his gaze lowered to her pebbled nipples, outlined by the thin fabric of her nightgown. Blood surged to his loins. He forced his attention back to her face, his heart hammering.

He could feel her heat. Her breath whispered over the suddenly sensitised skin of his face and neck. An intense feeling of protectiveness washed over him and he raised his hand to caress her cheek—soft and smooth. Her eyelids fluttered down and she drew in a tremulous breath.

'Goodnight, Eleanor,' he whispered. He dropped his hand and forced himself to turn for the door.

'Wait!'

He paused, his hand on the latch, not trusting himself to look round. There was a rustle and his jacket was thrust into his arms.

'It would not do for Lizzie to find this in the morning.'

Matthew opened the door.

'Thank you, Matthew.'

Her words stayed in his mind long after he had climbed into his cold, empty bed. He could not decide whether she was thanking him for what he had done, or for what he had not done.

And she had called him Matthew.

She had long dreamed of falling in love. She would not give up her independence for anything less. What she had never considered was this confused state of mind that accompanied her feelings about Matthew Thomas.

Desire.

Yes, she desired him, and she recognised it and admitted it for what it was, despite her innocence. Was it possible to feel desire without love? Men certainly did.

Think of it the other way round. Could I imagine loving a man without desiring him?

She thought not.

Desire.

The following morning, Eleanor studied Matthew, who was seated on the far side of a dozing Aunt Lucy, from under her lashes. He stared broodingly out of the chaise window at the passing scenery. The bump on his nose was more noticeable in profile. How had it been broken? Fighting? How little she still knew of him.

Last night… In her mind's eye she saw him

again, clad only in his nightshirt, the neck open, revealing bronzed, smooth skin. It reached to just above his knees and she had drunk in the sight of his naked calves and feet—muscular, hair-dusted, so very different from her own pale, smooth limbs. She, thank goodness, had been totally covered by her nightgown and, apart from her hair being loose, she had been no more exposed than if she had worn a day dress. Less, in fact, as the fashion now was for a scooped neckline and her nightgown buttoned chastely to her neck.

Matthew moved, shifting round to prop his shoulders into the corner and refolding his arms. He stretched his legs out, crossing them at the ankle, and glanced across to Eleanor. She did not look away, but held his stare as his blue eyes darkened and his jaw firmed. He looked away first.

Desire.

He felt it, too. That fact gave her an inner confidence she had not imagined before they met. Even her own mother had abandoned her...that pain still ran deep. And Donald...his silken words and treacherous kisses...he had lied without compunction...told her he loved her...and she had believed him because she wanted to, until the truth had smacked her in the face and she could no longer fool herself with the pathetic fantasy of her own making. Being desired by an attractive man like Matthew had salved her inner doubts about her allure as a woman and her self-esteem had blossomed.

It had not taken her long to become comfortable in his presence. It helped that he no longer teased or flirted. She appreciated his restraint, even though she felt she might now enjoy such banter and might even be able to join in the game without fear of ridicule. Trust. She barely knew him, yet she trusted him, not only to protect her against her unknown enemy but, and more importantly, to protect her against herself. Against her desire and her needs. Last night—if he hadn't left when he did, she shuddered to think of the consequences.

Now, she must look to her future. There would be many suitable men in London. She hoped she might meet one who would make her blood sizzle the way Matthew Thomas did. And that he might view her as an alluring woman and not as a walking treasure chest.

'We are almost there,' Matthew said.

The view from the window had gradually changed. Where before there had been fields and woods and heaths and pleasant market towns and small hamlets, they now travelled through a maze of busy, dingy streets, the wheels clattering over endless cobbles.

'It will be a relief not to have to travel again tomorrow,' Aunt Lucy said, stirring and yawning.

'Are you quite well, Aunt? You are very pale.'

'I have the headache, my dear. I shall be quite all right after a lie down.'

At Upper Brook Street, the servants sent on ahead had readied the house, and it was almost like arriving home, with Pacey, Eleanor's butler, and Mrs Pledger, her housekeeper, at the door to greet them. Matthew supported Aunt Lucy into the hall and then Mrs Pledger and Matilda took over, helping her up the white-marble staircase to settle into her bedchamber.

Eleanor surveyed the bright, welcoming entrance hall. If the rest of the house was of a similar standard, it would be more than adequate for their stay in London. She was resigned to spending the next few months, at least, in London, whilst Ashby Manor was made habitable.

Eleanor smiled at Matthew. 'Would you care for a dish of tea before you leave? Or a glass of wine?'

'Thank you—tea would be most welcome.'

Pacey showed Eleanor and Matthew into a back parlour, decorated in green and gold.

'Please leave the door open, Pacey, and instruct one of the maids to come and sit in here with us,' Eleanor said. She would start as she must go on, with a keen regard for her reputation and those vital vouchers for Almack's. After the butler left, she continued, 'I might not always seem it, but I am grateful for your help, Mr Thomas. And for your company. You have helped make a long, tedious and what might have been a dangerous journey infinitely better.'

'Have you any idea how soon you will be able to appoint new footmen?'

'No. I am sure Pacey will arrange that. There is bound to be a Register Office nearby.'

'Indeed there is, my lady,' Pacey said when asked upon his return to the parlour. 'Shall you require me to appoint additional staff?'

'Yes.' Eleanor told the butler of the happenings on the road.

'Lady Ashby will need two footmen to accompany her whenever she goes out,' Matthew said. 'Plus, you must treat the security of this house as of the utmost importance. External doors must be bolted and ground-floor windows latched at all times, no matter the inconvenience.'

'My lady?'

The butler turned to her for confirmation, allowing Eleanor to accept Matthew's instructions with more grace than she might otherwise have achieved. 'Yes, Pacey. It is as Mr Thomas has said.'

'And strong lads, mind. They need to be stout enough to protect her ladyship.'

'With your leave, my lady, I shall visit the Register Office immediately. The sooner we can appoint the extra staff the better, it would seem.'

Two maids brought in a tea tray and a plate of sandwiches, and one of the maids remained in the room afterwards. A rebellious part of Eleanor regretted her impulse to follow propriety so strictly, but she knew it was the correct thing to do. It forced their conversation on to everyday matters. Eventually, Mr Thomas stood to take his leave. Eleanor rose to her feet, her insides hollowing as she realised she might never see him again.

'I do hope you will call upon us from time to time, to let us know how you go on.'

He bowed. 'Of course.' He reached into his pocket and handed her a sheet of paper upon which he had written an address. 'If you have need of me, send word.'

Eleanor took the sheet with suddenly trembling fingers. 'Thank you,' she said, her voice strangling as her throat swelled. To her dismay, her eyes filled with tears and she hurriedly tried to blink them away. This would never do.

Matthew reached for her hand, and squeezed. He lowered his voice as he asked, 'Are you all right?'

Eleanor hauled in a deep breath. 'Yes. Yes, of course. I am sorry…so foolish of me. I dare say it's the journey…so very exhausting.'

She braved a glance at his face. His blue eyes burned into hers and she could not tear her gaze away.

'Day or night,' he said, 'if ever you have doubts, or you are scared, do not hesitate to send for me. I will get to you as soon as I can.'

Chapter Fifteen

Matthew stood in the shadows of King Street, opposite the house where his life had changed for ever. It looked smaller, somehow, and seedier than he remembered. Or was it the enthusiasm of youth that had coloured the place as glamorous and alluring? The sight of excitable young bucks, in twos and threes, swaggering along the street before lifting the knocker and gaining admittance, was profoundly depressing. *Nothing changes.* Young men…their bravado…seeking thrills…believing themselves up to any and every trick in the book.

If only they knew…

Thud…chest about to explode…king of hearts, fluttering to the floor… Henson, accusing, face dark, fists clenched…*thud, thud*…stammered denial, hands shaking, mouth sucked dry…faces, in and out of vision, disbelieving, sneering…voice hoarse, trying to be heard…needing to be believed…failing…alone…*thud, thud, thud*…anger, fury boiling over, challenging Henson…challenge accepted…men turning from him…no one willing to stand as second.

His breath juddered as he hauled it in and he was aware of sweat coating his brow and upper lip. He reached for his handkerchief, and passed it over his face. So real. He had sworn never to return. Why had he come?

A pair of large, tawny eyes materialised in his mind's eye. He had handed Eleanor his address as he took his leave of her and, for the first time in days, her outer shell of bravado had cracked. He had glimpsed the frightened girl inside, belying her rejection of his help. He had itched to take her in his arms and soothe away her fears. He would never have that right, but she needed protection and he could not deny that urge deep in his gut, no matter how hard he tried. He must find out who was trying to kill her. It was his duty to keep her safe, even if it meant facing his worst fear.

When he'd arrived from India, nigh on a month ago now, he would have cut his eyes out rather than start probing this old sore. Henson had been stabbed and robbed that same night, before their duel, snatching away Matthew's chance to fight for his honour and to clear his name.

Dishonourable conduct. He could not allow his scandal to taint Eleanor by association, which it would surely do once his true identity became

known. He must—somehow—prove his innocence. A lead weight settled in the pit of his stomach as he pictured Eleanor's growing trust of him
turn to scorn when she discovered the truth of his
exile to India.

He would gain nothing by going inside the
house opposite. All these hells were crooked—in
favour of the house, of course—but it was not the
house that had falsely accused him of cheating all
those years ago, nor the house that had believed
him responsible for attacking Henson shortly afterwards. The old resentment curdled his stomach. His own father. His own family. They had
believed him capable of both charges. They had
washed their hands of him. And now, if he was to
protect Eleanor, he would—inevitably—be recognised. Remembered. Accused all over again.

Henson.

Where to begin to look? Matthew ran through
the names of the men round the table that night—
names branded in his memory.

Henson, both Alastairs—Lady Rothley's sons,
Silverdale, Hartlebury, Perivale.

He would have to hope some of them were
in London for the Season. The older of the two
Alastairs, Lucas—now the Marquis of Rothley—
was not in town. That was no loss; he and Henson had been thick as thieves. But the younger
brother, Hugo…he might be a good place to start.

He must prove his innocence. Deep in his gut,

he believed others around that table must know the accusation to be false. They just hadn't spoken up against Henson—older, worldly-wise, a man the young bucks admired and wished to emulate. Maybe now, as more mature and, hopefully, responsible adults, they would take the opportunity to clear their consciences.

Matthew turned abruptly on his heel and strode away.

Three days after their arrival in town, Pacey opened the front door for Eleanor and Matthew was on the doorstep. Rendered temporarily speechless, she was grateful Aunt Lucy took charge.

'Mr Thomas! Why, what a pleasant surprise. How do you do?'

Matthew removed his hat and bowed, his blond hair glinting in the early afternoon sunlight.

'Good afternoon, Lady Rothley.' He bowed and then his blue gaze rested on Eleanor's face and her heart kicked into a gallop. 'Your servant, Lady Ashby. I am very well, thank you. Have I called at an inconvenient time?'

'Yes,' Eleanor said. 'We are—'

'No,' Aunt Lucy said. 'Your timing is perfect. We are going to call on Eleanor's cousin, James. Would you care to accompany us?'

'Aunt! I don't think…I beg your pardon, Mr Thomas, but—'

'I should be honoured,' Matthew said. 'Are you planning to walk?'

'Yes,' Aunt Lucy said. 'It is not very far, but it will be pleasant to have a gentleman's arm to lean on. Come, Ellie. Peter and William can still accompany us.'

Eleanor straightened her bonnet and sailed past Matthew on to the pavement. She could think of nothing worse than Matthew being present when she and James had their first meeting. Her irritation that James had not even had the courtesy to call on her in the three days since her arrival was bound to reveal itself and she was loath to give Matthew another reason to think ill of her cousin.

Eleanor winced inwardly at the spectacle they must present: it was bad enough having two burly footmen dogging her footsteps wherever they went but, now, to be seen in the company of... Eleanor looked beyond Aunt Lucy to Mr Thomas, strolling nonchalantly along the pavement, cane swinging. A cane? His blue superfine coat was well tailored, his tall hat set at a jaunty angle and—although he still presented a rugged and slightly dangerous appearance—no one would doubt him a gentleman. Mayhap he was wealthier than she had assumed. But he was still a merchant.

'...and we have spent much of our time shopping and with dressmakers,' Aunt Lucy was saying. 'The fire at Ashby destroyed much of Eleanor's clothing, of course, and it is a long time since I came to London. My dresses are sadly outmoded, I fear.'

Eleanor smiled to herself, recalling their argument over Aunt Lucy's need for some new gowns. Suspecting her aunt's funds were limited, Eleanor had refused to give way and eventually Aunt Lucy had conceded that Eleanor might treat her to a couple of new evening gowns. *After all*, Eleanor had argued, *you are only in London on my behalf. It is right and fair that I should bear your expenses.* Pride satisfied, Aunt Lucy had then thrown herself with enthusiasm into their shopping expeditions.

'What had your cousin to say about the carriage accident and the attack on that girl?' Matthew asked as they turned into Hill Street, where James and Ruth lived.

Trust him to settle upon the one topic she had hoped would not arise. Anger at James for not visiting her battled against her anxiety at seeing him again.

'We have not yet spoken,' she replied.

'Very discourteous of him,' Aunt Lucy said. 'Both Eleanor and I are disappointed by his neglect of his familial duty. It's been three days since our arrival and not even a note from him to enquire if the house is satisfactory.'

'I am sure he has good reason, Aunt.' Why she felt obliged to defend James, she did not know, when in reality she thought his conduct indefensible. She glanced behind, reassured by the stoical presence of William and one of the new footmen, Peter.

'No doubt his guilty conscience,' Matthew said.

Eleanor glared at him. 'Mayhap you should not come inside with us, if you are determined to stir the coals. James is hardly likely to attack me in his own house. Even if he is guilty.'

'Please do not desert us now, Mr Thomas. I feel so much safer with you here. I begged Ellie not to call upon James unannounced like this, but she would not listen to me.'

'Why did you not just send him a note and ask him to call on you?' Matthew said. 'Then you would meet him on your territory.'

'I cannot sit at home on tenterhooks waiting and wondering when he might appear. Surely that is understandable?'

'I understand you are impatient, Eleanor. Just like your mama.'

Eleanor stiffened. Just like her mama. That was exactly what no one must think any more. Apprehension had churned her stomach on and off all day, for tonight marked the beginning of her assault on society, at the Barringtons' ball. Aunt Lucy had been busy leaving cards with her old acquaintances and the invitations had started to trickle in.

Their new gowns had been delivered that morning and Eleanor was both looking forward to and dreading the moment she must enter the Barringtons' house and find all those eyes upon her. This time, however, she would not allow the whispers and innuendoes to overset her. She would hold her head high and prove she was not like her mother. At least visiting James gave her something else to worry about.

Aunt Lucy grabbed Eleanor's hand. 'I am sorry, Ellie. I don't know why I said that. I dare say I am nervous at the thought of facing James and what to say to him. I know you are nothing like my silly, selfish sister.' She halted outside a tall, narrow house. 'Look, isn't this James's house?'

'Yes,' Eleanor said, her stomach beginning to churn. 'This is it.'

She inhaled deeply to settle her nerves as Matthew rapped on the door.

'Mr Thomas, I know I do not have to say this, but please do not say anything to provoke James.'

'Me? Provoke?' Matthew's brows shot up.

Eleanor laughed. 'Of course, you would never dream of such behaviour, would you?'

For a long time there was no sound from within but, just as Matthew lifted the brass knocker to rap again, the door opened.

Eleanor stepped forward. 'Be so good as to inform Mr Weare that his cousin, Lady Ashby, is here and begs a few moments of his time.'

The footman stared at her with a doubtful expression and then stood aside. 'Good afternoon, Lady Ashby. I shall inform the master you are here. If you would care to follow me?'

They entered a dim hallway that, despite the good address and smart external appearance of the house, showed signs of wear and neglect. The house smelled in need of a good dose of fresh air, to blast away the stale cooking odours. The footman led them into a small reception room—equally musty and shabby, with heavy, dusty-looking dark green curtains framing the dirty glass of the window. Eleanor stripped off her gloves to await her cousin, trying to conceal her increasing unease.

Within a few short minutes, the door flew open and James appeared. Eleanor went to him, her hands held out in greeting, smiling, genuinely pleased to see him again. One look into those clear grey eyes banished many of her doubts. This was James—her beloved cousin, her childhood playmate.

'James, my dearest cousin, it has been much, much too long. Do please forgive us for calling unannounced, but I could not wait to see you. I do hope we are not putting you out?' She looked him up and down, then added, teasingly, 'You look very well, Cousin, but it seems you might have gained one or two pounds since last I saw you. You remember my aunt, Lady Rothley, do you not?'

'Indeed I do,' James responded, with a brief bow in Aunt Lucy's direction. 'How do you do, Lady Rothley?'

'And this is Mr Thomas.' Eleanor sent Matthew a warning look, which he returned with an innocent lift of his brows. How should she explain his presence? 'He kindly escorted us here.'

'In addition to the two footmen loitering in my hall?' James asked, but nevertheless shook Matthew's hand. 'You are looking very well, Eleanor,' he continued, 'but you should have informed me of your arrival. *I* would have called upon *you*.'

Eleanor frowned, puzzled by his manner. As James entered the room his surprise had been palpable, but there had been no sign of pleasure, and his greeting—although polite—held no warmth. Neither had he reassured her that they were welcome. Indeed, his words held more of a scold than a greeting. There was something about his manner—an edginess—she could not understand. Her doubts began to stir again.

Surely Matthew can't be right about James? No! I will not believe it.

Her stomach started to churn and she clenched her hands, digging her nails into her palms. 'You must have been aware we were to arrive on Saturday.' She squared her shoulders, steeling herself to keep her voice steady. 'It was you, after all, who made the arrangements for the journey. For which, by the by, I thank you.'

James frowned. 'I am sorry, Eleanor. I left the arrangements to my man and I seem to have lost track of the days somewhat.'

It is up to me to bridge this divide between us.

'Well, never mind now. It is not so very far to come. Oh, it is so very good to see you again, James.' Eleanor determinedly quashed her doubts as she clasped his hands again. 'We have become virtual strangers since you left Ashby. I do so wish it could be otherwise.'

James's face darkened at the mention of the Manor. 'There is nothing for me there, Eleanor, as you very well know. We are better off in town.'

Again, an underlying wariness. 'Is there anything amiss, James? You do not seem completely happy to see us and you have not even invited us to take a seat. Have we called at an inconvenient time?'

He had the grace to look ashamed, casting a fleeting glance at the door as he said, 'I'm sorry. I'm afraid I have an appointment in half an hour, one I cannot cancel. May I arrange to call upon you tomorrow instead?'

The door opened and Ruth—a slight woman with wispy, fair hair—entered the room. On seeing Eleanor, she stopped abruptly, her pale face set in its customary peeved expression.

'You did not tell me we were expecting visitors, James,' she said.

'I am sorry, my dear.' He hurried to her side, placing one hand under her elbow. 'Come and say hello to Cousin Eleanor. Her aunt Lady Rothley is here, too. And this is Mr Thomas. I was just explaining to Eleanor about our appointment.'

'I am sure they can have no interest in that,' Ruth said, as James urged her forward.

Reflecting that uncivil behaviour in another did not mean one should forget one's own manners, Eleanor smiled at Ruth, extending her hand.

'Cousin Ruth, how do you do? I hope we find you in good health?'

Ruth touched Eleanor's hand fleetingly. 'I am well enough, thank you.'

She dropped a brief curtsy to Aunt Lucy, 'Lady Rothley,' and nodded unsmilingly at Matthew, 'Mr Thomas.' After a brief pause, she added, 'I am sorry, Cousin Eleanor, but we must leave now if we are not to miss our appointment. I hope you will forgive us.'

Aunt Lucy caught Eleanor's eye and raised an elegant brow.

'There is no need to apologise, Ruth,' Eleanor said. 'We took a chance in calling upon you uninvited and I understand you cannot tarry if you have an appointment. I hope you will both call upon us soon so we can have a proper catch up with all the news.'

Ruth smiled again and inclined her head. 'We shall bid you goodbye, then.' She tugged her arm free from James's grip and moved to stand by the open door, leaving the visitors no choice but to leave.

Chapter Sixteen

'Well! How very peculiar.'

Lady Rothley shook her head as she gazed back at the firmly closed front door. Eleanor tucked her hand through her aunt's arm and turned her in the direction of home and Matthew fell into step beside them. The two footmen followed behind.

'Indeed,' she said. 'I thought James very ill at ease and Ruth looked...unwell.'

Probably the result of being married to a man like James Weare. Matthew was wise enough not to voice that opinion. Eleanor had been so happy to see her cousin again. She would be devastated if he did turn out to be responsible for the attacks. Matthew vowed to keep a sharp eye on Cousin James.

His quest to prove his innocence of cheating had not started well. Not one of the other players in that long-ago game were currently in town and Henson—that lying bastard who had accused him of cheating—had long been in exile, forced abroad by unpaid gambling debts. The irony would have amused Matthew had the matter not become—suddenly—of the utmost importance.

He had discovered, however, that his brother Stephen was in town. Two years Matthew's senior, they had always been closer than either of them had been with their eldest brother, Roger, Viscount Claverley—the heir and their father's son through and through. Stephen would be Matthew's next port of call. He would find out exactly how the rest of the family felt about him. Unanswered letters were one thing; if Stephen rejected him face to face…

He switched his attention back to Eleanor's words.

'I must talk to James on his own when they come to call and try to discover what is wrong. I cannot believe his coolness is solely due to my inheriting the title, although he did react badly to my mention of the Manor. It makes no sense, though—he has always known he would not inherit, even if Ruth did not. I can only think that she has turned him against me.'

'He was not happy at our calling in like that, Ellie.'

'I know, but that does not mean he was behind the fire or the accident.'

'Don't forget injuring that girl,' Matthew said.

Eleanor speared him with a glare. 'In fact,' she

continued, her nose firmly in the air, 'if anything, it makes me believe he knows nothing about any of the incidents, for would he not have better concealed his feelings if he were responsible?'

'I was hoping you would tell your cousin about those incidents,' Matthew said. 'I should have liked to see his reaction.'

'There was no time to discuss anything of note. You saw what he was like. Besides, he already knows of the fire.' Eleanor's voice was strained.

Matthew sympathised. He knew how hard it was to accept your own family turning against you.

'I will tell James about them when he calls upon us. Surely he will now come tomorrow? It is not his fault they had a prior engagement today.'

'It will do us no harm to be on our guard with him, Ellie,' Aunt Lucy said, as they crossed over South Audley Street. 'Mayhap it isn't about the title after all, but the money? Ashby is a wealthy estate and that house of James's looks in sad need of refurbishment. Ruth, I noticed, was dressed in the height of fashion and I'll wager she is a demanding spouse. I almost feel sorry for him—being wed to that sour-faced madam is enough to turn anyone peculiar.'

'I would not argue with that,' Matthew said. 'In fact, I—' He slammed to a halt. Two gentlemen were strolling along the pavement towards them. His heart pounded in his ears.

Stephen.

'Is something wrong, Mr Thomas?' Eleanor asked, stopping and looking back at him.

'I…I beg your pardon, ladies. I have this minute recalled a matter of the utmost urgency. I regret, but I must attend to it right away. You have the footmen for protection and it is not so very far to Upper Brook Street.' Stephen and his companion were getting closer. 'I will call on you very soon, to enquire how you go on. Goodbye.'

He doffed his hat and walked rapidly back the way they had come, angling across the road. He intended to face Stephen. But not here. Not now. Not in front of others and, most particularly, not in front of Eleanor.

'Well! How very abrupt,' Aunt Lucy said. 'I wonder what can have been of such importance?'

'I do not know,' Eleanor said, watching as Matthew paused to speak to a stranger on the other side of the road. He pointed back along South Audley Street, then glanced in Eleanor's direction before disappearing round the corner, back into Hill Street. 'It cannot matter to us,' she continued, determined not to reveal any hint of disappointment. 'Mr Thomas has his business to run, and we, dear Aunt, have a ball to attend.'

They resumed walking and Eleanor recognised, with a lurch of nerves in her stomach, two acquaintances from her come-out. Would they remember her? Would they snub her because of her mother?

Aunt Lucy had no such qualms. 'Lord Derham,' she said, smiling up at the taller man of the two. 'And Mr Damerel…' she nodded her head at the other '…how delightful to see you both.'

The two halted and bowed.

'Good afternoon, Lady Rothley. It is entirely too long since you have graced us with your presence for the Season,' Lord Derham said.

'It is indeed. I am here to chaperon my niece, Lady Ashby. Are you acquainted with his lordship and Mr Damerel, Eleanor, my dear?'

Eleanor smiled at them and dipped a curtsy. 'We have met, Aunt, but—like you—it is some years since I have been in London. I cannot be so bold as to hope the gentlemen might remember me.'

There was an immediate flurry of protest from the two men, with no hint that either recalled her mother's scandal.

'Do you go to the Barringtons' ball tonight?' Mr Damerel asked.

Upon being told they would be there, each gentleman immediately engaged Eleanor's hand for two dances. They parted company and Eleanor and Aunt Lucy continued towards home.

'I am pleased Mr Damerel has engaged me for the first,' Eleanor said. 'It will save me from the lowering prospect of sitting with the chaperons and attempting to look happy.'

The memories of her come-out still had the power to make her shudder. This time, surely, was going to be very different. She had even conversed with the two gentlemen without blushing. But…her surge of confidence dwindled as her self-doubts threatened to overwhelm her again. Mr Damerel and Lord Derham had been pleasant and polite, but they didn't know the real her—her mother had abandoned her; neither her father, before his death, nor Aunt Phyllis seemed to notice her unless it was to criticise; James had completely withdrawn from her; and, as for Donald and any other would-be suitors, they were only ever interested in her fortune.

'Have you heard from Hugo?' she asked, in an attempt to distract her thoughts from her own shortcomings.

'I sent one of the footmen to his lodgings. Evidently he is out of town and no one knows when he is likely to return,' Aunt Lucy replied. 'Really, it is too bad of him…'

Aunt Lucy happily grumbled about her younger son all the way to their front door, distracting Eleanor from her newly resurrected worries about the ball that evening.

Knowing Stephen was in town was one thing, tracking him down quite another. No good revealing himself in a public place—who knew how his brother might react? Matthew pulled the collar of his greatcoat around his ears and settled down to wait outside the house in Jermyn Street, where Stephen had bachelor rooms.

He had called at the house several times since he had seen his brother on South Audley Street, only to be informed Mr Damerel was not home. A coin pressed into the porter's palm had elicited the information that Stephen was expected to return home before going out again that evening.

It was two days since he had first seen Stephen. Two days in which he had not spoken to Eleanor, although he had watched over her from a discreet distance, alert to anyone behaving suspiciously.

He had already decided to revert to his family name even if Stephen rejected him. He had nothing to be ashamed of, but he did not want to reveal his true identity to Eleanor until he knew Stephen's reaction. He wanted to be prepared. If Eleanor rejected him…if she believed he would ruin her efforts to be accepted by the *ton*…then he must continue to protect her from afar, as best he could. He was more determined than ever to roust out whoever had put her in such danger, cousin or not.

The wind gusted, battering his hat and fingering his coat, looking for gaps.

Splat.

Hell, that's all I need.

Splat, splat. Huge raindrops burst on to the pavement, scattering the dust and tapping on the brim of his beaver hat.

Why am I skulking outside in the rain instead of waiting in Stephen's rooms?

He knew why, though. If Stephen had the same valet—Pring—he would recognise Matthew in a flash. He would forewarn Stephen and the news he was back in the country would wing its way to Rushock, the family's estate, and to his father and that he most definitely did not want. When he faced his father again, it would be on his terms.

The clip-clop of hooves on the cobbles grabbed his attention. A curricle drew up outside the house opposite. The gentleman driver leapt down and hurried to the front door whilst his tiger scurried round to climb into the vehicle and drive the horses away.

'Nine o'clock on the nose, Col.'

Stephen's voice. No mistaking it, even after all these years.

'Nine of the clock it is, guv.' The voice floated back as the curricle and pair clattered away.

Stomach on a mission to climb into his throat, Matthew strode across the road.

'Stephen.'

His brother froze on the threshold. He turned. Older, of course, but otherwise unchanged. Tall, rangy build, hawk-like nose—he got that from Father—keen grey eyes.

Ignoring the now-persistent rain, Matthew removed his hat. His brother's only reaction was a blink and the firming of his lips.

'You'd better come in,' he said and opened the door. 'First floor.'

Matthew led the way upstairs, thrusting down the nervous questions crowding his mind. Stephen would do what he would do. The die was now cast. On the landing, Stephen indicated a door.

'Sitting room,' he said. 'I'll tell Pring to bring some wine.'

Matthew shrugged out of his greatcoat and, after a second's hesitation, draped it over a ladderback chair set before a writing desk. The room was masculine—to be expected in this popular area for bachelor lodgings—all dark-green damask, polished wood panelling and leather seats. The fire was lit, as were the candles, dispersing the gloom of the murky late afternoon and Matthew used the poker to stir the coals. At the sound of the door closing, he turned.

Stephen's eyes narrowed. 'Defence or attack, little brother?'

'I doubt I would need a weapon in either case.' Matthew placed the poker back on the hearth.

'That I can believe. You have the look of a man who knows how to handle himself. How long have you been back in England?'

'A month or so.'

'And I owe the pleasure of this visit to…?'

'Courtesy call only.'

'It is usual to leave a card.'

'I have forgotten the niceties. You will have to forgive me.'

Like a pair of dogs, hackles raised, walking stiff-legged around each other.

The door opened and Stephen—who had not yet moved away from it—turned. There was a murmured exchange. When Stephen toed the door shut, he had a tray with a bottle and two glasses in his hands.

'You'd better sit down.' He put the tray on a table by the window and poured two glasses of rich red wine.

Matthew took a chair by the fire. Stephen remained standing.

Never mind—allow him the upper hand for now. My decision to come here; my responsibility to come to the point.

'I intend to make my home in England,' Matthew said. 'I had no intention of making contact with anyone from my past—'

'Not even your family?'

'My family—' Matthew placed his glass on a nearby table '—have made it abundantly clear they want nothing more to do with me.'

Stephen frowned. 'Where have you been?'

'Since I returned?'

'Since you left!' Stephen strode to the window

and stared through the glass. His tailored coat clung to the contours of his shoulders and back, revealing every breath he took. They were many and deep. 'We did not know if you were alive or dead.' A crack of emotion in his voice.

'But… Stephen… Father knew. And Claverley. They sent me to India. To Great-Uncle Percy.'

Stephen turned, frowning. 'You'd better tell me all of it.'

Matthew told Stephen about that night. As he talked, Stephen sat down opposite, his attention never wavering from Matthew's face. When he had finished, Stephen leaned back in his chair, his fingers steepled.

'So, Father sent you off to India. Why did you not write?'

The past had begun to reform into a coherent picture. Father and Claverley had not told the rest of the family where he had gone. He had been bundled on board ship and dismissed from their minds. Disowned.

'I wrote. Many times. No one—none of you— replied.'

Stephen's grey eyes searched Matthew's face.

'They never arrived,' he growled. 'Father must have made sure of it.'

'He was too ashamed to acknowledge I even existed after he disowned me.' Matthew could hear the sharp bitterness in his own voice. 'I did not do those things—cheat, or attack Henson.'

'He did try to clear your name. After you left.'

'I did not leave willingly.'

'I know that now. At the time, it seemed as though you had run away. It seemed like an admission of guilt.'

'You said he tried to clear my name. Did he discover the truth?' Knowing Father had at least tried kindled a tiny glow in his heart.

Stephen rose to pace the room. 'About the cheating, no. About the attack and the robbery, yes.'

'I already have the proof about the attack, thanks to Uncle Percy…although I suppose he and Father must have been in contact about that, which is how he knew. But the cheating…' Matthew had relived that night so many times, wondering what had happened, what he might have done differently. 'I know that extra card did not come from me. I have long thought about it. Henson was next to me and losing deep. He was already on the rocks before that night, according to the gossip. I think he meant to palm that king and he fumbled it. When the card fell on the floor, he immediately accused me. I'd been winning—it was an easy accusation to make stick. Have the other men at the game never said anything about that night?'

Stephen stopped pacing. 'I was never even told who was present that night. Father made certain it was all hushed up and forbade any of us to discuss it—or you—again. You know his views on codes of honour and gentlemanly behaviour. Of course, Claverley would never go against Father's decree, but Mother, Sarah and I—and Caro, now she is older—have talked about you and what had become of you. I've never heard the slightest whisper to suggest the accusation of cheating is common knowledge.'

That news was welcome. When he began to use his family name there would be no immediate scandal to taint Eleanor, unless any of those men returned to London. He would deal with that problem when it arose. He needed to speak to at least one of them, to try to uncover the truth of that night.

'You said you had no intention of making contact with any of us,' Stephen said. 'What changed your mind?'

'I'm a merchant, Stephen. I make my living through trade. This world…the world I grew up in…holds no lure for me.' That wasn't entirely true. Not any more. Eleanor's face materialised in his mind's eye. Was she safe? He needed to get back to her, to make sure. 'And neither would that world accept me. I don't belong any more.'

'You still haven't told me why you are here.'

Matthew leaned forward, under the pretence of stoking the fire. 'I have lived and worked with the name Matthew Thomas since I was eighteen.

It is now my intention to revert to my real name. Damerel.'

Matthew Thomas Damerel. His birth name, his family name. He could not move around in society without acknowledging it. He could not protect Eleanor without using it. He could not clear his name without reclaiming it.

'Why?'

Matthew shrugged. 'I will not live my life ashamed of something I did not do. I intend to clear my name. I will find proof.'

Stephen grinned suddenly, and thrust out his hand. 'Welcome home, little brother. Let me know how I can help.'

Chapter Seventeen

Eleanor sat at the table in her first-floor drawing room, writing a guest list for a soirée she was planning. It was difficult to concentrate. Her mind kept wandering to Matthew Thomas. He was annoyingly evasive. It was three days now since he had accompanied them to James's house and, since then, not a word. Although…she tapped the end of her quill pen absently against her cheek… there had been a time or two she had caught sight of him. Or thought she had.

In the distance.

Watching.

As soon as she noticed him, however, he had melted into the crowd and she was left wondering if it was the product of an over-active imagination. Or wishful thinking. Was it his way of ensuring she was safe, despite her rejection of his offer? Did he feel obligated to watch over her? Some masculine notion of honour…having once taken responsibility for her safety, did he feel unable to walk away?

If only he would call. She missed him. He had become a friend. One she could talk to. One she felt comfortable with. Unlike the men who had hovered around her like wasps around a ripe plum when she attended her first ball. Since then, there had been a procession of male callers, presenting her with flowers, reciting poetry, generally making cakes of themselves. She had learnt to bite her tongue, but she found herself wishing Matthew was there to share the joke.

And the others: the prowlers, the dangerous ones, the rakes. She shivered at the memory of some of those looks of dark determination. Thank goodness for Aunt Lucy, who was alert to their wiles and gave them all short shrift. Thoroughly distracted, she gazed from the window, overlooking the street. And frowned. Surely...that man... had she not seen him before? The man in question—medium height, slight build, unremarkable other than a pointed nose—paced slowly past on the opposite pavement. As Eleanor watched, trying to place where she might have seen him, he glanced at the house, perusing the frontage from top to bottom. Then his pace quickened and he soon disappeared from view.

Had he seen her watching him? Who was he? He was dressed like a clerk, in a nondescript brown suit. Where had she seen him before? She searched her memories.

The door opened.

'Mr Thomas has called, my lady.'

Her heart stuttered, then raced.

'Thank you, Pacey. Please show him up and inform Lady Rothley.'

Matthew…an image flashed into Eleanor's mind. The last time she had seen him, before he had disappeared around the corner. He had stopped and spoken to someone: the same man Eleanor had just seen outside.

Matthew followed Pacey up the staircase, mentally rehearsing the words to reveal his true identity to Eleanor. She would not be pleased at being misled. He knew her well enough to know that.

'Good morning, Lady Ashby. I trust you are well?'

He knew she was. He had been watching over her, making certain of it. Timothy, Eleanor's footman, had been most helpful in keeping him informed both about Eleanor's outings and her increasing number of gentlemen callers. He had thrust aside his jealousy; whether he was Matthew Thomas or Matthew Damerel could make no difference to his eligibility. He was a third son, making his living in trade. He was proud of his achievements, but that same pride dictated he was not a suitable match for a wealthy peeress.

'That day we visited James,' Eleanor said.

Matthew felt his brows shoot up. 'No greeting? No enquiry after your visitor's health? Tut-tut, my lady.'

Eleanor flushed. 'I apologise. But this is important.' Her words tumbled out one after the other. 'You spoke to a man, after you left Aunt Lucy and me. Who was he? Have you set him to watching me?'

'What man?' Matthew paused; racked his brains. 'I left you and I walked back to Hill Street. I do not recall speaking to anyone. I had urgent business.'

Avoiding being seen by my brother.

Eleanor crossed the room to scrutinise his face. Her scent enveloped him, her tawny-brown eyes huge—and doubtful—in her dear face. Matthew clenched his fists to keep them by his sides, to stop himself cradling her cheeks and kissing those soft lips.

'It was on the corner of Hill Street. Have you set anyone to watch me? A man in a brown suit with a pointed nose?'

'Who is watching you, Ellie?' Lady Rothley had come in and paled with fright. 'Oh, do not say you have seen the villain who has tried to harm you.'

Eleanor's words had sparked a memory in Matthew. 'I do recall a man in brown, now you say that, but he was only asking for directions.'

Eleanor bit her lip. 'I am sorry, Aunt. It was nothing. I thought I recognised a passer-by just now. I make no doubt I was mistaken.'

She smiled at her aunt, but it was forced and her eyes were strained. Matthew made a mental note to talk to Eleanor about this again but, for now…the subject was distressing Lady Rothley and he had another, more serious, matter to discuss.

'There is something I need to tell you,' he said. The change of subject would no doubt drive all thoughts of lurking villains from Lady Rothley's head.

As Eleanor and her aunt sat down, Pacey returned.

'Are you at home to Mr Weare, my lady?'

Eleanor leapt to her feet again. 'Why, yes, of course, Pacey. Please show him up.'

Matthew cursed silently. His confession must wait.

She crossed the room to greet her cousin as he came in wearing a sheepish expression. He kissed Eleanor on the cheek. Their family resemblance was strong—James was tall with an abundance of thick dark-brown hair and the same tawny-coloured eyes—and yet he seemed somehow less vital than Eleanor; faded, almost.

'Before you say anything, Eleanor, allow me

to apologise once again for the welcome we gave you the other day. It was a somewhat trying day all told.'

'Oh, James, there's no need. I told you that I understood. Is Ruth not with you? Is she still unwell?'

'Yes, I'm afraid so,' he said. 'It's the strain, you know. That appointment on Tuesday was with her doctor. She finds these things intolerable, but I'm afraid they are necessary. He has given her a restorative for her nerves, so she'll soon be her old self again.'

James walked further into the room and started when he became aware of Matthew, shooting him a suspicious look from beneath bunched eyebrows. 'Mr Thomas, isn't it? Good day to you, sir. I didn't expect you to have a visitor this early in the day, Cousin. Please forgive my intrusion.

'Lady Rothley, your servant.' He bowed.

Matthew held James's gaze as he stepped forward and gripped the other man's hand, noting the deep worry lines around his eyes and mouth.

'I had hoped to talk privately with my cousin,' James said pointedly.

'You have had ample opportunity since we called upon you on Tuesday.' It was a provocative statement. Matthew knew very well—thanks to Timothy—that James had not called as promised, but had sent a note to Eleanor instead.

James's jaw tightened. 'Eleanor is well aware

that my wife has been unwell since then and that I could not leave her. What exactly is your interest in my cousin, sir?'

'James, really, there is no need for such a challenge. Mr Thomas has called in to assure himself that I am still alive.' Eleanor's voice wobbled, belying her attempted humorous note.

'Alive? What do you mean?'

'It is time you told James what has been happening,' Lady Rothley said.

'I know, Aunt, and I intend to. We had an eventful journey to London, James, and Mr Thomas came to our rescue. He appears to think that places him in a position of obligation to me.'

Matthew watched James closely as he elaborated. 'Your cousin and her aunt had the misfortune to be involved in a carriage accident just outside Ashton. One of the horses was shot and the carriage overturned.'

'Shot? Good God, Eleanor. Are you all right? Was anyone hurt?'

His shock was evident. If James had been involved, he was a convincing actor. But who else could be responsible? It was this man who stood to gain from her death.

'Everyone escaped unscathed, James, please don't worry.'

'And, following that,' Matthew continued, 'a young girl was brutally attacked in the very room that you reserved for Lady Ashby in Stockport.

Fortunately—although not for that poor girl—I had insisted that the ladies stay in Ashton overnight as they were already shaken by the accident.'

James blanched and groped blindly for the seat behind him, sinking into it. 'No...' he breathed. 'Oh, my God, Eleanor! And she was in the room I reserved for you, you say? I can't believe it. What a...what a terrible coincidence. But thank goodness you are all right.'

'You believe it to be a coincidence?' Matthew glared at James.

'Mr Thomas...please...' Eleanor said.

'What?' James looked wildly from one to the other. 'What? You believe...you mean...you think *I* had something to do with it?'

'James, of course not. It must have been a coincidence. Mr Thomas has merely taken some wild notion into his head. Of course I don't believe you had any hand in it.' Eleanor looked daggers at Matthew, who was unrepentant.

'You must stop denying the gravity of this, my lady. *You* are the common factor to these incidents. *Someone* attempted to kill you on three occasions. That—' he glared at James '—is no coincidence, and when I find out who—'

'And who, precisely, are you, sir?' James snarled, springing to his feet. 'Matthew Thomas? Where are you from? Can anyone vouch for *you*? It seems to me that you, also, have been a common factor to these events. I, on the other hand, have been right here in London. And I can produce witnesses to prove it. I repeat—where are you from? My cousin is a wealthy lady; do you hope to win her over by scaring her witless? Is that your game?'

Matthew's chest swelled with fury when he recognised the doubt that crept into Eleanor's expression, her original misgivings about him clearly reignited by her cousin's words. Now would be the ideal time to reveal his true identity, but he was damned if he would discuss his past and the reason he used a false name in front of this weasel.

Surely Eleanor can't believe I am involved in some way?

He fought to keep his temper under control but, before he could utter a word, Lady Rothley leapt to his defence.

'That is a preposterous slur, James. I am surprised at you.'

'Any more preposterous than your accusations against me?'

'I have no doubt Mr Thomas can prove he was nowhere near Ashby Manor at the time of the fire. And he drove away the man who attacked that poor girl.'

'He was there? At the time? What does that tell you?' James stared triumphantly at Eleanor. 'Ellie, have some sense, I beg of you. You cannot, surely, believe *me* capable of such a thing? You've known me all your life.'

'I don't believe you did anything, James. How could I? I love you.'

'This attack,' James said slowly, his eyes narrowing as he turned his gaze on to Matthew. 'How did you hear of it, Ellie, if you were in… Ashton, was it, you said?'

'Mr Thomas told us of it,' she replied. 'He caught up with us on the road—' her gaze flicked to Matthew and a delicate colour stained her cheeks '—and then he escorted us the rest of the way to London, as protection.'

'So you take the word of a complete stranger that a girl was attacked as she slept in the bed you were to occupy?' James said. 'And you do not think it odd that he conveniently appeared after the carriage overturned, and then weaved this Canterbury tale about an attack. You just believed him? Have you heard of it from any other source?'

Matthew had heard enough. He had been scarred enough by false accusations in his time. 'The attempted murder can be verified by the magistrate in Stockport,' he said brusquely, 'and, although I do not know precisely when the fire occurred, I have no doubt I can prove my whereabouts if *you* feel the need for such proof,' he added, looking at Eleanor.

Eleanor avoided his gaze and Matthew's heart sank. Her cousin's insinuations were feeding her doubts. His behaviour when he had caught up with her at Leek could scarcely have reassured her as to his motives. She had been in shock; he had seized the opportunity and kissed her. It was little comfort that he had been so very frantic, thinking she might be lying injured somewhere. The sight of her safe and well had triggered an eruption of such relief that his common sense had deserted him. He had acted on pure instinct.

It was even more lowering to view his actions when she had returned to the parlour later that night. He could find all manner of excuses for his behaviour: he was a little foxed, which lowered his resistance; she had seemed to invite his kiss; he had been vulnerable, thinking of his estranged family and craving company and closeness when she had entered the room. Not one of those excuses was worthy.

'I don't believe Mr Thomas was responsible any more than I think you were, James. I should hope that both Aunt Lucy and I are better judges of character than that.'

Eleanor's declaration penetrated his reflections and his heart lifted.

'Indeed we are.' Lady Rothley's black eyes glittered as she glared at James. 'I sympathise with Eleanor's support for you, James, but I tell you straight that I am not yet convinced of your innocence. Why have you avoided Eleanor these last few years? That alone raises my suspicions.

You may rest assured Eleanor will be very well protected from now on.'

At this, James spun to face Eleanor. 'I did not come here to be accused in such a vile manner, Eleanor. I shall be pleased to see you again whilst you are in town, but preferably without your companions.'

'I'll just bet you will,' Matthew growled.

'And as for you, sir. If I find these wild conjectures have been made public, rest assured that I shall come looking for you. And do not doubt that I shall be making my own enquiries.'

He strode from the room without a backward glance.

Eleanor, who had risen to her feet when James left, stared at the door, breasts heaving, eyes brimming.

'I hope you are proud of yourselves,' she said. 'I had hoped to rekindle my friendship with James whilst I was in town, but I fear there is no chance of that now. What on earth made you accuse him so blatantly? Could you not see the shock on his face when you told him about the accident? Was that the expression of a guilty man?'

She rounded on Matthew. 'And you, Mr Thomas. You appear to believe I am unable to take care of myself. Well, might I inform you, I have been taking very good care of myself for three years now and I intend to go on doing so for many years to come. I do not need a man to protect me or to guide me and I shall thank you, sir, to stay out of my affairs in future.'

Her hands were clenched into fists, sparks of fire lighting her tawny eyes. Lady Rothley clucked loudly and rose from her chair to go to Eleanor, taking her arm and leading her to the sofa, where she sat down next to her, taking one of those fists between her two small hands, petting and scolding in equal measures.

'Now, now, Ellie, you must calm down, for you know you don't mean that. I am sorry for accusing James, but I just couldn't help myself. You must not blame us for being protective of you, for it is only because we care.'

Eleanor averted her face. 'I cannot believe James would hurt me. You have both made up your minds and poor James will be guilty in your eyes until the real culprit is discovered,' she said, bitterly.

Matthew ached to take her in his arms and soothe all her troubles away, to murmur in her ear that he understood how it felt to be betrayed by the people who should love you most. Her rigid posture, however, suggested it might not be easy to placate her. He cursed James Weare roundly but silently for driving the wedge of suspicion between them.

'If it helps,' he said, 'I do agree that your cousin appeared genuinely shocked when we told him what had happened. All we are asking is that you take your safety seriously.'

'I do,' Eleanor said. 'I promise I shall stay alert.'

She looked exhausted, never mind alert. This was clearly no time to confess his real identity. He would call back this afternoon and tell her the truth. He dare not leave it longer, for he had agreed to attend the Lexingtons' ball with Stephen that evening and the truth would be out.

'I shall leave you in peace,' he said.

Eleanor held out her hand, raising haunted eyes to his.

He took her hand and, unable to resist, bent to press his lips against her sweet skin. 'I hope to see you again very soon. Farewell.'

Chapter Eighteen

'Her ladyship is in the drawing room,' Pacey said, when Matthew called at Eleanor's house in Upper Brook Street that afternoon. He had delayed his visit until as late in the day as possible, in the hope that Eleanor's usual pack of admirers had been and gone.

'Does her ladyship have any callers with her at present?' he asked the butler as he led the way up the stairs.

'Indeed she does, sir. The door knocker has been busy all afternoon.' The butler's voice rang with satisfaction.

Matthew's heart sank. That meant he must kick his heels, waiting for the chance to speak to Eleanor and her aunt in private. Not a comfortable prospect when he had little hope Eleanor had yet forgiven him for the argument with James that morning. As they reached the top of the stairs, however, Matthew slammed to a halt, sick realisation twisting his stomach.

'Pacey!'

The butler looked round enquiringly.

'My apologies, but I have recalled an urgent matter I must attend to.'

That is becoming a too-familiar excuse—the sooner I reclaim my own name the better. I cannot continue like this. Spending time around the fashionable areas of London was proving riskier than he had anticipated.

'I'm afraid I will not even have time to pay my respects to the ladies,' he continued.

Pacey bowed. 'Very well, sir,' he said, and began to descend the stairs again.

'Do you know if Lady Ashby is to attend Lord and Lady Lexington's ball this evening?' Matthew asked, as Pacey handed him his hat in the hallway. If they weren't, maybe he could risk not speaking to Eleanor until the next day.

'As far as I am aware, sir, their ladyships' only engagement this evening is to dine with Lord and Lady Ely.'

Welcome news indeed.

Back out on Upper Brook Street, Matthew leapt aboard his curricle and drove away, breathing heartfelt thanks that he had seen in time the trap that lay in wait for him in Eleanor's drawing room. He pictured the scene: Pacey entering;

announcing Mr Matthew Thomas; faces, studying him, sizing him up; the curiosity about this stranger in their midst.

And then, when he was subsequently introduced as Matthew Damerel at the Lexingtons' ball that evening, the gossip and conjecture as to how they met, and whether she had known his true identity all along, would be bound to encompass Eleanor. It would inevitably harm her campaign to banish the memories of her mother's disgrace and her ambition to gain admittance to Almack's.

The past few minutes had emphasised the precariousness of his position. If he had any sense, he would cry off from the ball tonight, but could he delay any longer, knowing his father would arrive in London very shortly? Pring had recognised Matthew as he had left Stephen's lodgings the previous evening, prompting Matthew to write to his parents and also to his sister, Sarah—now married—to inform them of his return. It was better for the news to come from him than from some interfering busybody. Now, he sensed that the sooner he established his presence in society the better. His father—ever wary of sullying the family name—would not publicly disown Matthew which, in turn, would help protect Eleanor's reputation.

When Matthew had returned to England, he'd

had a definite plan. He had never intended to revisit that card game—his reputation and clearing his name hadn't been a priority. Once those next two ships had docked, and their cargoes were sold, he had planned to repay his father and then fade back into anonymity as Matthew Thomas.

But now…his plan had changed. Clearing his name had, suddenly, become urgent because Eleanor was in danger, and he had sworn to protect her and he could no longer do that from a distance.

'Mr Damerel and Mr Matthew Damerel.'

'Oh, my.' Aunt Lucy clutched at Eleanor's forearm with urgent fingers. 'I always thought there was a familiarity about him. He favours his mama, of course, and his brother is his father's son. No wonder I missed the connection when we met Mr Damerel with Derham the other day.'

Eleanor excused herself to the group of ladies she was chatting to, and turned to her aunt. They were at the Lexingtons' ball, their dinner engagement with Lord and Lady Ely having been cancelled.

'I beg your pardon, Aunt, what was that you said?'

Aunt Lucy tugged Eleanor round to face the door. 'Look who is there, talking to our hosts.'

Eleanor perused the knot of guests at the ballroom door. As she spied a familiar shock of dark-blond hair, she gasped.

'It's Matthew… I mean Mr Thomas,' she whispered.

'Mr Damerel, it would now seem,' Aunt Lucy said. 'I wonder… I do seem to recall some scandal, years ago. Oh, tsk. My memory is not what it used to be. I have been buried in the country for far too long.'

Eleanor struggled to make sense of what she saw. Matthew—tall, handsome…elegant, even—in immaculate black evening clothes. *What is he thinking? He will never get away with…but… Stephen Damerel? Has Matthew somehow persuaded him to take part in this charade, or…?* She could not think straight. Matthew was looking around, that keen blue gaze sweeping the throng.

Eleanor turned away. 'Aunt Lucy, I am feeling a little faint. Might we go into the other room and sit quietly for a few moments?'

She struggled to keep her expression neutral as Aunt Lucy peered up at her. 'Of course, my pet. Come, let us slip out of this door.'

They made their way into a room that had been set aside for the older, less lively guests who enjoyed a quiet gossip away from the banter and bustle of the ballroom.

Eleanor sank into a chair with its back to the door.

'Who is he?' she demanded, as her aunt sat opposite her.

'It would seem his name is Matthew Damerel.'

'He was with Mr Damerel, so…are they related?'

'I think they must be brothers…it is coming back to me…there was a third brother…he was a wild youth, expelled from school, a black sheep. Left England under a cloud, although his father—Rushock, you know—hushed it all up. He was ever a stickler—couldn't abide scandal. Disowned the boy, I seem to recall. I wonder if he knows Matthew has returned.'

Eleanor listened with a sinking heart. Anger…hurt…humiliation…she could not sort one emotion from the other…they flooded her and she wanted to sink through the floor and never have to face Matthew again. Her behaviour had been shocking enough…succumbing to the hot looks and honeyed words of a man she believed beneath her station in life. But now…that man was one of her peers. The son of an earl, albeit disgraced. How he must have laughed at her naivety. What a disgust he must feel for her, knowing her to be so lacking in morality that she had encouraged… nay, instigated…such intimacies with a man such as she had believed him to be.

And to think…she had even confessed her desire to be accepted into society and her desire to gain approval to attend Almack's in order to

banish the memory of her mother's shameful behaviour.

*Oh, how he must have chuckled, to hear my
hopes and aspirations, when all the time he had
his own shady past to conceal. Scandal, Aunt
Lucy said. The very last thing I need.*

She wanted to disappear. She wanted to die…
to crawl into a dark corner and lick her wounds
like an injured animal.

But she wouldn't.

She stood up. 'Come,' she said to Aunt Lucy.
'Mr Th—Mr Matthew Damerel might have made
a fool out of both of us, but I will not hide away,
afraid to face him.'

'Ellie, my dear. I beg of you, do not do anything you may live to regret.'

*Too late for that, dearest Aunt, if you did but
know.*

Eleanor headed for the ballroom, Aunt Lucy
on her heels.

I wonder what he did.

*I do not care. He is not a suitable acquaintance
for me and that is that.*

As they reached the door, Aunt Lucy clutched
at Eleanor's arm.

'Do not forget that nobody, other than James
and Ruth, knows we are already acquainted with
Matthew Damerel. Just follow my lead when we
are introduced.'

Eleanor patted her aunt's hand. 'Do not fret. I

am not about to ruin my chances of acceptance by enacting a vulgar scene. I shall be above censure at all times, you may trust me on *that*.'

'Lady Ashby.' A tall, russet-haired gentleman was bowing before her. Lord Derham. 'We meet again. If you are not engaged for this dance, would you do me the honour?'

Eleanor smiled. 'Thank you, my lord. I should be delighted.'

This is more like it. An earl. Tall. Very handsome.

Eleanor gazed into green eyes…eyes that did absolutely nothing for her. No shortened breath. No quickened pulse.

Mayhap I simply prefer blue eyes? It means nothing.

As she skipped down the line of dancers, a figure at the edge of the floor—talking to Aunt Lucy—caught her attention. Her heart squeezed, then lurched, and she missed her step. She hastened to catch up with the music, concentrating fiercely on the steps of the dance until the end.

Lord Derham returned her to Aunt Lucy, still standing with Matthew and his brother.

'My dear, you remember Mr Damerel?' Eleanor could hear the anxious undertones in her aunt's voice.

'Indeed. Good evening, Mr Damerel.'

'And this is his brother, Mr Matthew Damerel.'

Eleanor forced a gracious smile as she nodded

her head at both men. She could feel the trace of those ice-blue eyes as they travelled from her head to her toes and back again. *How very impolite!* She tilted her chin and focused on Lord Derham.

Only to find a wide-shouldered figure blocking her view.

'Might I beg your hand for this dance, Lady Ashby?' Matthew leaned in, lowering his voice. 'As long as you do not consider a third son beneath your touch?'

Had she imagined that hint of a warning? Could James be right? Was he another fortune hunter? After all, what *did* she know of him? She was a fool—she had kissed him, told him her secrets and, in return, he had given her a false name and now she discovered he was hiding a disreputable past. Well, she was wise to him now and this one dance would give her the opportunity to tell him so, and to caution him to keep his distance from her. After that, she would banish him from her life and her thoughts, for the sake of her reputation if nothing else.

'Of course, Mr Damerel.' She stretched her lips in a sweet smile. 'I should be delighted.'

It was a country dance. As soon as the opportunity arose she whispered, 'You lied.'

As he opened his mouth to reply, she carried on. 'No, I do not want to hear your excuses. From now on...' The steps of the dance forced them apart. When they came together again, Eleanor continued, '…you are to leave me alone. I do not want my name associated with yours in any way, shape or form.'

His lips thinned. 'That was not your view when you thought me a humble merchant.'

Oh! How ungentlemanly, to throw that at her, even though it was exactly what she had feared he would think.

'I have my reputation to think of,' she whispered at the next opportunity.

'And you want vouchers for Almack's…and association with the likes of me might spoil your chances?'

The steps of the dance separated them. They came together again. Eleanor hissed, 'Precisely!'

Then, after a brooding silence from Matthew, she said, 'Why didn't you tell me the truth?'

They parted. Came together again. His fingers curled around her gloved palm as he took her hand.

'We cannot talk here. Meet me upstairs. I will tell you everything.'

'No! How can you even ask…what if we were seen?'

So far, her evening engagements had gone well, with only one or two barbed comments about her mother, which she had fended off with ease. She had even exchanged pleasantries with Maria Sefton and Emily Cowper, both patronesses of Almack's, and although there had been no promises made, Eleanor harboured the hope that their approval of her membership would be forthcoming. Her confidence had begun to grow.

'We can be careful—'

'No! Do *not* ask again.'

They finished the dance in tight-lipped silence and relief flooded Eleanor when it ended.

A succession of partners—and supper—came and went. Eleanor was in control of her emotions and her behaviour. Not one person could point an accusing finger at her and say *'Like mother, like daughter'*. It was not so bad—now she was over the initial shock of Matthew's appearance in the ballroom and the fact he had lied to her, even though she could not quite suppress her conjectures over the scandal Aunt Lucy had mentioned. Surely the scandal couldn't have been *too* dreadful, or Matthew's brother would not openly acknowledge him like this.

And then Arabella Beckford appeared. Or, as some kind soul informed her, Arabella, Lady Tame, as she now was—a wealthy widow. Of all the girls who had tormented Eleanor during her come-out, it was Miss Arabella Beckford who had stuck in her memory. The acknowledged beauty of the day, Arabella had been—and still was— petite and delicate, with golden curls, big blue eyes and pouting rosebud lips. In London for the first time, Eleanor had towered over Arabella, feeling utterly unfeminine—all clumsy angles and awkward silences—and she had suffered many unkind gibes from the other girl.

No wonder, thought Eleanor sourly, as she watched Arabella pouting up at Matthew—gazing at him through fluttering eyelashes—she had hated her come-out. The old feelings of inadequacy washed over her.

Why can I not be feminine, like Arabella? Why would any man prefer a huge lump like me?

Eleanor turned abruptly from the sight of Arabella flirting with Matthew.

'Excuse me, Aunt.'

Aunt Lucy looked round from her engrossing conversation with Sir Horace Todmorden, a dapper gentleman with luxuriant side whiskers. 'Yes, dear?'

'I am just going upstairs to the ladies' retiring room.'

'Shall I come—?'

'No. There is no need. I shall sit in the quiet for a few minutes, to catch my breath. I declare, I am quite out of practice and all this dancing has exhausted me.'

'Very well, my pet.'

Eleanor left the ballroom and climbed the stairs to the retiring room. Finding it blessedly empty, other than the maid on duty, she sat for a short while, relaxing back in a chair, settling her thoughts and emotions.

Anyone but Arabella. Surely Matthew will see through her to the spiteful little cat she has always been? She stifled those thoughts. What did it matter to her who Matthew talked to? Or danced with? Or…?

She stood up, suddenly furious with herself. She was hiding again. If she was not careful, it would become a habit. She would not allow anyone to drive her away this time.

She stepped out of the door to return to the festivities, then froze, sensing a movement in the passageway behind her.

'Eleanor.'

The quietest of whispers, but she would know his voice anywhere. And his scent. His unique maleness, plus the tang of citrus. She spun round to face Matthew Damerel.

'I must talk to you.'

'And I must *not* talk to you.'

He stood by the open door into the next room. He held out his hand, beckoning.

The chatter of female voices impinged on Eleanor's awareness. A quick glance over the gallery rail to the floor below revealed a cluster of young ladies mounting the stairs, presumably on their way to the retiring room.

'Quick. Or we shall be seen.'

Eleanor reached for the handle to the retiring-room door. She would be safe in there.

'I will follow you if you go back inside,' Matthew warned, reaching for her hand. 'Come. Please.'

The voices were louder. Even if she headed for the stairs, the young ladies would see Matthew and wonder... The gossip would spread from mouth to mouth...

Wretch! Scoundrel!

With no choice left, Eleanor swept past Matthew and through the open door.

Chapter Nineteen

'Despicable!'

They were in a small sitting room, furnished in a feminine style. One candle, set into a candlestick on the mantelpiece, flickered, throwing shadows around the room.

'You must allow me to explain.'

'Must I indeed? You could have explained this morning. You could call on me tomorrow to make your excuses. You did not have to…to…blackmail me into coming in here with you.'

'Blackmail? Don't be absurd.'

'Absurd? How dare you? You come into my life—I start to trust you, to rely upon you. You make me—' Eleanor bit her lip, appalled by what she had almost said.

You make me love you.

She gulped, her throat burning with the effort of stifling the hot tears strangling her voice and blurring her vision.

Stupid thing to even think. Just the heat of the moment.

'I think I know you and then I find I do not even know your name. Then you threaten me with exposure if I do not do what you want... and you call *me* absurd for calling it blackmail? What would you call it, Mr Thomas, or Damerel, or whoever you are?'

Her chest heaved. Her outburst had stolen the very breath from her lungs. She hauled in a desperate breath.

'I don't even know who you are.' The cry burst from her, searing her throat.

'Eleanor—'

'And *do not* call me Eleanor. You have no right.'

'No right? By God, what wouldn't I give to have that right? You have no idea...'

The grip on her shoulders tightened and she looked up through her tears into blazing eyes that churned with emotion. His face swam closer. He was going to kiss her. She felt his breath, harsh on her skin, as his lips sought hers.

'No. I cannot. I *must* not.'

Eleanor stumbled as Matthew tore his hands from her and strode to the window. She sank into a chair by the unlit hearth, dropping her face into her hands. What had just happened? He had been about to kiss her; she had *wanted* him to kiss her. It was he who had come to his senses and stopped before his lips touched hers. How could she be so weak-willed, so unprincipled? She gritted her teeth, determined to hide her bruised feelings. If Matthew should even begin to guess how she felt about him her pride would never survive—it was in tatters as it was.

Matthew stared out into the void, battling the urge to sweep her into his arms and to hell with the consequences. But it was the consequences for Eleanor that gave him the strength to control himself. He had set out on this path, and he had no choice now but to continue if he were to protect her from her evil cousin.

'Why are you even here?' he said, his back to her. He had been struck with horror when he caught sight of her—stunning in pale-yellow silk—in the Lexingtons' ballroom. 'Pacey said you were engaged to dine with the Elys tonight.'

'Lord Ely was taken ill so we dined at home.' She sounded dazed. 'Then we came...' Her voice sharpened. 'What are you saying? That you would not be here, announcing yourself as Matthew Damerel, had you known Aunt Lucy and I would be present? What a fine joke you have played on us, sir. I hope we have provided you with plenty of amusement.'

He faced her. 'You are upset with me...with every right... I will explain.'

'Go ahead.' Her voice was icy. 'I suggest you do it quickly, before my aunt comes looking for me.'

Matthew crossed the room to stand by the fireplace. Eleanor sat ramrod straight, hands gripped in her lap. Sitting in judgement. On him. Resentment churned his gut. Who was she, to look down on him? Why hadn't he had the sense to walk away that first day?

'My name is Matthew Thomas Damerel. I am the third son of the Earl of Rushock.'

'So you are not a merchant after all?'

'That part was true. I am a merchant; it is how I earn my living.' He had been proud of his independence. Now it felt as though he was admitting to something shameful. There was no shred of encouragement on her face. Her eyes were unreadable, her lips set in a hard line.

'Why lie about your name?'

'Thomas is my middle name. I've lived as Matthew Thomas since I went to India. My own name is too distinctive and I did not wish to invite speculation about my past.'

'But when you returned to England...surely, with your family here—'

'No!' Matthew scrubbed his hand across his jaw. How could he make her understand? 'That is the point. I am...was...' He stared down into the empty grate. Revealing his past—humbling himself—to Eleanor was harder than he anticipated, particularly in the face of her cold demeanour. But the truth was the only way if he was to regain her trust. 'My father disowned me when I was eighteen. I was rebellious in my youth—heedless of the troubles I left in my wake as I pursued my own pleasures. I was expelled from Harrow, sent down from Oxford, I drank too much, gambled, ran up debts…'

'Not so very different to many young men,' Eleanor said into the silence as he hesitated.

Matthew heaved a frustrated breath. 'No, not so very different. But then, at eighteen, I was falsely accused of something. My father believed my accuser's word against mine. He and Claverley—my eldest brother—decided I must go to my great-uncle in India. I refused, determined to stay and clear my name, but they wouldn't listen.' He fingered the bump on his nose—a constant, bitter reminder of their betrayal. 'Claverley took me by surprise. Knocked me out cold. When I came to, the ship had set sail and I could do nothing about it.'

'What were you accused of?'

'Does it matter?' He was loath to admit the sordid details. 'Will you trust me when I say the accusation was false?'

'Trust you? How can I trust you?' The words burst from Eleanor as she shot to her feet. 'You have lied and made a fool of me.'

'How have I made a fool of you?' He fought to hold the reins of his temper. 'And I did not lie… You are not listening—I have lived as Matthew

Thomas for eight years. My use of that name had nothing to do with you.'

'Nothing to do with me?' Her voice rose. 'Even after you *kissed* me?' Her cheeks flushed, but she held his gaze.

'Why,' he growled, 'should I tell you something I had no intention of ever revealing to anyone, ever again?'

'So why have you revealed it now?' She jabbed her finger at him, poking him in the chest. 'Why have you changed your mind?'

She was like a dog worrying at a bone…why could she not just accept what he was saying without challenging him?

'Is it to prove you would be an acceptable match for me by birth? Is that it? Was James right? Are you just another fortune hunter?'

The lid blew off his self-control. *'Fortune hunter?'* The words erupted from his mouth. Yet another false slur! Was it not enough he had been labelled a cheat all these years? 'How dare you? There is no force on earth that would persuade me to court a woman who not only outranks me but has tenfold my wealth.'

Her eyes narrowed and her jaw jutted forward. 'Then why are we here?'

'What do you mean? I told you…I needed you to understand.'

'But why me? Why not…oh, I don't know!

Aunt Lucy? Or…or *Arabella Tame*? Why have you singled *me* out for your explanations?'

'Because *they* do not need my protection,' he ground out. 'You do. I cannot leave you vulnerable. Good God, I have never met such a stubborn, infuriating woman. I tried to talk to you downstairs, but, no! You would not listen.' He grabbed her shoulders. 'I *had* to change my name back. How the he—*deuce* can I protect you when I was constantly afraid to show my face in society in case I was recognised? That is the only reason I am reclaiming my true identity. Obligation. And believe me when I say I am beginning to regret embarking on this whole nightmare.'

'Oh!' Eleanor jerked out of his hold. *'Obligation?'* She inhaled, then straightened her shoulders, lifted her chin and shook out the skirts of her ballgown. She raised both hands to smooth down her hair. 'I see. Well, you had no need to bother. I release you from any obligation…I have all the protection I need, thank you, Mr Damerel.'

She didn't quite know how she got there, but Eleanor found herself out in the passageway, heading blindly towards the staircase, the crush of the ballroom awaiting her. As she descended the stairs, her wits began to reassemble. Anger and humiliation still bubbled, tempered only slightly by her guilt at flinging that vile accusation at Matthew.

Moistening dry lips, swallowing convulsively,

she fumbled for her dance card to discover the name of her next dance partner. The space was blank and she gave thanks for that small mercy. She walked into the ballroom, head high, feeling as though every eye in the place was on her; as though every person knew what a fool she was; and as though her name was on every lip and it was spoken with scorn.

'Aunt Lucy, I am sorry, I have the headache. Would you mind if we go home?'

Aunt Lucy was still deep in conversation with Sir Horace. 'Oh dear, you do look rather pale, my pet,' she said, worry creasing her forehead. 'Of course we can go. Please do excuse us, Sir Horace. I hope we shall meet again soon.'

A delicate pink tinged Aunt Lucy's cheeks as Sir Horace kissed her hand. 'You can be sure we will, dear lady,' he said.

Chapter Twenty

He had two choices. Again. He could follow his head or his instinct. His head told him to leave her to her fate. She had rejected his offer of help enough times now. And she had insulted him. Those two words…circling in his head, like buzzards…is that what she truly thought of him? Of his reasons for returning to her side again and again? A fortune hunter? Had her cousin succeeded in poisoning her mind against him? No one could blame him for walking away this time.

Or he could harden his soul against those words and follow his instinct, which was to protect her come what may. And that meant he must proffer an olive branch. His temper had got the better of him, but he had not said anything untrue. She was stubborn. And she was infuriating. And there *was* no way on earth his pride would allow him to court her—no matter how his heart leapt at the mere sight of her and no matter how his hands curled into fists every time another man spoke to her, or smiled at her, or took her hand and led her on to the dance floor.

He simply could have said those things more diplomatically.

'You are very quiet,' Stephen commented as he drove his curricle into Hyde Park at five o'clock the following day.

'Sorry,' Matthew replied. 'I was wondering how long it would be before the rest of the family arrive in town.'

It was not a lie; he had been wondering what their response to his letters would be. His family hadn't been uppermost in his mind, though.

He had called at Eleanor's house in Upper Brook Street, determined to make amends for the night before, only to be informed by Pacey that the ladies were walking in the park. A short time later, Stephen had driven past—on *his* way to the park—and taken Matthew up.

'Not long, I should imagine, although I would hazard a guess our father will come on his own at first,' Stephen said. 'How will you play it?'

Matthew shrugged, his gaze skimming the clusters of walkers, searching. 'I'm not sure yet,' he replied absently. 'I suppose it will depend on his attitude. I am looking forward to seeing Mama and the girls, though.'

Not only was Sarah now wed, and a mother, but Caroline was to make her bow to society next spring. Little Caro…all grown up. How strange to find their lives had moved on without him. He had much catching up to do.

His heart gave a sudden lurch; speaking of catching up, there was his quarry. Eleanor, stylishly clad in a peacock-blue walking dress, with ivory spencer and bonnet, was strolling with Lady Rothley, who was leaning on the arm of a slight, very upright gentleman. As Matthew watched, they stopped to speak to another group walking in the opposite direction.

'Hey!' Stephen nudged Matthew. 'You need to clean out your ears, little brother. That's twice I've asked you the same question.'

Matthew tore his attention from Eleanor. 'Sorry. Wool-gathering. What was it?'

'I asked you what had grabbed your attention over there, but I've worked it out for myself. The Baroness Ashby? Are you serious?'

Matthew glared at his brother. 'What is that supposed to mean?'

'Whoa, there. Don't raise your hackles at me.' Stephen reined his pair to a halt a short distance from the group that included Eleanor. 'It was no reflection on the lady's charms. Look, Matt, you've only just arrived in town, so I'll drop you a hint. Don't set your sights on that particular lady. She's only been in town a week or so herself, but already she's been declared the Catch of the Season, despite her age. The deuce knows how she's still single, with all that wealth…those northerners must be a group of slowtops not to have fixed their interest with her by now. And it's not just the money…her husband will have the right to sit in the Lords on her behalf, you know. The Betting Book at White's is already filling up with wagers as to which lucky fellow will breach her defences first.'

'I am well aware of her circumstances,' Matthew growled, his muscles rigid. 'We met on the road to London.'

Stephen whistled. 'Did you now…you kept that very quiet. Well, well. Thinking of donning leg shackles, are you?'

'No!' Matthew hauled in a breath. He must tell Stephen the truth, or he would end up drawing his cork. 'My sole concern is for her safety.' He recounted the circumstances of his meeting with Eleanor and his discovery of the danger she was in.

'Nasty business,' Stephen said. 'You'll be hard put to protect her on your own, though. I'll pass the word to some of the other fellows—only the ones I can trust—and tell them to keep an eye out for any ne'er-do-wells sniffing around.'

'Ha! Plenty of them to be found, but not necessarily ones intent on killing her.'

'Uh-oh…do I detect a sour note, little brother? Seems to me you've developed a soft spot for the lady. It won't do, you know. You'd never stomach a wife that much richer than you, not with that stiff-necked pride of yours.'

Matthew jumped out of the curricle, ignoring his brother's knowing smirk.

Let him think what he pleases.

'I'll see you later,' he said.

'Keep that heart of yours well fenced, Mattie,' Stephen called after him. 'I can see it from here... glowing on your sleeve.'

Stephen's laughter faded as he drove away and Matthew grimaced. Had he really lamented the loss of his brother's banter and company all these years?

Matthew thrust Stephen from his mind as he approached Eleanor, who stood apart from the rest of the group, talking with a fashionably dressed lady whose back was to Matthew. Eleanor's eyes widened momentarily when she saw him and her lips firmed before her gaze slid on past him. Other than that, she gave no sign of recognition.

Matthew reached the pair just in time to hear Eleanor's companion—whom he now recognised as Emily Cowper, one of the influential patronesses of Almack's—saying, 'From what dear Lady Rothley has told me, it seems you had a horrid time of it during your first Season, my dear. Let me take your name to the Committee and see what I can do.'

Here was a fortunate coincidence. Eleanor

could hardly cut him dead in front of her ladyship, not without risking that all-important voucher. He smiled at Eleanor and lifted his hat.

'Good afternoon, Lady Ashby. We meet again.'

She managed a wintry smile. 'Good afternoon, Mr Damerel. Have you met Lady Cowper?'

'I have not yet had that honour.'

'Lady Cowper—Mr Matthew Damerel.'

'Charmed, my lady.' Matthew bowed, summoning his most winning smile.

Lady Cowper's cheeks took on a pink hue. 'Goodness me, yet another stranger in our midst—we *are* being spoilt this year. Where have you been hiding yourself all these years, sir?'

'Oh, I was a wicked youth, my lady… I have no doubt you were well protected from the likes of me. Alas, as a third son, I needs must earn a living and have lived in India for several years past.'

'Well, I am pleased to make your acquaintance now, Mr Damerel. You were pointed out to me last night, but you disappeared before I was able to gain an introduction.' She smiled teasingly at him. 'Infamous behaviour, sir.'

'I am mortified, dear lady. Had I but known of your presence, I would most certainly have contrived an introduction. Now we are old friends, however, I shall have no compunction in begging a dance the next time I see you, for I have it on good authority there is no other lady in the *ton* so light on her feet.'

'You, sir, are a shameless flatterer, but I shall look forward to it. Oh! There is Lord Plymstock. Please do excuse me, for I have something I most particularly want to say to him. I shall do what I can for you, Lady Ashby. Goodbye.'

Eleanor watched her leave. 'Well,' she said, without so much as a glance at Matthew. 'I had no idea you could act the flirt so convincingly, sir.'

He lowered his voice. 'I know how much gaining approval for Almack's means to you, Eleanor. It cannot hurt to keep the lady sweet.'

A muscle in her jaw clenched and she lowered her gaze to study the ground.

'I owe you an apology. For the things I said last night,' Matthew said.

'Which things, precisely?' She glanced around, then pierced him with an unforgiving glare. 'Do you mean you do not consider me stubborn? Or infuriating?'

A short laugh burst unbidden from his lips. 'By Jupiter, you get right to the point, don't you? My choice of words was poor. My apology is more for my behaviour than for the things I said. And, more importantly, for not telling you the truth of my identity beforehand—although, in my defence, I did try.'

'You did? Might I suggest you did not try very hard?'

'You may believe that if it makes you feel better, but when I called upon you yesterday morning it was my intention to tell you all. Then your cousin arrived and you were, understandably, upset. I called back later, but you were engaged with callers. And, yes. You are stubborn and infuriating. But I suspect you would say the same about me.'

She caught his eye. 'I might,' she said. 'But not in public,' she added, tilting her nose. 'I have too much care for my reputation. Now, I must return to my aunt.'

Before she could move, Matthew took a stride towards her and crooked his arm.

Eleanor raised a haughty brow. 'I do not think—'

'Lady Cowper is looking. Do you want her to suspect we have quarrelled?'

'My returning to Aunt Lucy will not look as though we have quarrelled.'

'It will when I follow you. She will wonder why we do not walk together.'

'Blackmail again, Mr Damerel?' Despite her words, Eleanor laid rigid fingers on Matthew's sleeve and her two footmen—who had halted at a discreet distance from their mistress—fell into step behind them.

'Do not imagine this means I have forgiven you,' she hissed even as her expression remained serene.

'Oh, I know you have not,' Matthew countered.

'I am curious, though. Why, precisely, *are* you still so angry with me?'

'Oh!' Eleanor halted and stared at him. 'Do you have to ask?'

'Well…yes, I'm afraid I do. You see, I cannot decide if you are still cross over my not telling you my real identity or because of my behaviour last night or because of what happened with James yesterday.'

They resumed their stroll, Eleanor staring straight ahead. Lady Rothley appeared to have finished talking with her friends. She looked round and, seeing Eleanor was with Matthew, she gave a little wave and then walked on ahead, her hand on the upright gentleman's arm.

'And if I say it is all three?' Eleanor asked eventually.

'Then I shall have to humbly apologise for all three,' Matthew said promptly. 'But you will understand that I am reluctant to apologise for something you may not still be angry about—there is only so much humble pie I can manage at one sitting.'

He was encouraged to hear a stifled giggle as Eleanor's fingers tightened on his sleeve. A sidelong glance revealed her lips pursed tight.

'There now, that is better, is it not? Do you think we might be friends again, or should I grovel some more?'

Eleanor almost burst with the effort of not

laughing. 'G-grovel? C-correct me if I am mistaken, but I have seen little s-sign of grovelling from you, sir. Cajoling, yes. Grovelling? I don't believe so.'

It was difficult to maintain her righteous indignation in the face of Matthew's teasing, but Eleanor was not yet ready to fully forgive him. The truth was that her feelings were much more complex than mere anger. There *was* anger—smouldering still—after his behaviour last night. Her heart quailed when she thought of the implications had they been seen; her reputation would have been ruined for ever. And she was hurt by his lack of trust. Why had he not told her the truth earlier, particularly after she had confided in him about her mother? And then there was the humiliation over those kisses and the lowering realisation that—even last night, when she was so furious—she still would not have rebuffed his kiss.

As for his argument with James—

'Tell me you do not place any credence on your cousin's suspicions,' Matthew said.

She shot him a startled look. How could he know what she had been thinking?

'No,' she said.

'Your eyes tell a different tale,' he said. 'You doubt me and my motives. I can see how you might suspect a sinister agenda after everything that has happened to you, but please believe that

I told you the truth last night about my reasons for not using my real name.'

Eleanor hesitated. Her doubts about Matthew, raised by James and fuelled by last night's events, had shaken her to her core, but a restless night had brought some perspective. Should she judge him through James's eyes, or through her own experience? His actions—those times on the journey to London when he had saved her from her own naivety—were surely not those of a fortune hunter? Even last night, it had been Matthew who had stopped before their lips had touched.

'I will admit that yesterday did raise doubts in my mind,' she said, still not ready to completely let him off the hook.

'I can only hope you will not allow those doubts to fester,' he replied. 'I thought I could protect you as Matthew Thomas, but I was wrong— the risk to your reputation if I was exposed was too great. Believe me when I say that is the *only* reason I have reclaimed my own name now. You remain in danger. I have sworn to protect you, and I hope you will accept my continuing protection and allow me the opportunity to expose your attacker.'

Calmness settled over Eleanor at his words. She could not deny her feeling of vulnerability with only footmen in attendance, but she would not admit that to Matthew.

'Very well,' she said. 'I accept. If only to keep

Aunt Lucy happy; she feels much safer when there is a gentleman around.'

'For Aunt Lucy's sake,' Matthew repeated, very slowly.

Eleanor glanced at him, suspecting he was poking fun at her, but he remained straight-faced.

'Very well,' he said. 'I am pleased that is settled. Now, I've been dying to ask…who *is* the gent with the splendid whiskers?'

Eleanor bit back a smile as she looked ahead to Aunt Lucy and her escort. 'They are quite magnificent, are they not? He is Sir Horace Todmorden and I believe he is courting Aunt Lucy. Is that not delightful?'

Chapter Twenty-One

Two days later, Eleanor and Aunt Lucy returned to their house in Upper Brook Street, having enjoyed another pleasant walk in Hyde Park escorted by Matthew and the increasingly attentive Sir Horace Todmorden. Eleanor sensed Pacey's disquiet as soon as he opened the front door. Her normally unflappable butler gave every impression of having to restrain himself from chivvying everyone inside.

'What is it, Pacey? Is there something wrong?'

'There has been An Incident, my lady.' His precise enunciation of those two words spoke volumes.

Eleanor removed her spencer and bonnet and handed them to Lizzie, barely noticing the squirm of apprehension deep in her belly, it had become so familiar.

'You had better come up to the drawing room

and tell me what has happened.' She led the way
to the room.

'One of the kitchen maids was accosted on her
way home from running an errand this morning,'
Pacey said.

'This morning? But why did you not tell me
earlier?'

'The silly girl was too scared to say anything
at first, but Cook finally managed to wheedle it
out of her,' Pacey said. 'In the normal course of
events, I would not bother you with such a triv-
iality, my lady, but in view of the goings-on I
thought I must apprise you of the incident immediately upon your return.'

'Goings-on?' Sir Horace queried. 'What goings-on?'

'I think you had better tell us exactly what happened to the maid, Pacey,' Matthew said.

'Wait!' Eleanor said. 'Before you do…' She
turned to Sir Horace. She had no wish to become
the subject of gossip, so the fewer people who
knew of her misfortunes, the better. 'I am sorry,
Sir Horace, but—'

'You must not object to Sir Horace knowing
what has happened, Ellie,' Aunt Lucy said, settling into a chair by the fireplace. 'He is most
discreet. You must not think he will bandy your
business about in the clubs. He was a cavalry officer, you know. He is used to all sorts of dangerous situations. He will be a valuable ally.'

A cavalry officer? Eleanor bit back her cynical retort. Quite what use a cavalry officer might be against her unknown assailant she could not imagine, but Aunt Lucy seemed smitten, and Eleanor had not the heart to deny her.

'Of course,' she said. 'Pray continue, Pacey. Which girl was it? Is she all right?'

'Yes, she is now. Once it was all in the open, she calmed down. It was Agnes, one of the kitchen maids. Cook sent her to the grocer's at Shepherd's Market for some almonds and spices. She noticed a man outside the house and he followed her. Then, on her way home, he began to walk beside her. She wasn't suspicious at first. She said he seemed harmless enough and pestered her about when she had time off and so forth. But then he began to ask about the house, and the routines, and about you, my lady. Agnes got scared and told him to go away and that our household was none of his business. He threatened her then and said if she told anyone about him, he would find her and hurt her.'

'I wish she had told us immediately,' Eleanor said, 'although no doubt the man would have run off as soon as she came indoors. Did she describe him?'

'Yes. She said he was about five and forty, and medium height with mousy brown hair. He was dressed respectably, in a brown suit.'

'A brown suit.' Eleanor's stomach clenched.

It sounded like the man she had seen. Who was he? Why was he watching her? Was it he who had tried to kill her and had attacked that poor girl in Stockport.

'Yes,' Pacey said. 'And a pointy nose.'

Eleanor sank on to the sofa. 'Thank you, Pacey. That will be all, but please ensure one of the men accompanies any of the maids if they have to go out on errands, will you? I do not want any of my household put in jeopardy.'

'Pacey,' Matthew said, as the butler walked to the door, 'just to be certain…did Agnes tell him anything about the house or Lady Ashby that might endanger her?'

'She says not, sir. But I cannot be certain she did not let something slip without realising its significance.'

'Very well. Thank you.' When the door closed behind Pacey, Matthew continued, 'Does that sound like the man you saw the other day, El… my lady?'

Eleanor nodded.

'Will someone please tell me what all this is about?' Sir Horace demanded.

'May I tell him everything?' Aunt Lucy asked Eleanor. When Eleanor nodded, Aunt Lucy said, 'Come here and sit by me, Horace, and I shall tell you what has been happening.'

Sir Horace settled into the chair opposite Aunt Lucy and Matthew sat on the sofa next to Eleanor.

Their conversation in the park seemed a lifetime ago. All she could feel now was relief that he was here and that he hadn't walked away in the face of her suspicions and doubts.

'Are you all right?' he asked in a low voice.

All right? Would she ever be all right again? All she wanted was to feel safe.

'Yes. I am fine,' she said.

She squirmed under his sceptical blue stare. 'No,' she admitted finally, 'not really.' She bit her lip, thinking. 'Would you do something for me?'

'It depends.'

Hmmph. In her head, his response had been unequivocal. *Anything*, he had said. She might have known he would not simply dance unquestioningly to her tune.

'Well? What is it you want?'

'A pistol,' she said, 'a small one that will fit into my reticule.'

'No.'

Was that unequivocal enough, Eleanor? Her lips curved into a smile despite her best efforts to maintain a straight face. She had—really—expected no other response.

'You do know,' she said, 'that I could simply go out and buy a pistol myself? Or send one of the servants to do so?'

'Do you know how to shoot? Or even how to load a pistol, or to care for it?'

'No. That is why I am asking for your help. I want you to teach me to shoot.'

'Why?'

'Because I do not feel safe!' In her agitation, she swivelled to look at him. 'Because you cannot always be here. Because, sometimes, in the dead of night, I lie awake and I think about what happened to that girl in Stockport.'

A low growl rose from deep in his chest. Heartened, Eleanor pressed on. 'It would be safer, surely, for you to guide me in the choice of pistol. And you will be able to reassure yourself that I am capable. And competent.'

'And bl—*impossible*!'

'That, too,' she said, smiling her satisfaction. 'So you will do it. Excellent. Shall we say tomorrow morning? At eleven?'

The thunderous knocking on his front door continued unabated. Where was Henry? Matthew put down his book and went to answer the door.

'Did you not take the hint?'

'Come in.' Matthew stood aside as his eldest brother, Viscount Claverley, swept past. He indicated the sitting-room door, which opened from the small hallway.

'Go on through.'

Henry appeared, red-faced and breathing hard, from the direction of the cellar steps. 'Sorry, sir. I was—'

'It is quite all right, Henry.'

It wasn't, not really. If Henry had been around to answer the knock at the door, he could have denied Claverley admittance, told him Matthew was from home.

On the other hand, this meeting had to take place at some point. Perhaps it was best to get it over with. At least he would know what he was facing. Judging by the scowl on Claverley's face and his opening salvo, it was not destined to be a warm 'welcome home, brother'.

Matthew followed his brother into the room. 'To what do I owe this honour?'

Claverley rounded on him with a cold glare. Matthew was gratified to see that he now topped his eldest brother by a good couple of inches.

'You were told never to return. Father—'

'Did he send you to tell me that?'

Claverley's mouth snapped shut. Matthew waited. Unless he had changed a great deal, he knew his brother would not lie. It was about the only thing to admire about him—his innate truthfulness.

'No,' he said. 'He does not know I am here.' He looked around the room with a curl of his lip. 'Is this the best you could afford to lease? I knew you would never amount to anything.'

Matthew held his temper in check. Claverley. Same smug, self-serving swine he had always been. Matthew's nose throbbed in an echo of the pain of that lucky punch...he would never forgive Claverley for the cowardly way he had caught Matthew off-guard and knocked him unconscious.

'Why,' he asked, suddenly overcome with curiosity, 'have you always disliked me so much?'

'You have to ask? You are a *cheat*. I despise any dishonesty.'

'Good God, you are *such* a pompous bag of wind. You haven't changed a jot, have you? Did it ever—?' Matthew thrust his face close to his brother's and gained some small satisfaction from the leap of doubt in Claverley's eyes as he recoiled.

Good! Let him wonder what kind of man I have become. Coming into my home and throwing his weight around.

'Did it *ever*,' he repeated, 'occur to you that I wasn't guilty of cheating?'

'You would say that. Father tried everything to prove your innocence. I told him he was wasting his time.'

'And I'll wager you were delighted he could not find that proof, were you not? Why have you always resented me?'

Claverley stiffened. 'I do not have to explain myself to you, Matthew. I have come to tell you to leave. Before Father finds out you have returned. You are not wanted.'

Matthew grinned mirthlessly. 'Not by you,' he

said, 'but I knew that, anyway. Besides, my being here is not negotiable. This is my house. Yes,' he said in response to Claverley's look of surprise, 'I own it. Outright.'

'If you are indeed that flush in the pocket, you are in a position to repay Father for the debts you left behind for him to settle.'

'And whose fault was it that I was not here to settle those debts myself? You made damned sure I had no choice.'

'Do you think we should have allowed you stay here and continue to taint the family name?'

'But I had done nothing.'

'You had done plenty, even before that night. Debauchery and profligacy. You were a disgrace to our family.'

Matthew clenched his jaw. 'In your eyes, maybe, but then you always were a sanctimonious bore. You are wasting your breath and my time, brother. I have business interests here in London and I am here to stay.'

Claverley's face darkened. 'Do what you have to do, but don't think Father will forgive you, for I shall do my utmost to make sure he does not.'

He stalked from the room, leaving Matthew staring at the half-open door. Claverley had become even more self-important and self-opinionated in the years Matthew had been away. What was it about some people that their opinion of themselves grew out of all proportion to reality as soon as they were placed in a position of authority—even if that position was simply due to the random chance of being firstborn?

Still, his brother's visit had achieved one thing. For the first time since his return to England, there was a glimmer of hope that his father might forgive Matthew. Surely Claverley would not be so agitated otherwise?

Whether Matthew could forgive his father… well, that was another question.

Chapter Twenty-Two

'This,' said Aunt Lucy, as they wound their way up the magnificent staircase at Beauchamp House in Grosvenor Square, 'is *the* ball of the Season. Everyone who is anyone is invited, and no one—unless they are on their deathbed—refuses.'

'It was good of the duke to send us an invitation,' Eleanor said, as they waited their turn to be greeted by their host—the widowed Duke of Cheriton—and his family.

'It was indeed. Although he could hardly hold the ball of the Season without the Catch of the Season gracing his ballroom with her presence, could he?' Aunt Lucy took great delight in teasing Eleanor about her newly minted title.

Eleanor was saved from replying by the duke himself.

'Indeed I could not,' he said, his deep voice warm with amusement. 'And grace my ballroom you most certainly will.' His silvery-grey gaze skimmed Eleanor in her blue-silk gown, his appreciation clear. He bowed. 'You are both very welcome.' His expression sobered and he leaned towards Eleanor, lowering his voice. 'I have doubled the footmen on duty, Lady Ashby, so you need not fear for your safety in this house.'

'I...' Words failed Eleanor. How did he know?

'And if there is anything I can do to help, you have only to ask,' he added. 'Now, please allow me to introduce my son, Avon—' the youthful Lord Avon was the spitting image of the duke as he bowed elegantly '—my sister, Cecily, and my brother, Vernon.'

Lady Cecily and Lord Vernon—both unwed, as Aunt Lucy had informed Eleanor in the carriage on their way to the ball—smiled as they greeted Eleanor. They were very alike, with auburn hair and green eyes, in contrast to the duke's dark colouring.

'Most of our guests have arrived by now, Leo, so you won't miss me from the line-up,' Lord Vernon drawled, eyeing Eleanor with as much appreciation as his brother. He stepped forward and crooked his arm. 'Might I escort you into the ballroom, Lady Ashby?'

'Why...yes. Thank you, my lord.'

Eleanor shot a look at Aunt Lucy, who merely raised her brows in response. Lord Vernon Beauchamp's caution in never allowing his name to be linked to any woman was common knowledge, as was his determination never to marry. Was he, like the duke, privy to her personal business?

As they descended the short flight of steps into the glittering ballroom Eleanor frowned as she noticed a seemingly casual, but consistent, movement of the people nearest to her. What was going on? A distinct area of clear space materialised at the foot of the steps. Stationed— really, there was no other word for it—around the perimeter of the clearing were five tall, broad-shouldered gentlemen whom she recognised as some of the most eligible bachelors in the *ton*. Not one of those gentlemen had formed part of her court since her arrival in London—they were the older bachelors, the most pursued and, from Eleanor's observation, the most determined to avoid matrimony. She had danced with some of them, but it was clear none were on the lookout for a wife. They had indulged in a little light flirtation with her—as was to be expected from men of their ilk—but none had subsequently called upon her, or sent her flowers.

So *why* were they now so focused on her? For focused they were. Even as their gazes ceaselessly scanned the other guests, she could *feel* their attention.

'What,' she whispered to Lord Vernon, 'is going on?'

Vernon glanced down at her, eyes crinkling, as he led her deeper into the ballroom. The other men formed a rough circle around them, keeping the other guests at bay.

'We take care of our own. Ah, here comes Damerel. I shall leave you in his capable hands.'

He bowed and sauntered over to speak to another of Eleanor's self-appointed guardians.

'Well! Really!' Eleanor hissed to Aunt Lucy. 'What on *earth* do they think they are doing? And *who*, I should like to know, told them about me? I *knew* we shouldn't have told Sir Horace what has been happening.'

'Ellie, please do not throw such accusations around without good reason,' Aunt Lucy said. 'Why, it could have been...well, it might have been the servants. You know how they gossip between the households. Or Mr Damerel, even. Why do you not ask him?'

'Ask me what?' Matthew said, as he reached Eleanor's side. 'Good evening, ladies. May I say how very charming you both look this evening?'

His eyes lingered on Eleanor's *décolletage*, igniting sparks that flickered along her veins, heating her skin. She curled her fingers against the desire to tug her neckline higher.

'Why, I appear to be the centre of attention of some of the most powerful gentlemen in the *ton*,' she said. 'Please tell me you have not told them of my...my *predicament*.'

'Of course I have not. I...*oh*! Deuce take it! Stephen?'

Stephen Damerel stood chatting with Lord Derham, who also formed one of Eleanor's 'guards', as she had come to think of them. At the sound of his name, Stephen strolled over to Matthew and Eleanor.

'Matthew?' He raised an elegant brow.

'You told your *brother*?' Eleanor hissed. 'What made you think it would be acceptable to me for *anyone* to know my business? And now...*look*!' In her agitation, she swept her arm aloft, indicating the surrounding gentlemen. 'The very last thing I wish is to be the centre of attention like this.'

She glared at Matthew, whose jaw firmed. 'I told Stephen because he was full of conjectures as to why I appeared so interested in you and I needed to nip them in the bud.'

Of course, it would never do for anyone to presume he was interested in her as a woman, would it? She could quite see how embarrassing *that* would be for him.

'And besides...' he lowered his voice and dipped his mouth close to her ear '...how did imagine you could *fail* to be the centre of attention in that dress?'

His breath tickled her neck and his scent surrounded her, sending her senses reeling. She stepped away, intent on clearing her head, and looked accusingly at Stephen Damerel.

'You are in danger. You need protection,' he

stated unrepentantly. 'I only told a few of my most trusted friends—it is not common knowledge.'

'What do you imagine could possibly happen to me in the duke's ballroom?'

Stephen shrugged. 'They will be discreet—you need not worry. Look, they are mingling now. They only wanted to ensure your safety until Matthew was here to look after you. They will still keep an eye out, but from a distance. No one will know. If I am honest—' a charming smile lit his face '—we are delighted to be of service. It makes a change to have a purpose to these gatherings.' He bowed and wandered away.

'You will not persuade them otherwise, you know,' Matthew said. 'They see it as their duty to protect a lady in need.'

'I know. Which is why I wished to keep this whole débâcle out of the public eye,' Eleanor said.

'Admit that you will feel more secure, knowing there are several pairs of eyes watching over you instead of just mine,' Matthew said. 'You've been feeling vulnerable ever since we arrived in London, I know you have. You wouldn't have asked me about a pistol if you weren't scared.'

'A pistol?' Sir Horace Todmorden had joined them. 'What is this?'

'Hush,' Eleanor said, glancing at Aunt Lucy whose attention, thankfully, had been claimed by old Lady Ely. 'I asked Mr Damerel to help me purchase a small pistol. For protection.'

'Oh, my dear lady, no. I really cannot condone…what? A young lady such as yourself with a firearm? No, no, no. It is far too dangerous. Why, what if the rogue should disarm you? Where would you be then?'

'No worse off than if I had no weapon,' Eleanor said. 'At least if I buy one, I will sleep better at night. There are no *tonnish* gentlemen around at that time to watch over me,' she added, with an innocent look at Matthew.

His eyes narrowed and he shook his head at her as Sir Horace barked a laugh.

'You've got your hands full there, my lad,' he announced, slapping Matthew on the back.

Eleanor's breath caught in her throat as her cheeks burned. Were their names already being linked? She must take care not to gain a reputation for being fast if Emily Cowper was to succeed in adding her name to the list for Almack's. She raised her fan and, under cover of cooling her face, glanced around the ballroom. Nobody was paying them attention. Her breathing eased.

'Sir Horace,' she said, 'I think you may be suffering under a misapprehension. I know I may speak freely, with you being such a particular friend of my aunt's. Mr Damerel is just a friend who is kindly helping me through this difficult time. That is all. There is no romantic intention on either side, I assure you.'

'None,' Matthew confirmed. 'I am a merchant

who works for his living and, once we unmask the culprit, I shall return to my own life. I should hate for any untoward rumours to circulate. There is Lady Ashby's reputation to consider.'

'Of course. My profound apologies, dear lady. Damerel, pray forgive me. I did not mean to imply…oh, dear me, no…I know you only…but your aunt did express a hope…'

The poor man was mortified. Eleanor smiled at him. 'There is no harm done. I am persuaded you understand the situation now. Let us forget all about it.'

Sir Horace, still beetroot-red, bowed. 'You are most gracious. Now, if you will excuse me…?' He left them to join Aunt Lucy and Lady Ely.

What had Aunt Lucy been saying? For that matter, what did she think? Was she harbouring romantic notions about Eleanor and Matthew? Eleanor's heart fluttered against her ribs. Until yesterday, any future had seemed impossible but…now…might there be hope? They were equals by birth. Might there, possibly, be a chance they could…?

Her thoughts faltered. This was foolish think-ing. He was a third son and in trade. Her hopes of living down her mother's scandal would be lost for ever. Besides, there was his pride to consider. *I could never accept a woman who outranks me and has tenfold my wealth.*

No, we can only ever be friends.

'Eleanor?'

Her name caught her whirling thoughts. 'Sorry. Did you say something?'

Matthew was watching her, a frown creasing his brow. 'I was saying, on the subject of your protection, I felt I should warn you that your cousin and his wife are present tonight.'

The news set her stomach roiling. She had not seen James since he had slammed from her house in a temper after realising he was under suspicion. What would he say? How would he react? Here was another reason to regret that others were aware she was in danger for, surely, they could not help but suspect James, the same as both Matthew and Aunt Lucy.

Eleanor licked at suddenly dry lips and Matthew signalled to a passing waiter for a glass of wine. She sipped at it gratefully. 'Thank you for the warning.'

'About that pistol,' Matthew said.

Eleanor raised a brow, encouraged that he had broached the subject voluntarily.

'You need a lady's muff pistol. That will be small enough to carry in a reticule or, as the name implies, conceal in a muff. There is an excellent gunmaker on Shoemaker's Row, in Blackfriars. Richard Fenton. I shall buy you one tomorrow and teach you how to shoot.'

'I understood the gentlemen of the *ton* always patronise Manton's?'

'Ah, but you forget. I am no gentleman of the *ton*. My associates frequent different haunts.'

'Oh!' Eleanor pictured a seedy workshop in a dark alley. 'I am not sure…would it not be safer…? I mean, I hope he is *reputable*.'

Matthew laughed. 'Of course he is reputable. What do you take me for? He is simply not quite as fashionable as Manton or his brother.'

'I see.' Eleanor fidgeted with her fan. 'It was my intention to choose my own pistol.'

'Trust me,' Matthew said. 'I shall find you the perfect pistol. A gunmaker's shop is no place for a lady.'

Chapter Twenty-Three

The musicians, clustered on the balcony, struck a chord. The chatter died and the crowd began the ebb and flow that would result in the dancers remaining in the centre of the floor and the onlookers arranged around the perimeter, some standing, some sitting. Gowns and jewels shimmered as they caught the light from the many chandeliers and Eleanor thought she had never seen so many sumptuous dresses and beautifully coiffured heads before.

'Is it not a magnificent sight?' she said to Aunt Lucy, who had finally escaped the clutches of Lady Ely. 'How I wish I'd had the confidence to enjoy my come-out instead of hiding amongst the chaperons.'

'Do not waste time regretting the past, my pet,' Aunt Lucy replied, squeezing Eleanor's hand. 'You made the right choices, for you, at the time. You are here now. Enjoy the moment. There is not a lady in this ballroom to outshine you, so make the most of it.'

'And I second that,' a deep voice murmured in her ear. 'I believe this first dance is mine?'

Her skin seemed to tighten until it felt too small to contain her flesh and her insides quivered.

Matthew. She glanced at him through her lashes as they took their place in one of the sets. His broad shoulders and square jaw allowed no doubt as to his strength and his masculinity. A glance at the other men in their set failed to flame her senses in the same way. His fingers closed around hers and fire flickered along her veins.

Who would choose smooth urbanity and polished address over Matthew's rugged capability and down-to-earth manner? Probably, she mused, many ladies of the *ton* would value those qualities higher. But not her. She did not want pretty words with no heart behind them. She wanted… Matthew. She might as well admit it. She had wanted him since that first kiss. It had just seemed so impossible.

Now…

She looked up and caught his eye. He looked…

'What is wrong? You look preoccupied.'

'As do you,' he said.

'But I was preoccupied in a happy way,' Eleanor retorted. 'You look precisely the opposite. Why?'

He did not reply.

'If you did not wish to dance, why did you ask me?'

His startled blue gaze bored into her. 'Please do not imagine you know what is going on inside my head.' He fell silent until they were near enough to converse again. 'If you must know,' he continued, 'I had a visit from my eldest brother earlier. I was wondering what reception I might expect from my father when he arrives.'

Eleanor pondered his words. Matthew was adamant he had no wish to accept his rightful place in society but...could reconciliation with his father change his mind? Ideas of how she might help ricocheted around her brain but, if she were to help, it stood to reason she must discover the cause of their estrangement: the reason his father had banished Matthew to India.

They joined hands for the next movement of the dance. She barely noticed, dancing by rote. A swift tug caught her attention.

'What are you plotting? I can see it in your eyes. You are up to something.'

Eleanor tilted her chin. 'I am not. I was thinking about supper.'

She avoided his narrow-eyed study of her face. At the end of the dance, she said, 'May we sit this one out, Mr Damerel? I find I am rather tired.' Matthew had marked her card for the first two.

'After one dance?'

'It is the worry. The thought of meeting James and Ruth has quite overset me.' She ignored Matthew's quiet huff of disbelief. 'I would appreciate finding a quiet corner to rest. To prepare myself.'

'Very well.' Matthew offered his arm and led Eleanor across the floor to where a set of French windows stood ajar. 'Would you care for a breath of fresh air? There are others out there, so we cannot be accused of being unchaperoned. You cannot afford to take any chances; the patronesses of Almack's are present. I saw Lady Cowper and Lady Jersey earlier.'

Eleanor glimpsed several guests outside on a well-lit, flagged terrace, where they were taking advantage of a cooling breeze. Perfect...enough in number to provide respectability, but few enough to enable them to converse without being overheard.

'Indeed.' Now to wheedle the truth out of Matthew.

They walked slowly to one end of the terrace, which ran the full width of Beauchamp House. Matthew held his tongue—Eleanor would speak her mind soon enough. Until then, he was content to enjoy the peace. As they turned to retrace their steps, Eleanor drew breath.

'Your father,' she said.

'Ah, now we get to it. I *knew* you were up to something.'

'I am *not* up to something. I am...interested.

Your brother Stephen has accepted you back. Why do you imagine your father will not? What did your other brother say?'

And if she thought he was going to tell her about that interview, she was mistaken. 'He was hardly overjoyed to see me.'

'And yet he visited you. Why?'

Matthew shrugged free of her hand on his arm and strode over to the balustrade. He gazed blindly into the dark garden beyond the terrace.

Tenacious.

It described her perfectly.

She's only trying to help.

As if she had heard his thoughts, she said, 'I only wish to understand.'

'I know.'

He turned to look at her. *Gorgeous.* His blood heated instantly. Her glorious dark tresses, piled on to her head, artful ringlets framing her beautiful face. That gown…the colour of a summer sky, over a white satin underdress…the low neckline revealing an enticing glimpse of full breasts and emphasising her fragile collarbones and swan-like neck, adorned by an elegant string of pearls. His hands curled into fists against the urge to reach for her.

She touched one of those fists…a fleeting contact, but enough to trigger that vibrant spark that arced between them whenever they touched. His resolve hardened. He must stay strong. Eleanor might believe her feelings lay hidden, but they shone from her eyes. He must disillusion her— she must understand there was no future for them, for her sake and her standing in society as much as for his pride.

'I was caught cheating at cards,' he said. 'My accuser was then attacked and robbed. That is why my father sent me to India. My accuser was badly injured and Father feared he might die.'

'But you didn't do it.' Her declaration rang with conviction.

'I was long ago cleared of the attack,' he said.

'Why did you not come home, then?'

'I am not wanted here.' Claverley's scornful words had pierced deeper than he realised. *Damn him. And damn everything.* And, in particular, damn his youthful indiscretions…his thoughtless, careless certainty that nothing could touch him. 'Not then. Not now. I have a debt to repay to my father. Once that is discharged, I shall return to my previous existence.'

'You are still bitter about his rejection of you. Is it not time to put that bitterness behind you and think of the future?'

'Am I not justified if I do feel bitter? Would you not feel the same had you been rejected by your…?' Too late, he bit his tongue. 'I'm sorry. I forgot. I should not have said that.'

He saw her swallow. 'It is true my mother left me. I don't think I have ever been bitter about it, though.' She took his arm. 'Come, let us walk and talk. It is easier to speak with honesty when you cannot see the other's face.'

They continued to stroll.

'Mayhap I was never bitter because I still had my father,' she said.

'But it must have affected you.'

'Of course it did. It devastated me. But…but…' From the corner of his eye he saw her shrug in a helpless fashion. 'I thought it was my fault.'

He had to strain to hear her. His heart swelled. He had been eighteen—old enough to rationalise his father's behaviour. Eleanor had been eleven years old. Still a child. No wonder, at times, she doubted herself. No wonder she concealed that inner doubt behind a shell of determined independence. He covered her hand with his and squeezed gently.

'You know now it was not your fault, I hope?'

She inhaled sharply. 'Of course. But we were talking of you and your father.'

Her voice was bright and positive. He bit back a smile. She was the most courageous woman he had ever met.

'May I tell you what I think, without annoying you?'

And here was a first—asking if he wanted her opinion before voicing it. 'Go on.'

'I think you should meet your father with an open heart. Listen to what he says and, more im-

portantly, how he says it. Do not barricade your
heart behind a wall of pride.'

That's easy for her to say. 'I will try,' he said.

'Did you prove you did not cheat at cards?'

'Who says I didn't cheat?'

'I say. I know you, Matthew Damerel. You are
too honourable to do such a thing.'

A lump formed in his throat and his eyes
smarted at her absolute conviction. She believed
in him, unquestioningly, when his own father had
not.

'Come.' His voice was gruff. 'We must go back
inside. I do not want you to catch a chill.'

'Cousin Eleanor, how are you?'

It was some time later when the familiar voice
roused Eleanor from her reverie and she turned to
see James standing over her, Ruth clinging to his
arm. Eleanor's heart faltered. She studied James's
face. Could he really be responsible for those attacks? But, if not him, who? And why?

'I am delighted to see you without that guard
dog of yours in tow,' he continued.

At least he hadn't noticed her new guardians.
Despite her earlier annoyance, the sight of Lord
Derham and Lord Vernon Beauchamp, hovering
watchfully, eased her apprehension. They had appeared shortly after Matthew—with a wink at
Eleanor and a whisper of 'Think of Almack's'—
led Lady Cowper on to the dance floor. Eleanor,

grateful for a respite from dancing, and for some time to ponder Matthew's earlier revelations, had sunk into a vacant seat next to Aunt Lucy and several of her friends.

Conscious that Aunt Lucy had stopped talking and was looking over in a none-too-friendly fashion, Eleanor rose to her feet, keen to avoid a repeat of the unpleasantness when James had called into Upper Brook Street.

'I am very well, thank you, James, and Mr Damerel—for I must presume that is to whom you refer—is merely a friend concerned with my well-being.'

'Damerel?' James's brow wrinkled. 'I thought he was called Thomas. You don't mean to tell me there are two of them?'

Eleanor inhaled deeply, determined to remain calm. 'He is the son of Lord Rushock,' she said. 'He uses another name for his business.'

She ignored the disdainful curl of James's lip. 'It is delightful to see you both,' she said, including Ruth—who looked pale and anxious—in her smile. 'I was about to take a turn around the room. Would you care to join me?'

They fell into step, with James in the centre, and made their way slowly around the edge of the dance floor.

'Have there been any further incidents?' James asked quietly.

'Yes.' Eleanor told him of the man she had

seen outside the house, and the man who had accosted and threatened Agnes, and described him to James.

Rather than further the conversation, James turned monosyllabic, his arm under Eleanor's hand rigid. What had caused him to clam up? A guilty conscience? Matthew would surely say so if he were here. Eleanor gave up trying to make conversation and spoke across James to Ruth, who clung to her husband's other arm.

'I trust you are fully recovered now, Cousin Ruth.'

Ruth shot a nervous glance at James before replying, 'I am quite well, thank you, Eleanor.'

James nodded approvingly at Ruth, who smiled tremulously. What did that look mean? The tension that simmered between husband and wife was palpable, but Ruth appeared to gain in confidence and proceeded to chat to Eleanor in an unusually friendly manner. She quizzed Eleanor about the forthcoming parties and events to which Eleanor had received invitations and offered advice as to which were likely to be the most enjoyable and which might prove a bore. Eleanor began to wonder if she had misjudged Ruth at their previous meeting. Perhaps Ruth *had* simply been on edge due to her imminent visit to the doctor, as James had claimed?

'James,' Ruth said, fanning herself, 'it is exceedingly hot in here and I do not see any footmen nearby. Would you be so good as to fetch us some wine?'

James hesitated. 'I don't…are you sure you will be all right?'

Eleanor stared in puzzlement. As James met her gaze, his jaw clenched. 'Eleanor?'

'A drink would be most welcome. Thank you.'

'Very well.' He found them two vacant chairs in an alcove. 'Do not move from here,' he said in a warning voice.

Eleanor raised a brow. James caught her look and reddened. 'It is very crowded. I am afraid I will not find you easily,' he said before hurrying away.

As soon as they were alone, Ruth turned to Eleanor and, taking her hand, regarded her earnestly.

'I am pleased to have this opportunity to apologise to you, Cousin Eleanor, for I fear I might have appeared unfriendly when last we met.'

'Think nothing of it, Ruth, for it is quite forgotten.'

Ruth's intensity unnerved Eleanor. She leant so close as she spoke that Eleanor had to force herself not to recoil. She could not help but look around for reassurance that her guardians were in view. They were. She relaxed.

'I was anxious about the appointment with my doctor.'

'Yes. James did explain.'

'Oh, James.' Ruth chewed at her lip, momentarily silent. 'He has changed, Eleanor. I do not know… Oh, it is nothing really.' She swayed closer and Eleanor, despite her best efforts, drew back. Ruth tightened her grip on Eleanor's hand and lowered her voice to a whisper. 'I know I can unburden my heart to you, dearest Eleanor. If only things had been different, we would be sisters now and I know my beloved Donald would urge me to trust you. I know that you love James and will not allow my worries to alter your regard for him, but I have no one else I can talk to.'

Eleanor swallowed hard. Where was James with their wine? What was Ruth implying? She had never liked Eleanor and had blamed her for her brother's death, yet here she was, introducing Donald into the conversation without a blink of emotion or blame.

'It is a sensitive subject—' Ruth continued.

'Then I implore you to say nothing,' Eleanor said, pulling her hands free. 'To be honest, Ruth, if you and James have problems, they should be resolved between the two of you. Do not forget I have loved James from childhood— I am unlikely to take your side in any marital squabble.'

'No, no! You misunderstand me.' Ruth grabbed Eleanor's hands again. 'I do not seek to drive a wedge between you, but I need to talk of this, in case…in case…the worst comes to pass.' She gave a low sob and held a handkerchief to her lips. 'I am sorry. I am a little overwrought.'

'Very well.' Eleanor saw that she was unlikely to escape Ruth's confidences. 'What is the matter?'

'James is desperate for a son. But…but…I have been unable to get with child. Oh, Eleanor, he blames me, I know he does. Our appointment the other day was to determine whether anything can be done to help, but the doctor offered no hope. And now…I am so afraid… What if he should… what if he decides he wants a new wife? Mayhap you can understand the strain I have been under and forgive my unwelcoming attitude?'

'I am so sorry to hear that, Ruth, and of course I forgive you.' Eleanor buried her instinctive dislike for the other woman under her very real sympathy and patted Ruth's hand. The woman was so brittle it felt as though she might shatter into a thousand pieces and there was still a fervent glitter in her eye that made Eleanor uneasy. 'I am always available, if you should feel the need to confide in someone, but I am convinced your worries are without foundation. James is an honourable man. He would never cast you aside.'

'It is not being cast aside that I fear,' Ruth said.

'Then—?'

Ruth turned her head away and Eleanor strained to hear her words. What she said made Eleanor's blood run cold.

'It is James.'

Chapter Twenty-Four

Matthew cursed—with fluent inventiveness—under his breath as he watched a succession of wealthy, handsome, titled men dancing with Eleanor. A lead weight anchored in his chest as yet another of her self-appointed guardians led her from the dance floor. He was reconciled—most of the time—to never being worthy of Eleanor, but it was agony to watch her with these men, any one of whom would be a perfect match for her.

'You're back.'

Matthew whipped round at the sound of that familiar voice. Every muscle tensed and his chest swelled as he drew in a seemingly never-ending breath. Familiar hard grey eyes assessed him and it was as though the last eight years had dissolved, leaving his eighteen-year-old self facing the man whose love and approval he had craved above all else. He held his father's gaze as his brain battled for control of both his body and his speech. The colourful, noisy ballroom receded until there was just Matthew, facing his father.

Breathe out. Now.

He willed his voice into the open. 'You got my letter, then.'

'What are your plans?'

No welcome. No softening of those stern features. No pleasure in seeing his youngest son—now a man grown—after eight long years.

'I'm back for good.'

Matthew swung away, but...suddenly, Eleanor was by his side, with a swish of satin and the scent of jasmine. She grabbed his arm, pushed him back round to face his father.

'Mr Damerel,' she said. 'Would you do me the honour of introducing us?'

No! The silent roar reverberated around his head. He scanned the nearby guests; curious faces had turned in their direction. His jaw clenched so hard his teeth ached as he looked his father in the eye again. He stilled, momentarily breathless. Was that uncertainty in those familiar grey orbs?

Not out-and-out rejection, then.

Maybe? Possibly? Hopefully?

'Eleanor, Lady Ashby, this is my father, Lord Rushock.'

Eleanor dipped into a curtsy. 'I am delighted to make your acquaintance, my lord. Your son has proved *such* an invaluable support to me over the past few weeks. He is, if I may say, a son of whom any father would be proud.'

Matthew fought his inclination to close his eyes in despair. What on earth was she thinking?

His father inclined his head. 'Good evening, Lady Ashby.'

He said no more. The silence loomed around them, prodding Matthew to say something…anything…to fill that void.

'I am sorry to speak to you of such things in company, but you must know that I intend to pay the debts I owe you.'

A frown creased his father's brow. 'That is not necessary.'

'It is more than necessary to me—it is essential. I…you need not fear I shall ask anything of you, but I should like to see my mother and sisters.'

'I have not told them you are back.'

'You did not tell them where I went. You allowed them…all of them…to believe I would leave without a word. They did not even know if I was alive or dead.' His voice shook; the words near choked him. He swallowed convulsively, and drew strength from Eleanor as she—under cover of her skirts—feathered his hand with warm fingers.

'No doubt Stephen told you that.'

'Why would he not? He was as shocked at your actions as, no doubt, Mama will be. You should know, sir, that I have written to Sarah, so it will do you no good to try to prevent Stephen from telling Mama the truth. Besides—' Matthew gestured at the onlookers '—you know how fast news travels.'

'I did my best for you. If Henson had died—'

'But he did not. And... *I...was...innocent.*'

'But not of cheating.'

Eleanor's gasp soothed the wound to his heart. As did the sudden realisation that his father had the look and the sound of a man who suspected he was in the wrong, but was desperate to justify his actions.

Matthew reached a decision: this should not, *could* not, be resolved in a crowded ballroom.

'I will call on you tomorrow,' he said. 'With the money. And we can discuss how we move on from there.'

His father opened his mouth, then snapped it shut.

'Very well,' he said, after a pause. 'I shall await your visit.'

Matthew watched his father walk away, the tightness in his chest relaxing as his galloping heart eased to a trot.

'I am sorry you had to witness that, my lady,' he said, without looking at Eleanor.

'Are you angry with me?'

She did not sound particularly contrite. More...

interested. Was he angry? Yes…and no. He felt a reluctant smile tug at the corners of his mouth.

'What made you imagine it was your business?'

'I was interes—'

'Interested. Yes. I gathered that. Interested; or interfering, depending on your perspective. Or…' he glanced at her, and her expression dispelled the remaining shards of any anger he had felt, '…or a friend, trying to help.'

She smiled. 'Thank you. One question.'

'Go on.'

'How shall you repay your father?'

His spine stiffened. *This*, surely, was a step too far, even for her.

'Do you have enough funds readily available? If not, I can—'

'No!'

She recoiled, a wounded look on her face. 'You do not know what I was going to say.'

'I can guess.' He gripped her arm and steered her into an empty alcove nearby. 'Do not insult me by offering me money. I am no pauper. I can pay my own debts.'

But he couldn't. Not yet. Not until Benedict arrived with those two ships and their cargoes were sold. After that, he would have the wherewithal to pay his debts, invest in further imports and to live comfortably. Until then, however…

'I was only offering a loan,' Eleanor said, in a hurt voice.

Matthew groaned inwardly. He must raise the money somehow. His pride would never allow him to admit to his father he was not yet able to pay his full due, but neither would it allow him to accept money from Eleanor, loan or not. It would have to be the bank. Or, if the bank failed him… he had always thought of moneylenders as the last possible resort but, now, Eleanor had supplanted them.

'I'm sorry,' he said, 'but I will not accept money from you, even as a loan.'

'Very well. I cannot force you to accept, but the offer is there if you have need.'

'Thank you.'

'Lady Ashby? I believe this is our dance?'

Matthew fought the burning jealousy that scorched his gut again as he watched Eleanor walk away on the arm of yet another self-assured, titled and no doubt wealthy member of the St James's set.

His mistake had been to secure her hand for the first two dances. He could not dance with her again without causing gossip. It was bad enough they had spent so much time already in one another's company, although the continued attentions of the cream of society's most eligible bachelors would no doubt preclude any criticism. No one would risk upsetting *them*.

He was now condemned to spend the rest of the evening either watching Eleanor from the edge of the ballroom or dancing with another lady. Neither option particularly appealed. With a muttered oath, he spun on his heel and headed for the card room.

In the hallway he passed two jaded-looking elderly gentlemen, making their slow way to the ballroom. The name 'Baroness Ashby' caught his attention and he slowed.

'I only said that I don't know as *I* should care for a wife who is mistress of her own property,' said the one, as he availed himself of a liberal helping of snuff. 'An independent wife? Goes against the natural order of things, don't you know. How's a man to keep his pride?'

'You'd be too lily-livered to stand up to her, anyway,' his companion retorted. 'Why, she must be six inches taller than you for a start. Besides, you wouldn't get a look in, old fellow. With her wealth, she can look as high as she pleases for a husband. I doubt she'd settle for a paltry baronet like you, not with all the rich blood in town at the moment.'

They moved out of earshot and Matthew entered the card room with a heavy heart.

'Milady!'

Eleanor jerked awake, heart clambering into her throat, mind groping to identify that voice.

Her maid's anxious face was lit by the wavering flame of a candle, the shadows casting her normally unremarkable features into a macabre mask.

'Lizzie. What is it?' Eleanor pushed herself into a sitting position and gathered the bedcovers to her chest. 'You frightened me. What time is it?'

'Nigh on four. Mr Pacey told me to come in here and not to leave the room no matter what.' The urgency in her whisper set Eleanor's scalp prickling. 'Peter's standing guard outside the door.'

'Standing…?' Panic clutched at Eleanor. 'Is everyone all right? Aunt Lucy?'

'Matilda is with her.'

'Tell me.'

'Peter heard a noise in the dining room.' One or other of the footmen were always on duty in the hall during the night. 'He went to look and there was a window open.'

The sound of Lizzie's chattering teeth broke the silence of the night. And it was silent, Eleanor realised. The servants must be searching very quietly.

'Come here and get under the covers, Lizzie,' Eleanor said, not sure if the maid's violent shivers were from cold or fear or a combination of both.

Lizzie scrambled into the bed. 'Oooh, milady. Everyone is up now and searching for him. Mr Pacey said I was to come to you and I was that pleased…what if *I'd* happened to come across that monster?'

'Surely the maids aren't searching? Why, what if—?'

'Not on their own, milady. They've paired up with the men, to carry the candles. Ooh, milady, the men have all got weapons and everything.'

'Weapons? What weapons? I did not know we had any.'

''Twere Mr Matthew, milady. He made sure there were enough stout clubs for us all to hide under our beds.'

Everyone except me. And, I presume, Aunt Lucy. Hmmph. The sooner I get that pistol the better.

'Just in case, he said. And wasn't it lucky he did that, milady?'

'Indeed. Was Peter certain that window had been closed before?'

'Oh, yes. And Mr Pacey—he always does a last round after everyone has gone to bed.'

Eleanor had the sensation of thousands of ants swarming through her veins. The urge to get up… to take action…battered at her, but she ignored it. She would only make it worse if she left her room. At least in here she was easier to protect. It was difficult, though, as the seconds stretched into minutes. From time to time they heard the muffled thud of a door closing, or the creak of a floorboard, and at each noise Lizzie squeaked and huddled closer, comforting Eleanor and helping her to conceal her own terror.

'Did Peter see anyone?' she asked. Had anyone got inside? Was he, even now, in the house—hiding…biding his time? Or had Peter frightened him off?

'No. There was no one in the room. But he could have gone through into the parlour, couldn't he, milady? Peter came upstairs to wake Mr Pacey. Mr Pacey was very cross. *He* said as how Peter should have stood his ground and shouted. Now, Mr Pacey says, we don't know where he might have gone while Peter—'

A yell followed by the thud of running feet silenced Lizzie, who huddled even closer to Eleanor. Shouts echoed through the house. Doors slammed. Glass shattered. Then silence reigned once more. Eleanor pushed back the bedcovers and swung her feet to the floor. Lizzie grabbed at her, tried to tug her back into bed.

'Milady! No!'

Eleanor patted Lizzie on the shoulder. 'It's all right, Lizzie. I only intend to poke my head out of the door. Peter is outside, after all. I need to know what is happening.'

She wrapped a shawl around her, and approached the door. Despite her conviction that Peter—solid, dependable Peter—was on the other side, she hesitated. What if…? Lizzie was watching wide-eyed from the bed, knuckles white as she clutched the sheet.

'Peter?' she called, low-voiced. 'Are you there?'

'Yes, milady.'

'Is it safe for me to come out?'

The door inched open and Peter's familiar face appeared in the gap. 'I think so, milady. It was Mr Pacey that found him, but he couldn't hold him. Some of the other lads are giving chase.' He sounded disgruntled and Eleanor had to smile. What young man wouldn't yearn for some excitement in an otherwise mundane life?

'Has he left the house?'

'Yes, milady. Agnes came up to tell me and John—it was John was put to guard Lady Rothley. He wouldn't have got to either of you, milady. Not with us here.'

'If you are certain he has gone, you and John may go and help the others if you wish.'

Eleanor shook her head, smiling at the sight, moments later, of the two footmen bounding down the stairs with the eagerness of hounds on the scent.

Chapter Twenty-Five

'I don't think we should, Ellie. Why can we not wait until Mr Damerel is here to escort us?'

'I will not be made a prisoner in my own home, Aunt. We are only going to Hookham's and we will have the men with us.' As a concession to her aunt, Eleanor had agreed that three of the footmen should accompany them to the circulating library this time. 'It is broad daylight. No one would be reckless enough to try and attack me in public.

'Besides, Mr Damerel is not promised to his father until noon, so we shall not see him until mid-afternoon at the earliest.'

'That sounds encouraging,' Aunt Lucy said. 'The more time dear Matthew spends with his father, the more likely they are to resolve their differences.'

Matthew had undertaken to go to Blackfriars to buy a pistol for Eleanor straight after meeting Lord Rushock. Eleanor did not enlighten Aunt

Lucy. She still did not know about the pistol, although how Eleanor might contrive to practice shooting without her aunt knowing...mayhap she could enlist Sir Horace to distract her?

Later, as they walked along Bond Street on their way back from the library, Eleanor began to regret her insistence on having her own way.

The pavement was even busier than usual and tension spread its tentacles from Eleanor's stomach to encompass her entire body. People were too close, brushing against her as they weaved around each other. Occasionally a passer-by stepped between her and the two footmen behind her, and her heart would pound and her palms grow clammy. Why hadn't she simply postponed her visit to Hookham's? There were too many people, all hurrying about their daily business: too much jostling, too much noise, too much traffic. The din from the passing wagons, carriages and hackneys—rattling over the cobbles, their drivers losing patience, shouting at their horses and each other alike—was tremendous.

They were often forced into single file, with Aunt Lucy and William ahead of Eleanor and Peter and John behind. A sudden surge in the crowd forced strangers both in front and behind Eleanor, there was an outcry from the middle of the swarming mass of people and then a hard shove knocked Eleanor off her feet. There was a flurry of movement as a crew of urchins scuttled past, into the road, dodging the traffic, as a cry of 'Stop, thief!' rang out.

Eleanor landed with a painful bump on her bottom, her heart seized with fright. For one awful moment…she struggled to catch her breath, eyes screwed shut in an attempt to pretend it had not happened, knowing it was only by the merest good fortune she had not landed in the road itself, under the iron-clad, dinner-plate-sized hooves of the straining workhorses hauling a coal wagon past at that very moment.

An accident. That's all. Nothing to worry about, just a gang of pickpockets. She forced her lids open, looked in vain for her servants and Aunt Lucy. Nowhere to be seen. Strangers crowded her vision—all craning their necks to see what had happened.

'Allow me.'

Breathless, shaking, Eleanor turned her head to stare up into dark eyes lit with a sardonic gleam.

'Why,' the speaker proclaimed, 'if it ain't my little coz, Eleanor. Well met, my dear.' He smiled, his handsome face lighting up.

She stared at him. Recognition dawned. 'Hugo! It's you.' Her relief was indescribable. At that moment, she could have kissed him.

'It is indeed. And why, may I ask, are you sitting on the pavement in Bond Street? You could have afforded a hackney coach if you were that tired.'

'Do try not to be so ridiculous,' Eleanor retorted. 'That's just like you—always funning. Help me up, Hugo, please; we are providing everyone with quite a spectacle here.'

'You are, you mean,' he said. 'I was simply passing by, mindin' my own business.'

'Are you all right, milady?' She looked up to the welcome sight of William, Peter and John as they shouldered through the onlookers. 'The crowd…it was impossible…'

'I'm fine,' she said. 'Where is her ladyship?'

Peter plunged back into the surrounding throng, presumably to look for Aunt Lucy. Hugo helped Eleanor to her feet and helped her to brush the dust and debris from her clothes.

'*Three* footmen, my dear? I had not realised you were of such consequence.'

Eleanor bit her lip against a bubble of laughter. 'I will explain later,' she said as Aunt Lucy was shepherded through the gathered spectators by Peter.

'Ellie! What happened?' Her frantic gaze was glued to Eleanor's face.

Eleanor looked up. 'I was knocked over,' she said.

'Attacked?' Aunt Lucy shrieked. 'By him?'

'Not attacked, no.' Eleanor told her aunt what had happened.

'Good morning, Mama.'

Aunt Lucy shrieked again, this time a happy sound. 'Hugo. It's you.'

'It is, isn't it,' he agreed, 'as I have already confirmed to Eleanor. I was not aware you were coming to town, Mama.'

'I wrote and told you, Hugo.'

'Ah, did you indeed? That might explain it.'

'Explain what?'

'Why I didn't know, of course, m'dear. Been out of town. Rusticating. Only got back last night.' There was a pause. 'Now I come to think of it, there *was* a pile of letters and suchlike on my desk.'

'And you didn't think it important to look through them this morning?'

A pained expression appeared on Hugo's face. 'I thought they must be bills, m'dear. Far too unpleasant this early in the day. I was just heading to my club. To fortify m'self, you understand. But you still haven't told me what you are doing in town?'

'I came with Eleanor, to lend her countenance, you know, whilst the repairs were carried out.'

'Repairs? And, please do forgive my curiosity, but why would you think Eleanor had been attacked?'

'It's a long story.' Eleanor shivered, her legs suddenly like jelly.

Hugo put his arm around her and gave her a squeeze. 'C'mon, Coz, let's get you home.' He flagged down a passing hackney. 'Your men can walk back.'

Once inside the coach, Hugo eyed Eleanor with concern.

'I am unharmed, Hugo, truly I am.'

'If you say so, m'dear. I shall, however, expect a full account of what has been going on once you're safely home. Lucas'd have my guts for garters if anything happened to you—or to Mama—on my watch. Besides which, as you may have noticed, she's the only the mother I have.'

He winked at Aunt Lucy, whose cheeks glowed as she beamed. 'You are such a good, kind son.'

Hugo grimaced. 'Hush now, Mama; I do have a reputation to uphold, you know.'

Eleanor let their words wash over her and she breathed a sigh of relief as the carriage drew up in Upper Brook Street.

Matthew paced the drawing-room carpet in Eleanor's house. The news with which Pacey had greeted him when he arrived in Upper Brook Street five minutes before had shaken him to the core and driven his doubts over the wisdom of that bank loan clean from his head.

'Wise move, getting this for her ladyship,' said

Sir Horace, turning the dainty muff pistol over in his hands in the light from the window. He had arrived not two minutes before Matthew and was equally as troubled by Pacey's account of the happenings during the early hours of that morning. 'Fine workmanship.

'Pleased to admit I was wrong last night, m'boy. The ladies are more vulnerable than I realised.'

'More than I realised as well,' Matthew admitted, coming to a halt near the older man. 'I thought we had covered all the angles and they were safe in their own home. It seems I was mistaken.'

'But the scoundrel did fail to get anywhere near Lady Ashby,' Sir Horace said. 'No need to blame yourself. The measures you took were effective—it was just a shame it was Pacey who discovered where he was hiding. Had one of those strapping footmen winkled him out, I doubt he would have broken free so easily.'

Matthew resumed his pacing. 'Where are they?' He headed for the door. 'The blazes with what Pacey says, I'm going…'

Voices in the hall alerted him to Eleanor's return. Pacey had sworn they would be home any minute and it seemed he was right. Matthew flung the door wide just as Pacey was about to open it for his mistress. Two quick strides and he was in front of her, searching her dear face, taking her hands, raising them to press relieved lips against sweet-scented skin.

'Well, well. Matthew Damerel, if my eyes do not deceive me.'

Matthew froze. That voice…Eleanor tugged her hands free of his.

'I did not know you two were acquainted,' she said. 'Come, let us go into the drawing room. Pacey, some refreshments, if you please.'

Matthew, speechless, brain scrambling to order his thoughts, stood aside to allow Eleanor past. She was followed by Lord Hugo Alastair and Lady Rothley.

This was his chance. Alastair had been at that game.

'How do you two know each other?' Eleanor asked, after introductions had been made.

She sank into a chair by the fire with a re-lieved sigh. Lady Rothley settled on to the sofa, with Sir Horace on one side of her and Hugo on the other. Matthew took the other chair. Hugo's dark gaze switched from contemplation of Sir Horace to Matthew.

'You're back,' he said, ignoring Eleanor's ques-tion. 'How long has it been?'

'Eight years, give or take.'

'Never mind that,' Lady Rothley said. 'Tell Mr Damerel about your accident, Ellie.'

'Accident?' Matthew recalled the general grub-biness he had noticed, but not really registered, on Eleanor's primrose walking gown. 'What happened? Are you hurt?'

'I am a little bruised, no more. I was knocked over by some boys. Hugo came to my rescue.'

'Hugo? Pacey said you took three of the men with you. Where were they?'

'It was crowded. It was hard to stay together. I have discovered,' she added, with a rueful smile, 'the disadvantage of being escorted by one's servants. One can hardly walk along Bond Street on a footman's arm, can one? And you were right, Aunt. I should have waited for Mr Damerel to escort us. I only wished to return my book, it was hardly a matter of life and death.'

'Unlike last night,' Lady Rothley said.

'Pacey told us what happened,' Sir Horace said, patting Lady Rothley's hand. 'What a dreadful experience, dear Lady Rothley. You will pleased to hear, Lady Ashby, that Mr Damerel has acquired that pistol on your behalf, so—'

'Pistol?'

Matthew cursed under his breath. Why hadn't he reminded Sir Horace not to talk of the pistol in front of Eleanor's aunt?

'Matters of life and death? Pistols? Would somebody please tell me what, precisely, has been going on?' Hugo said.

Eleanor caught Matthew's eye. He interpreted her silent plea and told Hugo all that had happened since the library at Ashby Manor had been set on fire.

Hugo stirred and rose elegantly to his feet. 'It would appear that, despite my every effort to appear otherwise, I do have a sense of familial duty after all,' he said. 'Mama, Ellie, I shall see you both later.'

'Where are you going?'

'Why, to fetch a change of clothing, of course. I shall move in until after this villain is caught. As your sole male relative here in town, I am almost honour bound to join the fray, do you not agree? It should not be the responsibility of—' his gaze switched from Matthew to Sir Horace '—random strangers to protect you. However, I find I do have one question before I go—have you any idea who the culprit might be?'

Matthew stood, gritting his teeth against the other man's deliberate provocation, conscious he needed Hugo's co-operation if he were to have any chance of proving his innocence of cheating.

'You have one thing wrong, Alastair—you are not El— Lady Ashby's only male relative in town. James Weare, her other cousin, is our main suspect.'

Hugo's eyes gleamed. 'James Weare—well, I never. I had forgotten he was your cousin—and your rightful heir to boot, if I am not mistaken. The little worm,' he added, softly.

Matthew instantly warmed towards Hugo.

He might give the appearance of careless, plea-sure-seeking selfishness but with those three last words he had revealed his dangerous core—a good man to have on the spot, protecting Eleanor. But…Matthew's spirits plunged at the realisa-tion that his own indispensability was shrink-ing by the minute, what with Hugo moving into Eleanor's house and the watchful presence of Ste-phen's friends by night.

'That reminds me,' he said to Eleanor, 'what did Weare have to say for himself last night?'

Eleanor pulled a face. 'The conversation was… *stilted* is the best description. He did ask if I'd had any other problems, and I told him about the man I saw, and about Agnes. He was uneasy and Ruth seemed timid.' She paused, then continued in a quiet voice, 'James was reluctant to leave Ruth and me alone. And when he did…' she chewed at her bottom lip, her eyes haunted '… Ruth is scared of him.'

Hugo crossed the room to take Eleanor's hands in his. 'Do not fret, little coz—'twill all be settled before you know it, now that *I* am here,' he said, with a mischievous glint in his dark eyes as he flicked a glance towards Matthew.

Matthew thought if his jaw clenched any harder his teeth might shatter.

Remember. You need him.

Eleanor tilted her head, a sweetly loving smile on her lips as she regarded her cousin. 'Dear

Hugo,' she said. 'You have always been such a reliable fellow, has he not, Aunt? I declare, I do not know how I should have managed all these years without such constant, devout attention.'

Lady Rothley laughed as Hugo grinned.

'Minx,' he said and bent to kiss Eleanor's cheek.

'Before you go, Alastair, might I have a word in private?' Matthew said.

Hugo raised a brow. 'Secrets?' he murmured. 'Do tell.' But he followed Matthew to the far end of the room without further demur.

'That card game,' Matthew said, 'the one where Henson accused me of cheating. Do you remember it?'

'I do. And, before you say any more, and because I'm a generous sort of fellow, I do know it was a false accusation.'

A hard ball of anger lodged in Matthew's chest. 'If you knew,' he said, 'why the hell didn't you say so at the time?'

Hugo raised a brow. 'For the very good reason that, at the time, I did *not* know.'

'Then you can prove Mr Damerel was innocent,' Eleanor said. She had joined them, unnoticed. Matthew sighed. He should have known.

'Ellie, my dear, this is not for your ears.' Hugo attempted to usher Eleanor back to the other end of the room, but she held her ground.

One look at the determined set of her mouth

persuaded Matthew. If she did not hear what Hugo had to say now, Matthew would only have to repeat their conversation later. 'It is all right, Alastair,' he said. 'Your cousin knows about the game and the accusation, although she did not know you and your brother were present that night.'

'Lucas was there, too?' Eleanor said. 'Why did you not tell me?'

'Lucas. Yes,' Hugo said. 'And, as this appears to be important to my cousin, I will tell you. Luke is your man. He was friends with Henson, until *he* caught Henson cheating. He challenged him and Henson just laughed—congratulated Luke on being the first to catch him out. Luke was furious and then, not long after, they had a huge row. Over some woman, I believe. However, I digress. Luke told me Henson admitted it was he who had cheated that night. He—Henson, I mean—thought it highly amusing that you had taken the blame.'

'Why did he not say something to clear my name?' All that time, he could have been back home, with his family.

Hugo shrugged. 'No one knew where you'd gone. There didn't seem much point.'

That was true. Apart from his father and Claverley not one soul in England had known where he was, or what had happened to him.

'This is wonderful,' Eleanor said. 'Now you can prove your innocence to your father.'

'I shouldn't have to. He should have trusted me.'

'But he did not. And think of your mother and your sisters.'

She was right. Finally, he could hold his head up in the knowledge that nobody could point the finger at him.

'Hugo, will you write down what you have just told us? Or, better still, do you think Lucas would write a letter, setting out the facts?' Eleanor said. 'So that you have written proof, should anyone ever mention it,' she added, to Matthew.

Hugo shrugged. 'I can try,' he said. 'Lucas keeps himself to himself these days, but I shall use my best powers of persuasion. I will fetch my belongings and then, dear cousin, I shall write to my brother.'

'This is so exciting,' Eleanor said after Hugo had left.

She gazed up at Matthew with glowing eyes and Matthew's heart sank. Did she not know him at all?

'You can reconcile with your family,' she continued, 'and take your rightful place in society with no fear of those past lies lurking in the background to sully your name.'

She was all eagerness, her wealth and position giving her the confidence that her vision of the future was a rosy certainty. He knew what she felt for him: it radiated from her eyes whenever she looked at him, even when she was angry with him. And his feelings, also, had grown far beyond the initial attraction and the subsequent lust. But he would not allow those feelings to turn to love. She deserved better than him. She deserved to take her rightful place at the pinnacle of society. It had been her goal in coming to London and she was on the brink of achieving it.

'You forget, my lady,' he said. 'I have neither the desire nor the intention of taking *any* place in society. I have a life of my own and to that I shall return once the danger to you is past. Come, we should rejoin your aunt.'

He hardened his heart against the flash of hurt in her eyes. He could protect her from her unknown assailant, but he could not protect her from the pain of his snub.

It is for the best. But...if only...

No. Regret was pointless. He had kissed her. Twice. Those kisses burned in his memory. He should have resisted her. He should never have called upon her once they returned to London.

How easy it was to be wise after the event.

Chapter Twenty-Six

Aunt Lucy watched with interest as Eleanor examined the muff pistol purchased by Matthew. Surprisingly, her aunt had raised not a single objection to her having the weapon—a circumstance that made Eleanor even more fearful for her safety. Even Aunt Lucy thought her in enough danger to warrant having a weapon to hand for protection. When would this nightmare end? But…the end of the threat to her life meant the end of her association with Matthew. He had made that abundantly clear. Unconsciously, she sat straighter, lifting her chin. He must never know how his earlier words had plunged ice into her heart.

'I say we should confront that weasel now, Damerel—you and I together. What do you say?' Hugo had returned with a packed valise, his valet in tow, and an eagerness to act.

He was talking about James. The truth tore at her. The truth she could no longer deny.

'We have tried before,' Matthew said. 'He will only deny it and we have no evidence. We must get hold of that fellow who accosted the servant girl. That is the only way we might get evidence.'

Eleanor concentrated on the pistol, its curved walnut grip smooth under her stroking thumb. The pistol blurred and she blinked hard to prevent her tears from spilling. What a fool she was. Of course Matthew did not care for her. Who would? Her mother hadn't. James didn't—he was prepared to kill her, for goodness' sake.

Why should I care? She was at the pinnacle of her success, fêted as the Catch of the Season and her ultimate ambition was within her grasp— Emily Cowper had dropped her a hint just the other day, saying that her approval for Almack's was all but secure.

'Will you teach me to shoot this?' she asked Hugo, uncaring that she interrupted his quiet discussion with Matthew and Sir Horace.

'I am flattered you should ask, m'dear, but I'm afraid I won't have the time. We've come to the conclusion that, if confronting Weare is not the answer, he must be tailed, at all times. Sir Horace and I are to organise it, as Damerel has so few acquaintances in town. But never fear, I shall be back to escort you this evening and I told Pacey to place me in the next bedchamber to yours, so you may sleep easily tonight.'

Eleanor and Aunt Lucy exchanged startled

looks. This brisk-talking, resolute gentleman was nothing like the nonchalant and care-for-nothing Hugo they were familiar with, the man who never stirred himself on anyone else's behalf.

'Besides,' he continued, 'although it pains me to admit this, Damerel was always a far better shot than I. He will teach you.'

Not the news she wanted to hear, but she acquiesced, determined not to reveal any hint of dismay. From now on, she must look upon Matthew as a dear friend. Nothing—and never to be—more.

Hugo and Sir Horace said their goodbyes and left.

'Well, Mr Damerel? Where do you suggest we go to practise? To the park?'

'First, I shall teach you how to care for it and load it. Then…' he hesitated. 'I fear it will be too public in the park—you will not want to attract attention. And you will be very exposed. What about here? Not indoors, but outside in the back yard?'

'It is not very big. Will there be room?'

His lips twitched. 'It'll be big enough for our purposes. This—' he plucked the pistol from Eleanor's hand, leaving a trail of tingles where his skin brushed hers '—is not designed for long distances.'

She tried to bite back her gasp of consternation.

Matthew crouched beside her chair. 'Are you

certain you want to do this?' he asked. 'Now Alastair will be here overnight, and Weare will be followed, I doubt you will ever need it.'

He touched her hand. She raised her gaze to his, searching his expression. Compassion and concern: emotions prompted by fondness for a close friend.

'I hope I will never have to use it,' she said, 'but I want to learn. I will feel safer.'

'Very well. I suggest we go outside and begin.'

'Aunt Lucy. Will you come, too?'

'Oh, no, my pet. I can think of nothing worse than all that noise. Take one of the footmen with you—I am sure that will suffice for the proprieties.'

Outside, Matthew showed Eleanor how to load the gun by unscrewing the short barrel, seating the gunpowder and the ball and carefully screwing the barrel back in place, first ensuring no powder had spilt on to the threads. He showed her the action of the sliding safety catch and explained how to carry the pistol in the half-cocked position to prevent accidental discharge. She repeated the actions several times until she was confident. By then Timothy had joined them, carrying a tightly stuffed sack.

'What is inside it?' Eleanor asked, eyeing the sack with horrified fascination as Timothy placed it on an old stool brought outside from the pantry, the garden wall behind serving to prop the sack upright. That, according to Matthew, represented her attacker. The man she would have to shoot if ever he got close enough to her to threaten her life. She swallowed down the sour bile that flooded into her mouth. She must not flounder at the thought of shooting into a sack. If she could not do this, how could she ever defend herself?

'Old rags and the like, milady. Mrs Pledger gave them to me.'

Matthew stood behind her. Close behind her. Suddenly, it was hard to breathe…his scent and his heat enveloped her as he lifted her arm to demonstrate how she should aim at the target.

'Close your left eye.' His voice in her ear, the rumble of his words vibrating through his chest, through her muslin dress and reverberating through her body, deep into her core. She sucked in a breath, willing her hand not to shake. 'Steady now.' He covered her white-knuckled hand where she gripped the pistol, his fingers gentle; reassuring. 'Relax.'

It was easy for him to say, nigh on impossible to do. She tried to breathe more evenly; tried to relax her arm and fingers.

'Aim for the centre of the sack. Gently now. Squeeze.' His breath tickled her ear, causing a ripple of gooseflesh down her neck. Her arm jerked as she pulled the trigger.

Bang! Smoke puffed from the pistol and Eleanor stifled her scream as the recoil vibrated up her arm. She had braced herself for the noise, but had not realised the power of the kick of such a small weapon. She swallowed hard; turned to Timothy, who held the powder flask and spare balls; began to reload.

'I will do better this time,' she announced, to no one in particular, and took her stance as Matthew had showed her.

Matthew moved behind her.

'No. I will do this myself.'

She took aim, squeezed—striving to keep the movement smooth—and fired again.

'Yes!'

Matthew's triumphant shout bounced from the surrounding garden walls and Eleanor prised open her eyes, which she had screwed shut—quite without intent—at the moment she fired. A ragged, black-rimmed hole had appeared in the sack. Not in the centre, but at least she had hit the target.

'Well done,' Matthew said. 'Try again.'

She glowed with his praise. Donald had never praised her. He had always found fault.

She practised until the sack was in shreds and her right arm trembled with fatigue.

'That is enough for today,' Matthew said, gesturing to Timothy to clear everything away. 'You must be worn out. Let us go inside.'

Aunt Lucy was nowhere to be seen when they returned to the drawing room. A maid followed them in, bearing a tray laden with a jug of lemonade and a plate of sandwiches.

'Cook said as you would welcome some refreshments, milady.'

'Thank you, Nell, that is most thoughtful. Where is Lady Rothley?'

'She's gone up for a nap, milady. Would you like me to sit in with you?'

'No, that won't be necessary, thank you, but leave the door open on your way out, will you?'

Eleanor sat on the sofa, a glass of lemonade in her hand, whilst Matthew propped one arm along the marble mantelpiece.

'Thank you for teaching me,' Eleanor said.

Matthew sipped at his lemonade. The sweet yet sharp drink reinforced his bittersweet thoughts throughout this long day. What would the future hold for Eleanor? He knew his own future—the days would be filled with running his business. But what of hers? Would she wed? He tamped down the pain such a thought evoked. Maybe she never would marry. She certainly seemed content with her independent life.

'Why have you never wed?'

He hadn't meant to ask the question quite so bluntly, but he did not regret asking it. A memory stirred. Lady Rothley...talk of a betrothal. Or a near betrothal. He racked his brain, trying to recall her exact words, as Eleanor stared pensively into her glass, as though it might provide answers.

'I almost did,' she said eventually. 'Three years ago, just before my father died. I was on the brink of getting betrothed, when I found out...' She paused. 'I was fortunate I discovered his true nature before all the settlements had been agreed. I withdrew my acceptance of his offer.' She looked up, eyes glittering defiance. 'I have never regretted it.'

'And what was his true nature?' He could guess what was coming.

'Avaricious!'

'He was after your wealth.'

'He was. He was quite the expert at hiding his true intentions, though. He intended to live a life of luxury in London whilst I remained at Ashby, running the estate to fund his pleasures.'

Bitterness surfaced, breaking through that outer shell of confidence she customarily hid behind. No wonder she was so uncertain of her own allure as a woman.

Before he could probe further, she continued, 'It is the reason Ruth never liked me.'

'Ruth?' What did Ruth have to do with it?

'Donald was her brother.'

'Her *brother*?' Whatever he had expected, this was not it. 'Why have you never told me?'

Her brows snapped together. 'Why on earth should I tell you? It's in the past. All finished with.'

'But…could it not be him trying to kill you? Revenge is a motive.'

'No!' Eleanor jumped up from the sofa and crossed the room to the window. She stood rigidly, her arms wrapped around her waist. Matthew set his glass down and followed her.

'He is dead,' she said. 'He was a soldier. He had planned to leave the army but, when I refused to marry him, he had no choice but to return to the military life. He was killed in battle. At Talavera.'

'I am sorry,' Matthew said.

She turned to face him. 'It is in the past, as I said.'

Matthew cleared his throat. He must say this without a single tremor in his voice to betray him.

'You will find someone worthy of you, I am certain.'

Only the slightest flare of her nostrils revealed her emotions. 'I am sure I will,' she said, her voice flat as she stepped to one side and glided past him to gain the centre of the room. 'Thank you once again for obtaining the pistol and teaching me to shoot.'

Her dismissal of him was plain. It was for the best. He must concentrate on finding proof against her cousin.

'It was my pleasure. Are you engaged this evening?'

'No. We were to have gone to the theatre but,

after such an eventful night and day, we have decided to stay at home.'

'In that case, I shall see you tomorrow. I hope you will feel safer now, with your pistol and with Alastair staying in the house.'

Her pursed lips stretched into a semblance of a smile. 'I shall indeed. Goodbye, Mr Damerel.'

Chapter Twenty-Seven

It was the night of Eleanor's soirée, several days after the intruder had broken into the house on Upper Brook Street, and there had been no further incidents, to Matthew's relief. If she never had to use that pistol he would be a happy man—it went against his every instinct, to hand over even the smallest part of her protection to her or, indeed, to others. He had found fewer and fewer excuses to call upon her now Hugo was in residence and, although he still escorted her to her evening entertainments, the presence of her 'guardians' meant she was well looked after. His position was fast becoming redundant.

He arrived early at her soirée, hoping to snatch a few moments with Eleanor before her guests arrived. Pacey showed him up the stairs and there she was, her back to him, fiddling with a flower arrangement on a side table set into an arched alcove on the first-floor landing.

As Pacey stepped forward to announce his presence, Matthew stayed him, then crossed the landing to stand behind her.

'Good evening, my lady.'

Eleanor started, then turned to laugh up into Matthew's face, soft lips parted revealing white, even teeth, her eyes glowing, the gold flecks in her irises reflecting the candlelight.

'Goodness, you startled me.'

Matthew's heart turned in his chest. She looked so beautiful, her elegant pale rose gown displaying her womanly curves to perfection. He drank in the vision. How much longer would he be able to do so? How much longer could he remain part of her life?

Eleanor brushed a wisp of hair from her face. Her hands were bare, her gloves lying abandoned on the table behind her.

He sketched a bow. 'My apologies for my early arrival—I thought I would come early in case your cousin showed his face before the appointed time.'

'He is not attending,' Eleanor said, as she led the way into the drawing room, 'and neither is Ruth. I feel…such lightness of spirit. I shall be able to enjoy this evening without the constant apprehension of what James might say or do. I felt obliged to invite them despite my dread of seeing him again.'

The doors between the drawing room and the

sitting room beyond had been thrown wide, the furniture removed and the carpets rolled up ready for the dancing. The piano was set at one end of the room, the pianist already there, running his fingers up and down the scales.

'James sent a note round this morning to say he was going out of town on urgent business and Hugo has confirmed he left on the mail coach,' Eleanor continued, as she crossed to the front window, twitched the curtain aside and peered out into the twilit street. She laughed self-mockingly, and shook her head. 'It is foolish, I know, but I cannot help but look outside every so often, in case I see *him*.'

'It is not foolish. You are right to stay alert. Where is Alastair? Is he here?'

'Oh, yes.' She smiled at Matthew over her shoulder, eyes twinkling. 'He is upstairs, completing his *toilette*. He attends society events rarely and his pride dictates he is not found wanting.'

'He does not enjoy such gatherings, then?'

'No, and judging by what has remained unsaid, I suspect that, in my cousin's case, it is a case of mamas and chaperons beware.' She lowered her voice. 'He leads a reckless life and my uncle did not leave the family fortunes in a robust state. Not many parents would countenance an impoverished second son courting their daughter.' She flushed. 'Oh! That was tactless indeed. I am sorry, I did not mean…I hope I did not cause offence?'

'My shoulders are broader than that, I hope,' Matthew said. Her words might have stung if he had not already inured himself to that truth. 'Besides, Alastair's position as second son is positively charmed compared to mine. A third son is a far more hopeless proposition, would you not say?'

She looked up, laughing again. 'Only if those parents were fixed upon their daughter marrying for position. Or wealth.'

Their gazes fused. Matthew's waistcoat suddenly seemed too tight to draw breath as Eleanor's smile faded and her eyes questioned his. Without volition, he raised his hand to her cheek and trailed his fingers down soft, silken skin to her mouth.

'Eleanor.'

Her eyes widened, darkening as her lips parted. A quick glance to the pianist, who was absorbed by his trilling chords, and Matthew tilted her chin, lowering his head to touch his lips to hers. It felt like home. Where he belonged. With a deep groan, he gathered her to him, backing her through the curtains into the narrow bay beyond, ignoring the clamour of caution in his head.

Her arms snaked around his neck, her fingers threading through his hair as their tongues entwined. The rush of blood to his groin kept his conscience at bay as he plundered her sweet mouth. The press of her body to his, her full breasts squashed against his chest, her unique perfume—jasmine, interwoven with the tantalising scent of feminine arousal—flooded his senses as his hands roamed her voluptuous curves. Lost in the most arousing kiss of his life, he forgot time, place and propriety as Eleanor cupped his face, then slipped questing hands beneath his coat to caress his chest.

As her touch crept lower Matthew reluctantly resurfaced. A stolen kiss was one thing. Any more...

'Eleanor...' A harsh whisper from fevered lips as the enormity of his actions hit him. 'You are... irresistible.'

He could hardly bear to meet her eyes. Instead, he peeked through the slight gap between the curtains. The room was still empty. The pianist beyond was still absorbed in his music.

'Quickly,' he said, leading her back into the room. He stepped back. Examined her. No signs of ravishment, her hair still in place.

It wasn't her hair you were manhandling. Guilt shrouded his thoughts, penetrated deep into his heart. What had he done?

'Matthew...?'

'I am sorry. I had no intention...' He paused. It was not possible. The future. Could he...? Every ounce of his pride rose up to smother his guilt. No. He could not. 'You are so very lovely. But…'

She released him from the hook upon which he squirmed. 'But it can never be?'

He shook his head.

A frown creased her forehead. 'You will make up your differences with your father and the rest of your family, you will see. You only need the time and the opportunity.'

'And then what?'

He had not meant to sound so harsh, hated the hurt that surfaced in her tawny eyes before she dropped her gaze.

'I will not be a kept man.'

'You have your business interests—'

'They are nothing in comparison.'

'In comparison to what?' she snapped. 'You have worked for what you have, Matthew. How does that make you a lesser being?' She laid her hand on his arm. 'I would never view a gentleman who earns his way in the world as inferior to a gentleman who has inherited his wealth.'

'Then you are the exception to the rule,' Matthew said, 'for that is exactly how society views a man who has to work for a living.'

'Who cares what—?'

'*You* care. You came to London to erase the memory of your mother's scandal, to be accepted for Almack's. You care what society thinks of you. You want a position in society, and you have one. And *I* care what society would think of *me* if…'

His voice had risen. He stepped back and Eleanor's hand slipped from his arm.

'I am sorry,' he said, quieter now. 'I had no intention of raising false expectations. I will not be labelled a fortune hunter on the catch for a rich wife. My honour…'

'Your honour?' Her eyes flashed scorn. 'You speak of honour, yet you think nothing of stealing kisses from a maiden who, by your own admission, you would never wed.'

The bitter words hung in the air between them. Why could she not see how hard this was for him, too? Did she think it gave him pleasure to picture her with another man?

'You should go and find your gloves before your guests arrive.'

Eleanor left the room without another word, back straight, head high.

He had expected nothing less.

Although he had stated his case, Eleanor's words nevertheless came back to him at times during the evening. *I would never view a gentleman who earns his way in the world as inferior to a gentleman who has inherited his wealth.* He believed her. The problem was not with her views on the chasm between them, but with his. And with his pride. He might start with just a tiny feeling of inferiority, but what if it were to grow? What of Eleanor's penchant for having her own way? How long before their disparate circumstances reared up to cause trouble? *He* would never be approved to buy vouchers for Almack's—not that he would want them, but that was hardly the point. Would she grow to resent him and to regret shackling herself to a gentleman who would not be fully accepted everywhere?

She deserved better than him and, in time, she would see it.

On the other hand...love. He could think about her, and them, and all the reasons—very good reasons—why they should stay apart. It was the only outcome that made sense. But then, in his heart... Eleanor. She was so deeply entrenched he could not imagine a day without loving her. He had no interest in any other woman.

Confused, Matthew chatted, and danced, and played cards by rote as Eleanor acted the gracious hostess. He clenched his jaw against the pain of seeing Eleanor with other gentlemen, all more worthy of a wealthy peeress than he.

When will they get here? How will he react? Will he hate me for interfering?

Eleanor's nerves skittered as she chewed at her lower lip, hoping she had done the right thing. She looked around, seeking Matthew, and her stomach clenched in irritation at the sight of him dancing with yet another pretty miss. He had not danced with her and she could not blame him.

That kiss…she had been swept away by it… swept away by him…until anger had allowed her to gather her wits. She had returned to reality with a painful bump. Matthew was right. It was for the best. She could see it now. It could never work. She was better off without him.

There was a flurry of movement by the door, and Pacey appeared. He caught her eye and beckoned. *Oh, heavens.* Eleanor's heart raced as she walked to the door. Too late for doubts or regrets: the die was cast.

In the hall downstairs, William was divesting a scowling Lord Rushock of his hat and gloves. Eleanor's heart sank at his expression. Stephen had assured her their plan would work. She must trust him to know his own father. But Matthew… that stubborn pride of his…would it allow him to unbend enough to meet his father halfway in this attempt at reconciliation?

Stephen Damerel stood waiting for his father, with an anxious frown that cleared as he caught sight of Eleanor.

'Good evening, Lady Ashby,' he said, with an elegant bow. 'I apologise for our tardy arrival.'

'I am delighted you could both attend.' They exchanged a conspirators' smile. 'Good evening, Lord Rushock. I trust you are well?'

'Harumph!' Rushock's chest expanded. 'Yes, well enough, I suppose, although—'

'Father, you do wish to mend your fences with Matthew, do you not? Think of Mama.'

The older man subsided. 'Yes.'

His brevity surprised Eleanor. He had appeared an inveterate blusterer, but mayhap it was all show.

'Would you like to come through to the parlour?' she said. 'Mr Damerel, if you would be so kind as to—?'

'I'll go and get him.'

'Thank you. Pacey will show you which room.' And Aunt Lucy and Hugo had been primed to forestall any guests who might notice that both Eleanor and Matthew had disappeared.

They waited in silence in the parlour. Eleanor, full of trepidation now the moment was close, was unable to make small talk. Lord Rushock paced the room, hands clasped behind his back.

The door opened to admit first Matthew, then Stephen, who closed it and leaned back against it in a nonchalant manner; only the tight line of his mouth revealed his tension.

'What is the meaning of this?' Matthew's ice-blue gaze speared Eleanor. He turned to leave. 'Let me pass.'

'Not yet, little brother. Not until you and Father have a proper conversation. It is time you thrashed over the past and set it behind you.'

'We've talked. There is nothing left—'

'For your mother's sake, if not mine.' Rushock gripped Matthew's shoulder. 'Please, son.'

Matthew's indrawn breath was audible. 'Very well. Just family.'

It was as though he stabbed her in the heart. It could not be clearer that she did not belong. Eleanor walked to the door, trying not to show her hurt.

'I will see you later,' she said in a low voice to Stephen as he opened the door to let her pass.

Chapter Twenty-Eight

Matthew searched the room for his hostess. Ah…there! She could not help but stand out, with her burnished curls piled high, topping every other woman in the room by half a head. He strode across the room to where Eleanor stood with Lord Vernon Beauchamp and his sister, Lady Cecily. Her awareness of his approach was exposed by the sudden flush of her cheeks, despite her determined attempt to keep her attention on her companions.

Beauchamp…rake and darling of the *ton*. Resentment scraped at Matthew's insides. It mattered not that Stephen had assured him none of the gentlemen watching over Eleanor was hanging out for a wife…and why Stephen had even thought it necessary to tell him such an irrelevant fact, he did not know…! Grrr! He'd lost his train of thought. All he knew was the sight of Eleanor anywhere near any of these so-called gentlemen *burned* in his gut.

And the memory of her interference scoured his insides even more. How dare she? What business of hers was it if he and his father were estranged? If he had any doubts over not courting her, her interference had consolidated his decision. She always thought she knew best. She was a stubborn, managing tyrant.

And an utter peach.

His anger subsided—a little—as she shot him a wary glance through her thick lashes. A tremulous smile hovered for an instant on those full lips before she settled her focus back on Beauchamp.

As the conversation ebbed and flowed he thought back to the interview with his father. It had been awkward. Both men—he recognised from a distance—had been wary of offering too much, in case the other rejected that degree of conciliation. Thank God for Stephen and his patience and diplomacy in brokering their deal. For that is what it had reminded Matthew of. A business deal. With sky-high personal stakes. They had left the parlour with a new understanding and, in Matthew, the joy of knowing he would shortly be reconciled with the rest of the family. Claverley would be furious. That made the reward even sweeter.

Gradually, Eleanor's conversation with the Beauchamps drowned out his introspection.

'I am arranging a day out to Richmond next week,' Lady Cecily was saying. 'I do hope you will join us, Eleanor, with your aunt. I will send you an invitation.'

'Thank you, Cecily. I should be delighted.'

'And you, Mr Damerel? Might I persuade you to join our number?'

'If I am still in town, I should be delighted, my lady.'

'Are you planning to leave London?' Was that a hint of panic in Eleanor's question?

He summoned up every last vestige of his resolve. 'I am. As soon as you are in no further danger, my lady, I plan to visit my family.'

'Then you and your father—'

'Have reached an understanding.' He should thank her for her help, but his anger at her unasked-for interference was too raw. It was an uncomfortable clash of feelings and it was simpler not to give vent to either. Maybe when he had calmed down a bit… 'I am very much looking forward to seeing my mother and sisters again.'

Her eyes glittered. 'There is no need to remain in London on my behalf,' she said. 'Hugo is here and I am sure the other gentlemen who have been so kind in watching over me will continue to do so for as long as necessary. Is that not so, my lord?'

'Indeed,' Vernon said, in his rich, cultured

voice. 'We are at your service for as long as you need us.'

'So, there is nothing to prevent you going home tomorrow, if you so wish,' Eleanor said, her tone indifferent although the faint crease between her brows told its own tale.

He could not blame her...he was not the only one with pride.

'I will finish what I started,' he said. 'I shall call upon you tomorrow, at two o'clock, if that is convenient, to discuss your protection over the next few days. Alastair, as I understand it, has a long-standing commitment tomorrow so, if you need to go out, I shall be available to escort you in the afternoon.'

Eleanor nodded. 'Very well. I shall see you at two tomorrow. Now, if you will please excuse me, I have guests to attend to.'

A short time later, a heavy hand landed on his shoulder.

'Well, my boy—' his father's voice boomed in his ear '—I am pleased we have buried our differences.' He chuckled. 'We are too alike, that is the truth. Proud. Your mother would say stubborn, too, but I will not admit to that.'

'I am pleased to put the past behind us too, Father,' Matthew said. 'Although I must tell you again that I shall not give up my business interests. Quite apart from that pride you mentioned,

I actually enjoy what I do. I could never live an idle life.'

'You won't be idle, my son, not with that estate your grandfather left you.'

His father had earlier told Matthew that his mother's father had bequeathed an estate in Leicestershire to Matthew, subject to his return to England of his own free will.

'It may not enjoy a vast acreage, but your grandfather was able to live very comfortably off the rents,' Lord Rushock continued. 'It's prime hunting country, you know.'

'Despite that, I will continue in trade with my business partner. That was our plan in returning to England.'

'Plans can change.' His father nudged him and nodded in Eleanor's direction, where she was bidding farewell to some of her guests. 'It looks like you're in a fair way to fixing your interest already, you sly young pup—way ahead of the other bucks hanging out for a rich wife. She'd be a good match for you, worth a tidy fortune. She'd not be to everyone's taste, mind, too tall and robust for most, but a pretty enough face, I'll grant you. And that fortune will be more than enough to compensate. It's good to see the years away have given you some good sound common sense.'

Fuming, Matthew clenched his fists. Even his own father thought he would court Eleanor purely for her wealth. No longer thought a cheat, but now labelled as a fortune hunter.

The next day a frustrated Eleanor gazed at the clock in the drawing room, watching the minute hand creep past the six and tick its way up towards the hour again. It was already past half past two.

Where is he?

Hugo was out and Eleanor had declined to accompany Aunt Lucy and Sir Horace on their visit to friends because Matthew was due to call.

The clock struck three; she paced the floor.

Where is he? It would serve him right if I wasn't here when he arrives.

But still she waited, increasingly annoyed—not only at Matthew for his tardiness, but also at herself for staying meekly at home, awaiting his arrival.

She looked at the clock for the umpteenth time. Five past three. She wandered to the window and craned her neck to peer up and down the street below. A discreet cough drew her attention and she turned to see Pacey at the door.

'A message has been delivered for you, my lady.' He held out a folded and sealed sheet of paper.

'Thank you, Pacey.'

She did not recognise the writing so it was not from Matthew. She broke the wax seal and smoothed the single page, which was covered in a cramped and hurried script.

> *My dearest Cousin Eleanor*
>
> *Our recent conversation about my Troubles gave me such comfort and I would beseech you to come to my Aid. I am in such turmoil about your Cousin James. You are the only person I can turn to in my Distress and I must plead with you to come to me without Delay whilst he is from home.*
>
> *I shall be at Home all afternoon and I hope and pray that you will attend me here without Delay, for I shall be unable to answer to the Consequences if you do not come.*
>
> *Please do not Fail me. It must be Today, before your Cousin returns.*
> *Your Desperate Cousin*
> *Ruth*

Eleanor frowned as she finished the letter, then re-read it carefully, wondering what had caused Ruth to write such a hasty and muddled missive. The 'troubles' she wrote of suggested her agitation at her lack of a family. But her insistence that Eleanor attend her before James came home... Could Ruth have discovered something about the attacks?

Eleanor considered her options, eager to hear

what Ruth had to tell her. If she waited for Aunt Lucy—out shopping, with Sir Horace as her escort—to return, she would surely insist upon accompanying Eleanor to visit Ruth. Whilst that might be the sensible thing to do, would her aunt's presence prevent Ruth from being completely honest?

Also, the longer she delayed her visit, the more likely it was that James would return whilst she was there. Therefore, the sooner she went to Ruth, the better.

She could send word to one of her 'guardians', but the same objections to Aunt Lucy's presence applied equally to them. Ruth would be unlikely to speak openly in the presence of anyone else, particularly a man.

Which left Eleanor to rely upon her own resources, much as she had done for the past three years.

She would go in the carriage, right to the front door. She had her footmen. She would take her pistol. With James away from home, what possible danger could there be? Her mind conjured up the image of the stranger she had seen watching her. She had not seen him since that time outside the house. And Ruth would be there, after all.

She made up her mind. She *would* go and, if she sensed the slightest threat when the door was opened to her, she would simply refuse to go inside. She rang the bell.

'Pacey, I am going out in fifteen minutes. Can you send for the carriage and ask Lizzie to attend me upstairs, please? And tell three of the footmen—whoever you can spare most easily—they are to accompany me.'

'May I know where to, my lady?'

'To call upon Mrs Weare,' she replied. 'When Lady Rothley returns, please tell her where I have gone and what time. And tell her not to worry, for I have protection with me.'

Pacey hesitated. 'My lady, should you not wait until—?'

'*Now*, Pacey.' The butler bowed and withdrew.

Eleanor went to her bedchamber to change into her sprigged-muslin walking dress and to load her pistol. If James was the culprit, and he returned home unexpectedly, she would be ready for him. Lizzie helped her into her pomona-green spencer and bonnet, and she carefully placed the pistol into her matching reticule, ignoring Lizzie's gasp of horror.

'Come, Lizzie, fetch your coat, please. I wish you to attend me on my visit to my cousin's house.'

'Very well, milady.' Lizzie was stiff with disapproval.

As they trod down the stairs to join William,

Timothy and Peter, who were awaiting them in the hallway, Eleanor pushed her qualms aside.

Instead, she chose to focus on her satisfaction that the decision of whether or not to continue waiting for Matthew had been taken from her hands.

Chapter Twenty-Nine

The same mournful-looking footman from before answered the door in response to William's knock. Timothy assisted Eleanor from the carriage and she approached the entrance. The front door stood wide and, beyond the servant, she could see a maid busy polishing a console table. The hallway seemed brighter, the sweet scent of beeswax a pleasant contrast to the stale cooking odours that had given the house such a musty air on her previous visit.

Reassured that normality reigned, Eleanor called to the coachman, 'We will not be long, Joey. Please walk the horses around if they get restless.'

She stepped across the threshold into the hall.

'Mrs Weare is in her bedchamber, milady,' the footman said, eyeing William, Timothy and Peter askance. 'She has requested that you attend her there.'

'Is your mistress unwell?'

'No, milady. No more than usual.'

'Is Mr Weare at home?'

'No, he has travelled out of town. He is not due back until tonight.'

'Very well. Timothy and Peter, you will wait for me here in the hall. William—' he was the biggest and burliest of the three '—you can wait for me on the upstairs landing. And Lizzie will come with me.' She had already warned the men that, if James were to return, they must come to her immediately.

James's footman frowned, but raised no objection, merely indicating they should follow him. Eleanor relaxed a little as she climbed the stairs with Lizzie, William at their heels, the weight of her pistol providing comfort. Surely, if there was a plot to harm her here, the servants could not behave in such a humdrum manner. James was still away from home and the fact that the footman had raised no objection to William accompanying her upstairs reassured her.

Ruth's bedchamber was on the second floor. Eleanor entered to find a large, bright room, decorated in rose and cream, the tall windows open to allow the sunlight to stream in. The room was far better appointed than the shabby sitting room into which she had been shown on her first visit. Mentally, she shrugged. How James and Ruth chose to decorate their house was none of her concern.

The bedchamber had been arranged in two halves: to the right of the door was a bed, beyond which there was a door, possibly leading to a dressing room or even to James's bedchamber. An elegant chest of drawers and a vanity dresser in matching mahogany were arranged against the wall.

To the left of the door was a sitting area consisting of two bucket chairs, arranged either side of the fireplace. On the long wall opposite Eleanor, set between two of the windows, was an elegant *chaise longue*, upon which Ruth, haggard in top-to-toe black, reclined. Eleanor faltered. Was she in mourning? No, she could not be. Her parents and brother were all long deceased and no one else had died to Eleanor's knowledge. She crossed the room to greet Ruth, aware from the corner of her eye that Lizzie moved to stand near the fireplace.

'Eleanor, my dear, dear cousin, I am so pleased you have come. I have been in such turmoil.'

Ruth did look unwell, her cheeks gaunt, her eyes blazing with a fervency that brought to Eleanor's mind her discomfort when Ruth had confided in her at the Duke of Cheriton's ball.

It is too late to regret coming now, she thought, with a trickle of unease. *Find out what she wants, then leave as soon as you can.*

'Ruth, I hope I find you well? Tell me, what is

so urgent that you needs must summon me with such urgency?'

Ruth rose from the *chaise longue* and Eleanor exchanged a nervous look with Lizzie as Ruth circled the room before walking to the window and staring out, her arms folded around her torso, her narrow back and shoulders rigid. 'I told you I was desperate to get with child, did I not?'

'You did.'

Eleanor moved towards Ruth, angling to one side, so she could see Ruth's expression. It was oddly impassive. Eleanor tried to quash her growing fear. Lizzie was here. William was outside the door, with instructions to come in immediately if she called him.

Suddenly, Ruth spun to face Eleanor. 'It was him! James! I found him out. He was putting poison in my food. Poison to prevent my conceiving…to prevent my child inheriting Ashby. But I fooled him. I stopped eating. I am with child, although he does not yet know it.'

Eleanor's mind reeled. Could this be true? She couldn't believe…*poison*? No, not James. She stepped towards Ruth, vaguely aware of Lizzie, now by her side, clutching at her arm, trying to tug her towards the door. She strove to speak calmly, reaching out to touch Ruth, trying to build a rapport with her.

'Listen to me, Ruth, please. James longs for a

child, you know he does. He loves you. Why on earth would he prevent you from conceiving?'

'He doesn't want us at Ashby. He *never* wanted us at Ashby.'

Eleanor shook her head, scrambling to make some sense of it all, remembering the attacks on her. Could James really…? Her whirling thoughts skidded to a halt. *Ashby?*

'But… Ruth…your child won't inherit Ashby. It belongs to me, not Ja—' Her blood froze as pieces of the puzzle began to slot into place. *Ruth?* Could Ruth be responsible for…?

'It's not natural.' Ruth snatched her arm away. '*I* should be Lady Ashby, by rights. James tricked me. I didn't know, until it was too late. Even then, we could have stayed there and lived a comfortable life but, no…he insisted we come here and struggle. He never wanted us at Ashby.'

Did she mean the baby? Eleanor eyed Ruth's slender form. She did not look *enceinte*. 'Us? Who do you mean? Who doesn't James want at Ashby?'

'Me and Donald.'

'But…Donald is—'

'Dead! Yes, he's dead. And it's all your fault.' Ruth's eyes glowed with a fanatical light as she spewed out her accusations. 'Ashby could have been Donald's. Why do you think he proposed to you? For your *charms*? You killed my brother and now you're Lady Ashby, and you have all the money and *we*…we have nothing.'

Even though she knew it was untrue, it hurt. 'Donald died in the war, Ruth,' she said.

'He only went back because of you. Why didn't you just marry him? We could all have been happy then. At Ashby. It's your fault Donald is dead. He died horribly. In agony. And it is your fault. You might as well have pulled the trigger yourself.'

Rationally, Eleanor knew Donald's death was not her fault and yet, deep inside, there lingered a splinter of guilt. *If* she had married him, it was true he would still be alive.

She tried again to pacify Ruth, even though she suspected the other woman was beyond reason, ignoring Lizzie's hissed 'Milady!' and shrugging off the increasingly urgent clutch of her fingers.

'Ruth, you cannot know what really happened in the Peninsula. It is a war. Soldiers face injury and death every day. You must not torment yourself with details you cannot possibly know for sure.'

'I know everything! Garrett was there. He was with Donald when he died.'

'Garrett? Who is…?' Eleanor followed Ruth's triumphant gaze as she looked at the second door opposite the fireplace. Eleanor's stomach clenched in fear as she recognised the man she had seen outside her house, turning the key in the lock.

'William! Help!' Eleanor's scream mingled with Lizzie's.

There was a thump against the door Eleanor and Lizzie had entered by, which shook, but held. Ruth must have locked it, unnoticed, during her circuit of the room. The man—Garrett—smiled and walked towards Eleanor, who backed away, skirting around Ruth. At least she could now see them both at once. She pushed at Lizzie, in a silent attempt to tell her to go and unlock the first door, which was now unguarded, but the maid was more intent on staying close to Eleanor.

A gloating smile played around Ruth's lips. '*Now* you will learn the truth,' she spat, 'before you die. My child *will* inherit Ashby and there is nothing you can do to prevent it.'

Eleanor backed until the *chaise longue* prevented further retreat. *Her pistol!* She fumbled in her reticule but, just as her fingers closed around it, Garrett grabbed her, his hands closing hard around her upper arms.

As Eleanor struggled she was aware of Lizzie tugging at Garrett and more loud thumps coming from the locked door. Slowly, relentlessly, Garrett dragged her towards the open window.

She forced herself to look Garrett in the eye. 'You do not have to…you will hang…why would you risk—?'

'You killed my boy,' he snarled.

'Your boy?' Eleanor panted with the effort of resisting him. Surely William would break the door down soon? Garrett's arms were wrapped tight around her, but her pistol was in her hand and, if she got the chance, she would use it without a qualm. She gritted her teeth, struggling harder, aware of Lizzie now grappling with Ruth.

'I brought him and Miss Ruth up from little nippers. They deserved Ashby! Weare tricked her! Miss Ruth was *born* to be a lady.'

Eleanor's head spun and she gasped for breath as she struggled with all her strength to free herself. Although slightly shorter than her, he was immensely strong and slowly, inexorably, they neared the window. Her heart tumbled with fear. If they reached the low sill, one good push and she would fall. Hauling in a deep breath, she braced herself for one more effort to free her right arm and, somehow, use her pistol.

Suddenly, with a loud crash, the first door flew open. Garrett's grip loosened for a second, but that was enough for Eleanor. With all her remaining strength she pulled away from him, then spun around, holding her pistol up with a shaking hand. Garrett's attention was not on her, however, but on the man who had burst through the door.

'No, Eleanor!'

Eleanor's breath seized as Matthew charged at Garrett, who roared with fury, swinging wild punches. Eleanor's heart was in her mouth as she watched Matthew dodge Garrett's flailing arms, until one well-aimed punch to Garrett's jaw saw him slump to the floor, knocked out cold.

'Noooo!' Ruth's shrill cry resounded around the room. Shoving Lizzie aside, she advanced on Eleanor, fingers clawed.

'Ruth! Stop! I beg of you.' James had appeared. He pushed between Ruth and Eleanor, arms out wide in a placatory gesture. His voice gentled. 'Please don't upset yourself, my love—you know what the doctor told you. Come, come with me. I'll get your medicine for you—that will make you feel better.'

Ruth stared past James at Eleanor, eyes crazed, spittle spraying as her words tumbled over each other in frantic speech. 'Help me, cousin! He is trying to poison me. He doesn't want me to have a baby. Now you can see I am telling you the truth.'

Quick as lightning, she dodged around James and ran at Eleanor, who instinctively flung her arms wide and wrapped them tightly around Ruth's frail form. Matthew was by her side in an instant, but his help wasn't needed for, as soon as Ruth felt Eleanor's arms around her, all the fight seemed to leave her and she slumped. James then took his wife, murmuring to her, and led her from the room as Garrett, still on the floor with William standing guard, groaned and stirred.

With a sob, Eleanor turned into Matthew's

arms, feeling him remove the pistol from her slack grasp. Legs trembling, she leaned into him, his heart hammering in her ear, drawing comfort from his solid strength, wanting nothing more than to blot out the horror.

'Thank you,' she whispered, once her breathing had steadied and her legs felt capable of supporting her. She looked up at him. His hold tightened, and he bent his head to feather a kiss on her forehead.

Then she registered the blessed sound of Aunt Lucy's voice, drawing nearer, until, 'Ellie, Ellie, oh, my pet. Here, Mr Damerel, let me take her.' She put her arm around Eleanor and led her from the bedchamber. The maid who had been polishing in the hall showed them into a small parlour and then disappeared with the promise of refreshments.

James and Matthew joined them some time later. Eleanor, although still shaken, went immediately to her cousin.

'James, my dear...'

He heaved a sigh. 'You deserve an explanation, Eleanor. Ruth is ill. Her moods were always up and down, but controllable if she took her medicine. Then Donald was killed and Garrett returned and started putting fanciful notions in her head, and she got worse. One day she would be convinced the entire world conspired against her, the next it would be as if nothing was amiss, and she would go shopping and spend and spend. Nothing else seemed to make her happy. And, gradually, she focused her blame onto you. When she took the potion the doctor made up for her she seemed to improve, but lately…' He shrugged.

'I have just found out that it was Garrett who was responsible for the attack on that girl. I went to Stockport and showed this around.' He held up an artist's likeness of the man. 'There can be no doubt. The Runners have taken him away.'

He gathered Eleanor's hands to his chest. 'Ellie, I don't know what to say. I am so very, very sorry. I should have had Ruth committed long ago. I tried so hard to keep her happy and contented and to give her all she desired, but nothing worked for long. She would sink into the depths of despair at times.' He looked sadly at a portrait of Ruth that hung over the fireplace. 'I have no choice now. I must have her committed. I thought she could stay here, if we were vigilant. And I tried to keep Garrett away, but it seems the servants were too scared of her rages to stand up to her for long. They were meeting in secret.'

'But why was Garrett prepared to kill for Ruth? It doesn't make sense.'

'I thought the same. That's why, when I first knew of the attacks on you, I didn't think of him. But your description, when you spoke to us at Cheriton's ball…I knew then. That is why I was reluctant to leave you and Ruth alone together. And…when I asked him just now…before they took him…oh, dear God! He was their natural father! Ruth and Donald's.'

'Their *father*? But…*how*?'

'It's a sordid tale. Garrett was bailiff to Ruth's mother's family. They were in love. When she married Mr Aldridge, Garrett went, too, to work for them, and they continued their affair, right under the poor man's nose. It is quite the scandal.'

'I feel sick,' Eleanor said. 'What will happen to Ruth now? Are you truly going to have her committed?'

'I must,' James said. 'This has proved I cannot keep her safe. Nor keep others safe from her torrid imaginings. I see no alternative.'

His face was etched in misery and Eleanor felt her heart go out to him. To think he had been trying to keep Ruth happy and calm all this time—his reluctance to abandon her to a lunatic asylum did him credit. Eleanor longed to help.

'What do you *want*, James?'

He looked puzzled. 'Want? I do not know, but I know I cannot bear to think of her in one of those places. They are horrifying. Truly horrifying.'

'Then she shall not go to one. Come home to Ashby. Waycroft Farm is empty. The house is good, solid stone and it is isolated. We will make it secure and we will hire people to help care for

Ruth. You always loved Waycroft, James. Come, what do you say?'

'You would do that for Ruth, after what she has done?'

'I am doing it for you, my dear.'

'Eleanor…my lady…are you sure this is a good idea?' Eleanor started at the sound of Matthew's voice. She had almost forgotten anyone else was in the room. 'What if someone makes a mistake and Ruth gets out?'

'Mr Damerel is right, my pet. It is too much of a risk.'

'She will not. We will make sure she is kept securely—and comfortably—for as long as necessary. And it will be lovely to have you home, James. You can help me with the estate.'

'Thank you, Ellie. Your generosity…' James grasped her hands '…I do not feel worthy, but I am so very grateful. I will discuss it with Ruth's doctor. He is upstairs with her now.'

Chapter Thirty

'Her ladyship has commanded me to deny her to all callers, sir.' Pacey stood square in the open doorway of Eleanor's house in Upper Brook Street, blocking Matthew's way.

'It is all right, Pacey. I am sure her ladyship will make an exception for Mr Damerel.'

Lady Rothley had appeared behind Pacey, who reluctantly stood aside to allow Matthew to enter.

'Come with me.' Lady Rothley smiled at Matthew. 'Let us see if you are able to lift her mood, for I have never known her so low. One would have thought, with the danger now past, she would be in the best of spirits. But, no...she has hidden herself away and, as you heard, has instructed Pacey to refuse all visitors.'

It was the day after the discovery that Ruth Weare had been behind the attacks on Eleanor. And that final attack would never have happened if Matthew had not been late calling on Eleanor.

That there was a good reason for his tardiness did little to assuage his guilt over her ordeal and the distress she must still be suffering. It was only blind luck that he had arrived in time to prevent injury or even death and it would be a long time before he could forgive himself. And now... He pondered Lady Rothley's words as he followed her to the rear of the house; there was nothing he might say to cheer Eleanor up, for he had come to say his farewells.

Eleanor was sitting by the window in the parlour when they entered. She looked over at Matthew, expressionless, her eyes dull.

'I told Pacey no visitors,' she said, in a lacklustre tone, 'but good afternoon, Mr Damerel.' She smiled, humourlessly. 'If you have come to scold me for going to visit Ruth alone, please save your breath.'

'I have not come to scold you.'

'Good. All that remains, then, is for me to thank you for coming so swiftly to my aid. Aunt Lucy told me what happened.'

Matthew had arrived at Eleanor's house just as Sir Horace had set Lady Rothley down from his carriage. Pacey had immediately told them where Eleanor was and Matthew had driven them to Hill Street in his curricle, at breakneck speed.

'Yes, you were quite the hero,' Lady Rothley said. 'Heaven knows what I should have done if you hadn't arrived when you did, with Sir Horace having already driven away and Ellie having taken the carriage.'

Eleanor turned away as Aunt Lucy spoke and was again studying the sky, as she had been when they had come in.

Aunt Lucy nudged Matthew towards Eleanor. 'See what you can do,' she whispered. 'I fear she is still in shock.'

Matthew drew a chair close to Eleanor's and sat down as Aunt Lucy settled herself in a chair by the fireplace.

What to say? How to begin?

'It will take time for you to come to terms with what happened yesterday,' he said.

'Did Aunt Lucy saddle you with the task of cheering me up? I fear 'twill be a thankless task, judging by how I feel right now.' She glanced at him. 'You have come to say goodbye.'

He should be relieved she had made it easier for him. Perversely, he felt worse.

'Not simply to say goodbye. And it is only temporary, after all. I shall be back in London in a few weeks. It is, after all, my home. And I have my business…' The words dried on his tongue. After the news yesterday, how much longer would he have the business? How long before the bank foreclosed on that loan? He coughed, to clear the blockage from his throat. 'Not simply to say goodbye,' he repeated, 'but to apologise.'

'Apologise? For what?'

He gazed into her eyes. They looked…defeated. His heart lurched, thudding against his ribs. Why could he not cast aside his pride? His troubles would certainly be over then. No sooner had the thought surfaced than he thrust it down with an inner snarl. He would not live off any woman. Especially his wife. It was a man's place to provide for his wife and family.

'If I had arrived on time yesterday—'

'Then we would still not know who was behind the attacks,' she said.

'We would have known as soon as James arrived back from Stockport.'

'It is possible,' she said. 'But it is also possible that you…we…would not have believed him. Suspicion might always have tainted my feelings for him and my memories of him. For that, I am grateful that yesterday happened, if not for the way it happened. James is part of my life again and he will be back at Ashby, where he belongs.'

What need would she have of a husband now? She had proved herself capable of managing the estates since her father died. Now, she would have James by her side. Although… Matthew almost laughed as the thought occurred. What a reversal of the customary reason for marriage within the *ton*. Her only need for a husband would be to provide an heir for Ashby. James would never, now, have a child with Ruth, which left Eleanor the responsibility of continuing the barony. What man would settle for such a role? Not him. But— and he knew it with a sinking certainty—there would be plenty out there who would. And probably spend their married life resenting it and making their wife suffer.

It was not his concern. Not any longer. He was further from her than ever, after yesterday's news.

'I should like to explain,' Matthew said, raising his voice to include Lady Rothley in the conversation.

Eleanor's chest rose as she inhaled. 'It is unnecessary. It happened. But explain if you must.'

'I told you of the two ships sailing from India?'

'Yes. With your partner aboard one of them.'

His throat ached. Benedict—never again to see his quick grin, or to laugh at one of his dry remarks. 'One of them, the *Venetia*, docked yesterday morning. The other—the *Laura May*—they lost her in a storm off the west coast of Africa.'

Lady Rothley gasped and Eleanor straightened in her chair...the first sign of animation since his arrival. 'Oh, no! I am so sorry. Were there any survivors?'

'No. After the storm, the *Venetia* turned back to search, but found nothing other than some wreckage floating in the sea.' His voice cracked over his final words: 'All hands are believed lost.'

'And...Mr Poole?'

'He was on board the *Laura May*.' Matthew

surged to his feet and took a swift turn about the room. 'He is gone.'

The cargo was insured, but that was no compensation. And he had, maybe recklessly, presumed they would turn a large profit on the load, as they had done in the past, when he had secured his bank loan. His friend was dead and his business floundering.

'I am going to Rushock first thing tomorrow,' he said, halting by the door. 'I shall call on you when I return, but then I shall resume my old life, so our paths are unlikely to cross.'

'Then I trust you will have an uneventful journey,' Eleanor said, rising to her feet, but staying by the window. 'Goodbye, Mr Damerel, and thank you again for all your help.'

Matthew's heart contracted painfully. She had already distanced herself from him. Despite it being for the best, despite it having been his intention when he called this morning, it hurt. Badly. He hated to leave this cold distance between them but he must.

He left the house with a leaden weight suspended in his chest where his heart should have been.

The heart he had left behind.

'Well?' The thrill in Aunt Lucy's voice was plain. 'Is it all you expected it to be?'

It was ten days since Matthew had left Lon-

don and Eleanor had finally achieved her dream
of attending Almack's Assembly Rooms. Emily
Cowper, true to her word, had intervened with
the other ladies of the Committee and Eleanor's
name had been entered on the List, enabling her
to purchase a much-coveted voucher.

She gazed around the grand ballroom and put
as much excitement into her response as she could
muster.

'It is wonderful, Aunt Lucy. I am so pleased
to be here.'

Over the past fortnight she had developed a
certain skill in hiding her disillusionment and
despondency behind a mask of enthusiasm and
delight, but still from time to time she had caught
Aunt Lucy watching her with a troubled expression, swiftly erased. Nothing had been said—at
least, not to her. But she suspected neither Aunt
Lucy nor Hugo had fully swallowed her performance. Even James, preoccupied as he was with
Ruth's future care and safety, had commented on
her 'enforced gaiety'. He had put it down to the
trauma of what had happened and she was content for him to believe it.

The reality was that all pleasure had vanished
from Eleanor's world since Matthew's final visit.
Colours had leached into a uniform drabness; the
sweetest sounds were now shrill cacophonies; and
the parties and balls that had once been such a
delight were now a dead bore. But Eleanor had

thrown herself into the round of social pleasure with a smile plastered on lips that were numb and a false eagerness that saw her, night after night, out until the small hours. She groped her way through each day, counting the minutes until her head would touch her pillow and she might be alone with her thoughts. Her eyes burned with the effort of holding on to the tears she refused to shed, and from lack of sleep, but still she accepted each and every invitation that came her way.

Almack's… She danced every dance, her partners forgotten the instant their allotted dance was over…she sipped at the weak orgeat, hiding her grimace of distaste…chewed with dry teeth and tongue at wafer-thin brown bread and butter that tasted of sawdust…*this* had been the pinnacle of her desire. Her goal when she had set out from Ashby all those weeks ago. This cavernous hall, with its small orchestra on a balcony, playing interminable country dances; its gilded columns and enormous mirrors that reflected the light from huge chandeliers; the fluttering young ladies, mainly in their first Season; the gentlemen, resplendent in their black-satin knee breeches, either very much younger than Eleanor, or old enough to be her father.

'Good evening, my dear.' Emily Cowper stood before her. 'I am pleased to welcome you to our evening. I hope you are enjoying your first attendance.'

Eleanor smiled. 'Thank you for adding me to the List, my lady,' she replied, genuinely grateful to Lady Cowper for her help. It was, after all, what she had aspired to. It was hardly Lady Cowper's fault it had come to represent a hollow victory.

'Please, do not mention it,' said her ladyship. 'Now, are there any young gentlemen here with whom you are not acquainted? If so, I shall be happy to perform the introduction. At least here you may rest assured the gentlemen present have all met the approval of the Committee. A lady in your circumstances cannot be too careful, my dear.'

'Thank you, but I believe I am acquainted with everyone.' And not one of them matched up to the man who haunted her dreams.

'Very well. I shall leave you to enjoy the evening.' Lady Cowper tinkled a laugh and made her way back to the dais at the upper end of the room, where the other patronesses were seated, smiling and nodding at various acquaintances.

A young gentleman bowed before her. 'I believe this is our dance, Lady Ashby?'

Eleanor smiled by rote. They had been introduced, but his name quite escaped her. They were all interchangeable. She took the young man's hand and allowed him to lead her on to the dance floor.

'It'll cheer you up, Coz.' Hugo flung himself on to the sofa next to Eleanor and plucked the novel she had been reading from her hands. 'Say you will. It will be just the four of us. Well, to be frank, I had intended just you, Mama and me, but somehow Tidmungen has included himself. Not sure how that happened.'

'Todmorden,' Eleanor said. 'It's Sir Horace *Todmorden*.'

'Well, whoever he is, he's around here a sight too often for my liking.' A scowl marred Hugo's handsome face. 'Damme if I know what Mama sees in him.'

'He is kind to her,' Eleanor said. 'He listens to her opinion and he squires her about. She enjoys the attention.'

'Hmmph. Can't like the fellow, but don't suppose anyone'll listen to me. So, what do you say, Ellie? Is it to be Vauxhall tonight?'

'Very well, then. But I am not in need of cheering up.'

'If you say so,' Hugo said.

That evening, Eleanor gazed around her in awe as they entered the gardens, having chartered a river boat from Westminster to Kennington on the south bank of the Thames. It was magical, lit by thousands of colourful glass lanterns suspended from the trees that lined the gravelled walks, and Eleanor marvelled at the marble statues, the picturesque caves and grottos, the cascades and waterfalls, the canal with its elegant bridges in the Chinese style and the triumphal arches that spanned the South Walk.

By chance, they met with some of Sir Horace's acquaintances and were urged to join them for supper in their box. They feasted on cold chicken and wafer-thin ham, washed down with arrack punch and accompanied by the music of Handel, played by the orchestra. Afterwards, with Aunt Lucy and Sir Horace content to sit and natter with their friends, Eleanor accepted Hugo's suggestion they walk off their supper.

As they strolled, Eleanor noticed ahead of them a group of young bucks loitering at the entrance to a dimly lit side path.

'What is down there?' she asked.

Hugo laughed. 'Nothing suitable for your eyes, Coz. Wait until you've got a husband to stroll down there with. They're no places for unmarried ladies.'

'Well, if that is the case, I…' Eleanor stopped in her tracks. The breath left her lungs with a whoosh. Her heart somersaulted, like the acrobats who had entertained them earlier.

Matthew was strolling towards them, with Arabella Tame on his arm. As Eleanor watched, they halted and Arabella gestured to yet another shadowy side path, laughing up at Matthew. Arabella, with her dainty figure and her porcelain skin, her golden curls and pouting pink lips.

Eleanor turned on her heel, tugging her cousin

around with her. 'Hugo. I am sorry. I am not well. Could we return to your mama?'

'What?' Hugo glanced back over his shoulder. When he spoke again, the surprise had left his voice. 'Yes, of course.'

Eleanor swallowed her pain, gathered the cloak of her pride around her and walked away.

Back at their box, Eleanor pleaded the headache and they made their farewells. She looked neither right nor left as they returned to the mooring to take the boat back across the river. She didn't want to see. She didn't want to know. It was enough that he was here. In London. And he had not bothered to call on her.

She could no longer hang on to the fragile thread of hope that had been her only lifeline since Matthew had left London. It could be no clearer. She had no more hope, no more fight. The Arabellas of this world would always win.

It was time for her to go home. James was leaving for Ashby in the morning. She would go, too. There was no point in staying in London, for she had reached one definite conclusion. It was Matthew she wanted, or no one. Not one of the men she had met in London roused the feelings that Matthew could, just by looking at her with those bright blue eyes. If she could not marry the man she loved, she wanted nothing to do with marriage.

Chapter Thirty-One

Matthew turned on to the Cross Walk at Vauxhall Gardens, with Arabella, Lady Tame, clinging to his arm. Behind them strolled his brother, Stephen, escorting yet another Society beauty.

'Why don't you allow me to show you some of the other walks?' Arabella purred, her fingers tightening on Matthew's sleeve, indicating a dimly lit side turning. Stephen had told Matthew of them—Lover's Walk, Druid's Walk and others—perfect for privacy; for lovers' trysts; a stolen kiss, possibly more.

He looked down into her upturned, laughing face. She was beautiful. There was no doubt about it. Just not for him.

'Perhaps later,' he said, without meaning it.

There was only one woman he longed to hold in his arms. Only one woman whose lips he wanted to taste. And she wasn't petite, with golden curls framing a perfect heart-shaped face.

Eleanor. His heart groaned with the weight of his longing. He tried to push her from his thoughts, but the attempt was as futile now as it had been every day—and night—since he had last seen her. There she was. Constantly. Hovering at the edge of his mind, voicing her opinion, questioning his every move, reminding him she could not be so easily set aside or forgotten.

He had returned to London three days ago, happy to have seen his mother and his sisters, the raw ache that had plagued him for eight years finally soothed. He was back where he belonged. And yet...*this* pain was worse. Jagged. Sharp. A hole ripped in his soul. How many times had he nearly succumbed...swallowed his pride...gone to Eleanor and laid his heart at her feet? But he had resisted. He had to.

For her sake.

He knew, courtesy of Stephen, that she was as popular as ever. And, it seemed, making the most of that popularity. There was no event of note at which Lady Ashby—the Catch of the Season— was not present. She had even, finally, attended that most hallowed of all institutions. Almack's. Nothing emphasised the gulf between them more—he would never be deemed suitable for that temple of the *ton*, tainted by trade as he was.

Eleanor gave little appearance of missing him as he missed her. He knew, though—and better than most—how adept she could be at hiding her true feelings. But what if she was not acting a part? He was aware she had thought herself in love with him. But she was inexperienced. Had it been mere infatuation, fired by those few stolen kisses? Was she, even now, celebrating her lucky escape? He must stay strong. Keep away from her a little longer. Give her time to know her own mind. Her own heart. And then, when he did see her again, pride or no pride, he would tell her the truth of his feelings and beg for her hand, even though it chafed that he must come to her as a supplicant.

He could not support Eleanor—his business would barely scrape by following the loss of the *Laura May. Benedict.* He ached at the reminder of his friend's death. He still could not believe he was gone. It was far easier to imagine him still striding the deck, out there somewhere on the ocean, sailing the waves for ever.

He started. 'I beg your pardon?' He glanced down at Arabella, who pouted.

'I said, shall we rejoin the others?' She indicated the box that Stephen had secured for his birthday celebrations—full of happy, boisterous revellers, it was now two paces behind them.

Matthew felt his cheeks flush. He had been so lost in his thoughts that they had passed it by. 'My apologies, my lady.'

Supper was awaiting them in the box and Matthew did his best to join in the merriment. He felt a stranger amongst these people. They had different interests, different values. And none of them was Eleanor. He counted the hours until he could, without being damned as a killjoy, leave the party and seek his bed to lose himself in his dreams.

'Sir! Mr Damerel, sir!'

Matthew paused, his hand already raised to push open the door of Offley's tavern, where he had arranged to meet Stephen. Henry was hurrying along Henrietta Street, red-faced, waving a letter.

'This just came, sir.' Henry bent over, puffing, his hand on his chest. 'A seaman, sir. Just come into port last night.'

With a hand that shook, Matthew took the letter, moving to one side with an apologetic nod to allow a gentleman to enter the tavern. He gulped as he recognised the bold writing on the outside of the sheet.

Benedict.

He broke the seal and began to read.

A short time later, Stephen pulled out a chair opposite Matthew.

'You have the look of a man for whom life is good, brother,' he said, as he settled into his seat and gestured to a serving maid to bring him a tankard of ale. 'Finally summoned the courage to nail your colours to the fair Eleanor's mast, have you?'

In a buoyant mood, Matthew ignored his brother's jibe. Stephen had guessed his true feelings for Eleanor and Matthew had not denied them. Eleanor. He had been on the brink of following his heart. This news brought that decision closer, made it easier.

He had long dreamt of the day he might have his own family. Those dreams now danced within his reach, although he would have to swallow a quantity of humble pie before Eleanor might forgive him for his stubborn pride and for failing to understand, sooner, that love was all that mattered. But forgive him she must, whatever it took, for he could not envisage any other woman in the role of his wife and as the mother of his children.

In the meantime…

'I am celebrating,' he said, with a broad smile. 'This…' he waved the letter in Stephen's direction '…is the best of all possible news. Benedict is alive!'

'Where is he?'

'Somewhere in Africa.' Matthew bent his head to the letter, straining his eyes in the dim interior of the tavern. 'Lagos. The *Laura May* was badly damaged in that storm, but she survived. She was blown off course, which is why the *Venetia* couldn't find her when they went back to search. Benedict writes that they carried out basic repairs at sea, then headed for the nearest port. He wrote as soon as he could and handed it to the captain of another ship bound for England, to deliver to me.' Matthew leaned back, relief settling in, supplanting the race of excitement that had sent his blood coursing hot through his veins as he had read the letter.

'That,' said Stephen, raising his tankard, 'is news to celebrate indeed.'

'It is. And what is more,' Matthew said, 'I am now in a position to—'

A silky voice cut in. 'Damerel—your man said I'd find you here. Been lookin' for you all day.'

Lord Hugo Alastair stood over Matthew, who stiffened. This was a time for rejoicing. Hugo's expression did not suggest he sought a friendly chat.

'Congratulations.'

Hugo lifted an enquiring brow.

'You've found me.'

'Mind if I join you?' Hugo sat next to Stephen without waiting for a reply. He retrieved a letter from his pocket and put it on the table. 'Best get the business out of the way first. It came this morning. From Rothley.'

It seemed to be his day for receiving momentous communications, Matthew thought, as he read the words that confirmed it was Henson who had cheated in that long-ago card game.

'Thank you, and I will write to thank your

brother also. I'm grateful for your help.' Even as he spoke, he wondered what else was on Hugo's mind.

'Saw my cousin this morning…' Hugo said, then paused. Matthew's fingers tightened on the handle of his tankard. *Eleanor.* 'Just before she left.'

Matthew stilled, his eyes riveted on Hugo. 'Left? Where has she gone?'

'Home. And what I should like to know is— why?'

Gone? Why would she leave London when she was at the pinnacle of her success? With an effort, Matthew kept his expression blank. Any decision about Eleanor was his to make. He would not allow the likes of Hugo Alastair to push him around. Affecting an air of nonchalance, he raised his tankard and took a long swallow, before raising his eyes to look at his brother.

'As I was about to say—'

Stephen's grey eyes narrowed. 'You seem remarkably calm at Alastair's news.'

Matthew forced himself to shrug dismissively. He was good at hiding his feelings. He'd had a lifetime of practice.

'Or,' Stephen continued, 'you are remarkably good at concealing your feelings. I suspect the latter.'

'You may have noticed,' said Hugo, 'that I still await an answer.' His voice hardened. He leaned over the table, dark eyes hard. 'What happened between the two of you, that one glimpse of you at Vauxhall last night was enough to send her fleeing London, once again, in a state of despair?'

Matthew's stomach balled into a hard knot of fury, his eyes boring into Hugo's. 'I hope you are not suggesting what I think you are, Alastair.'

'I shall allow your conscience to provide the answer to that.'

'My conscience is clear.' *Apart from those kisses.* 'I'm sure I couldn't say why the lady left town. I have not seen her since my return from Rushock.'

Hugo sat back. 'Why not?'

Such a simple question. Almost impossible to answer. The tangled threads of reason barely making sense to him, let alone anyone else.

'I see no reason to justify my actions to you. Or to anyone else,' Matthew growled, glaring at Stephen, who was watching with a faint smirk. 'Lady Ashby leaving town has nothing to do with me.'

'My dear fellow, loath as I am to contradict you, my mother—who is, you will have noticed, exceedingly astute—is convinced your failure to even call upon my cousin is precisely the reason she decided to leave so suddenly.'

Matthew shrugged again. There was a protracted silence during which Hugo contemplated

Matthew, who tamped down his irritation. He would explain himself to Eleanor. No one else.

After several tense minutes, Hugo sighed, leaning back. 'I find myself in agreement with your brother. I believe you are concealing your true feelings...' He paused, his dark eyes calculating. Then, unexpectedly, he smiled.

'I'm goin' to regret this,' he said. 'Ask anyone and they'll tell you the same. Alastair? A bad lot—cares for nothing and nobody but his own pleasures and doesn't worry who gets hurt in the process. I don't permit interference in my life and I make it a rule not to interfere in anyone else's.'

Matthew exchanged a perplexed look with Stephen. What was Alastair talking about?

'It so happens that my cousin Eleanor is an exception to that rule,' Hugo continued, carefully examining his fingernails. 'I *do* care what happens to her. When I'm forced to watch her tryin' to be brave and pretend her heart's not breaking, then I'm persuaded it is time I intervened.'

His mouth quirked into another brief smile. 'Devil take it, there's something about you, Damerel. Trustworthy—that's what I thought when we first met. And you were good for Ellie, too—she was blooming when I first saw her in town and, when I saw you together, I knew why.

'So, what I fail to understand is—why have you let her go?'

There was a lengthy silence. Hugo studied

Matthew and Matthew forced himself to meet that knowing gaze.

'Deny that you love her and I shall leave right now.'

It was like a punch to his gut. It stole his breath. Hiding his feelings was one thing. Baldly denying them…

'I do not deny it. That is…was…precisely the reason why I cannot be part of her life.'

'Is? Was? Pray explain, for I fail to understand.'

'My brother's financial circumstances have vastly improved since yesterday,' Stephen said, 'although, to be blunt, I have always failed to see what difference that should make if you love one another.'

'I had nothing to offer her. She could do much better for herself than an impoverished third son. And I am no fortune hunter.'

Hugo wagged his head at him and Matthew set his teeth.

'Pride?' Hugo said. 'Is that it? You damned fool! You'll allow your pride to ruin both of your lives? No doubt you are congratulating yourself on your honourable behaviour in leaving the way clear for another man, Damerel, but let me tell you something.

'I know Eleanor well enough to know she will only ever marry for love, after the misery of her experience with Aldridge. She will never marry if she doesn't marry you. How can you deny her the chance to have a family?'

Matthew froze as Hugo's words hit him with the force of a lightning strike. Why had he never once considered Eleanor's point of view? Hugo was right. He had made his decision with no reference to her wishes, putting his pride first, denying her any choice over her own future.

'You have left her with no choice and no hope, Damerel.'

Chapter Thirty-Two

Eleanor was roused from her slumber by the liquid, warbling notes of a song thrush, singing its heart out outside her window. She listened, enthralled, caught up in the magic, until cruel reality flooded in, drowning the beauty of the song as the bitter truth of her life surged to the forefront of her mind.

She flung herself over in her bed, dragging the covers over her head as she buried it in the pillow, squeezing her eyes tight shut, in what she knew would be a forlorn attempt to go back to sleep. It was still early and she was in no hurry to face the day, or Aunt Lucy's pitying looks. At least James, who had travelled up to prepare Waycroft Farm for Ruth, was too preoccupied with his own troubles to concern himself with Eleanor's.

Finally, as sleep continued to evade her, she pushed back the covers, eased out of bed and shuffled over to the window to draw back the curtains. The weather was fine, with fluffy white clouds scudding across the cerulean sky, but the weather did nothing to lift her mood. She did not ring for Lizzie, but poured cold water into the basin from the pitcher on her washstand, washed quickly, then pulled on her shift and a lightweight pale-blue sprigged-muslin dress. She dusted a little rouge on her pale cheeks, determined to shield herself from her relatives' critical gazes.

Despite the early hour both Aunt Lucy and James were already at breakfast when Eleanor entered the morning parlour. Two pairs of eyes lifted to view her with concern as she sat at the table. She gritted her teeth. It was James who had suffered the most; why were they worried about her? Thank goodness Aunt Phyllis had declined to return to Ashby Manor until the renovations were complete. At least Eleanor did not have to face her at breakfast.

'Good morning.' She injected a bright note into her voice and plastered a smile on her lips. 'What a beautiful morning.'

'Indeed it is,' Aunt Lucy responded. 'You are up early, my pet. I was sure we would not see you until much later this morning.'

'Why ever not? I am not in the habit of lying abed half the day, as you well know, particularly when there is work to be done.'

'I thought—'

'You had a disturbed night,' James said. 'I heard you.'

Eleanor bit back her sharp retort. Even James had noticed. It seemed, since her return to her beloved Ashby, it had been nigh on impossible to stem the flood of tears she had successfully controlled whilst in London. In London there had still been hope, however slight. Now… Last night, she had cried herself to sleep. Again.

'I am looking forward to consulting with the decorator,' was her only comment as she picked at her breakfast.

By mid-afternoon, Eleanor's temper was teased to breaking point. Aunt Lucy, in her determination to lift Eleanor out of the doldrums, dogged her footsteps with such relentless cheeriness that Eleanor's nerves were in shreds. From viewing the renovations and discussing the decoration of the East Wing to visiting Joker—fully recovered from his fright when Bonny was shot—in the home paddock, Aunt Lucy was by her side.

Eleanor tried to be patient. She knew her aunt had been sad to leave London before the Season was over and also, she suspected, to leave Sir Horace. Aunt Lucy's heart was in the right place but, everywhere Eleanor turned, Aunt Lucy was there—watching her anxiously…taking her arm… patting her hand…attempting to coax a smile— until Eleanor was ready to climb the walls.

Finally, after partaking of tea and cakes in the drawing room, Eleanor headed for the door, announcing that she was going for a walk.

'What a splendid idea,' Aunt Lucy said, struggling to her feet. 'I shall enjoy some more fresh air.'

Eleanor stopped and looked around at her aunt, ready to snap her head off. But she bit her tongue, taking in Aunt Lucy's drawn expression.

'No, you would not,' she said instead. 'Just look at you—you are exhausted.' She took her aunt by the arm and drew her back to the sofa. 'Please, stay here and rest.'

Aunt Lucy sank on to the sofa with a small sigh and Eleanor crouched by her side, taking her hand. 'I know you are worried about me and I appreciate your efforts, but—'

'But you are plagued by the sight of me?' Aunt Lucy's dark eyes twinkled under arched brows.

Eleanor smiled. 'Oh dear; am I that transparent? I do beg your pardon, Aunt, but I truly would enjoy some time on my own. I shall walk around the lake and sit and rest a while in the summerhouse. It is always so peaceful there. I promise I shall be all right on my own. It is perfectly safe, you know, for the lake is in the middle of the estate and quite private.'

The weather was perfect for a walk. Eleanor strolled down the path that led to the lake. She was relieved to be free of the need to constantly school her expression in case anyone suspected she was unhappy. She sighed. Her life stretched before her in a never-ending round of duty and care. Soon, Aunt Phyllis would be home and Aunt Lucy would return to Rothley, and it would be as if the past few months had never happened.

On a whim, she turned and meandered through the woodland that skirted the path. The dappled sunlight filtered through the leaves and she watched, enchanted, as birds darted hither and thither, gathering food in response to the insistent cries of their young, crowded in the nest or, in some cases, perched in rows on branches, beaks gaping, demanding, never satisfied. Her loneliness—her aloneness—intensified.

She even caught sight of a vixen slinking through the undergrowth at the far side of a sunny glade, followed in procession by three cubs. That, too, emphasised her solitude—the whole world was happily playing families, and she was devastated she would never now have that chance. Angrily, she dashed away a lone tear that spilled on to her cheek, chiding herself for her self-pity. She joined another path, rounded a curve, then stopped to admire the stunning vista that lay before her.

It never failed to enchant her. The lake sparkled in the sunlight, gently rippling in the faint breeze. It was studded with water lilies, the bright green pads interspersed with white crown-shaped flowers, with the summerhouse on the far shore, facing south, framed by a wooded backdrop of majestic oaks and beeches, under-planted with silver birches and other smaller trees. Two huge weeping willows grew, one each side of the summerhouse, their dangling fronds sweeping the crystal surface of the water.

She turned on to the path that skirted the lake, passing dense clumps of reed mace—a few early dark brown velvety spikes providing a vivid contrast with the bright yellow of water flag irises in full bloom. She walked slowly, pausing frequently, breathing in deep gulps of fresh air, concentrating on the birdsong and the hum of busy insects, filling her thoughts with her beautiful surroundings, drowning out the painful memories that lay submerged. She watched, smiling, the amusing antics of a family of ducklings, then continued on her way until, eventually, she approached the first of the large willows that stood sentinel over the summerhouse, which it masked from view.

She had one foot on the narrow footbridge that crossed a stream gurgling down into the lake before she saw the figure on the opposite bank.

Matthew.

A torrent of thoughts and emotions cascaded through her mind. Heart and breath alike stalled. Numbly, dumbly, she stood frozen, greedily drinking in the sight. He was as handsome as ever: tall and broad-shouldered, his dark-blond hair reflecting the sun's rays. A muscle bunched in his jaw as he held her gaze. She couldn't read his expression. He was tense, but she could see neither pleasure nor apology in his look. Why was he here? Her stomach churned as she attempted to decipher his mood.

Then fury overwhelmed her. How dare he? How dare he stand there and make her feel all these swirling emotions, and not even try to ease the tension? Abruptly, she turned on her heel and strode back the way she had come. She heard running footsteps behind her and a hand grasped her shoulder, pulling her round to face him.

She wriggled out of his grip. 'Leave me alone!' She turned again, striding away as fast as she could.

He overtook her, stood square in her path.

'Eleanor. Please, wait. Let me explain.'

'There is nothing to explain. My understanding is quite adequate to the task of recognising a lost cause.'

'It was for your own good—you must see that. What can I offer you?'

'Nothing, clearly. And in that case, please let me pass.'

'No. Wait.' He raked one hand through his hair in the dear, familiar gesture that wrenched at her heartstrings. 'This has come out all wrong. Please, give me a minute. Let me tell you why I am here.'

'I *do not care* why you are here. You are nothing to me, apart from the fact you are ruining a perfectly pleasant walk.'

She could hear the tremble in her voice. She was desperate to get away before her emotions overwhelmed her. She *would not* let him see her cry. She clenched her teeth and crossed her arms, pinching the inside of one arm as hard as she could in an attempt to keep the tears at bay.

'Eleanor! Ellie, my dear, my love—do not, I beg of you. I have been such a fool! I have hurt you, I know. I had no intention—'

At those words Eleanor's temper reignited. 'Don't you dare to use those words to me again. Don't you *dare*. I know you had no intention. You told me so—no intention of kissing me, no intention of raising false expectations, no intention of making me fall in love with you, no intention of humiliating me. But you *did*. I thought you c-cared,' she ended, with a sob.

She lifted her fists to pound at his chest.

He caught her hands, gripping tightly so that no matter how she struggled she could not break free.

'I do! Oh, Ellie, I do care for you, more than you know. I *love* you, so very, very much. And I was wrong, when I said I have nothing to offer you. I allowed my pride to overcome my good sense. You were right. I do have something to offer—something that is more important than all the wealth and all the titles in the world. I have my heart to offer.

'My heart is what I offer you now, my darling Eleanor. My heart and, for what it is worth, every other poor, humble thing that goes with it—my body, my self, my soul.

'All that I am—it is yours, if you will have me.'

Eleanor stilled on hearing his words and her gaze lifted to fuse with his.

'This is not how I envisaged this meeting,' he said, with a tentative, rueful smile. 'I will explain myself properly, I promise, but I need to do this now.' He dropped to one knee, still clasping her hands in his.

Her heart lurched, then accelerated, pounding in her chest until she felt as though it would burst through her ribs.

'Eleanor, would you do me the greatest honour in the world? Will you marry me and make me the happiest man alive?'

He looked up at her steadily, but she could feel the tremor in his hands as he spoke the words and she knew that he spoke from the heart.

'Yes,' she whispered. 'Oh, yes.'

He surged to his feet and caught her into his embrace, lifting her as his mouth claimed hers. She melted against him, rejoicing in his safe, solid strength. She clung closer, winding her arms around his neck, responding to the urgency in his lips. Without breaking the kiss, he swung her into his arms and strode back to the bridge, crossing it to the summerhouse, where he sat on the day-bed, settling Eleanor on his lap. His arms wound around her waist, locking tight.

'I am not,' he announced, 'taking the risk of you running off again.'

She tilted her head back to look at him. 'How did you know where I was?' She peppered the words with light kisses feathered along his jaw.

He held her tighter. 'Your aunt told me where to find you.'

'I'm surprised she did not insist on sending someone to chaperon us.'

Matthew nuzzled her neck. 'She was delighted to see me, scolded me for taking so long to come to the point. Besides, she had other things on her mind. Sir Horace travelled up with me.'

'Sir *Horace*? Truly?'

'Truly. We met by chance as we were both hiring a chaise-and-four. He *said* he was coming north to visit relations and suggested we share the cost of posting up here. Your aunt was *exceedingly* happy to see him. She told me you were heading for this summerhouse and how to find it. I arrived here and I waited.'

Eleanor felt his chest vibrate as he laughed.

'I thought it the perfect setting for a proposal to the lady I love more than anything in the whole world.

'I thought it romantic.

'I *thought* to meet you at the doorway, where I would make my apologies and then propose properly. With decorum.'

He looked at her, his blue eyes glinting. 'I might have known you would set your own agenda. I thought I had missed you, you were such a long time. I was on my way to find you when I saw you at the bridge.'

'I was in no hurry. I needed to be on my own.' She paused. There was so much she didn't understand. 'You didn't call on me when you returned to town. I saw you. At Vauxhall. With Arabella Tame.' Try as she might, she could not disguise her hurt.

'It was Stephen's birthday. There was a group of us there, celebrating. I was not just with Lady Tame.'

He stroked her cheek, kissed her neck, ran the tip of his tongue around her ear. She shivered with desire.

'The Arabellas of this world mean nothing to me,' he murmured. 'Why would I want a self-centred creature like her when I could have my beautiful, intelligent baroness?'

Eleanor tilted her head, sought his lips. Several satisfying minutes later, Matthew said, 'I returned from Rushock a wiser man. When I saw my mother…the truth hit me. I could have been reconciled with my family when I first returned to England. Instead, I allowed my pride to stop me from contacting any of them. I let my pride win and my resentment sour me.

'I realised then that I was also in danger of allowing my pride to ruin any chance of happiness with you. I was in love with you, but baulked at the idea of being dependent upon my wife. Also—although I did not realise it at first—I was letting my concern about what others would think to dictate my actions. I had lived with the taint of "cheat" for a long time and I hated the thought of being labelled a fortune hunter.

'I returned to London with the intention of laying my heart at your feet. But...'

Eleanor stroked his cheek, his bristles rough under her fingertips. 'But...?'

Matthew huffed a self-deprecating laugh. 'I thought I was doing the right thing in not visiting you. You seemed to be happy. You had achieved your ambition of being accepted for Almack's. I thought...I wondered if your feelings for me had changed. I vowed to give you more time to know your heart and I tried to get on with my own life.

'The truth is...my courage failed me. I was afraid to find out that your love for me was mere infatuation.'

Eleanor straightened, eyes flashing indignantly. 'Infatuation? How could you think that, when I all but begged you—?'

'I know! I know...I was a fool. In my own defence, I was on the verge of throwing myself on your mercy the day after you saw me at Vauxhall. Then I received…the letter.'

The suppressed excitement in his voice was contagious. 'Letter? From whom? What did it say?'

'It was from Benedict. My partner.'

'*Benedict?* But he—'

'He is not dead, Ellie. The *Laura May* was damaged in that storm, but they made it into port, in Lagos. Oh, I can't describe my joy on reading his news.'

'That is wonderful indeed. I am so pleased… but…does that mean you have only proposed because you can now match my fortune?'

Matthew threw back his head and laughed. 'Match your fortune? I shall never do that, sweetheart. The profit I will make on that cargo will be a mere pittance next to your wealth, but I *will* have enough to continue in business with Benedict.' He bent a serious look on her. 'You do understand that I must continue my business interests?'

'Of course I understand.'

'And, in the interest of honesty, I should confess I was also on the receiving end of some blunt talk from your cousin Hugo.'

'Hugo? What has Hugo to do with us?'

'He talked some common sense into me.'

'*Hugo* did? Well, I'm sure it must have been for the first time in his life. '

He laughed, then sobered again. 'You do mean it, Eleanor? You will marry me?'

'Of course I will. I want nothing more in the world than to be your wife. But…are *you* certain?'

'More certain than anything…'

'You will not resent me in the future? You promise you won't allow your pride to come between us? '

'I could never resent you, my love. And, yes, I promise. I was a fool. A stubborn fool. Nothing is more important than loving you—and being loved by you. I am a very…lucky…man.' He interspersed his words with kisses. 'And now, my wife-to-be…'

Eleanor, her eyes riveted on his, saw them darken as he spoke, desire swirling in the blue depths. Her core tightened, a delicious longing awakening deep inside.

'…come here.' His finger slid beneath her chin and nudged it higher. He captured her mouth. Eleanor wrapped her arms around his neck as his lips demanded and she gave, moulding herself to him. He eased her back against the sumptuous cushions, his lips never ceasing their hungry demand.

Eleanor revelled in the weight of his body covering hers as his hand cupped her breast, his touch fiery through the fabric of her dress. Two fingers slipped inside her neckline and found her nipple, teasing the swollen bud until she could scarcely breathe.

She clutched fiercely, her fingers tangling in

his hair as he traced kisses down her neck to the upper swell of her breasts. She shivered with need, shifting restlessly beneath him...yearning...wanting...*needing*.

He raised his head and looked deep into her eyes.

'I want more,' she whispered. 'I want everything—all of you.'

He brushed her hair from her face, then placed his lips on hers in a long, soothing kiss as he moved aside and settled Eleanor beside him, cradled in his arms.

'Not yet, my sweet.'

The bitter memory of rejection rose from the depths of her past to pierce Eleanor's new-found contentment. She shifted to stare into his face. A frown creased his brows as his eyes searched hers.

'What?' he said. 'Why do you suddenly look uncertain? You surely cannot doubt my love for you?' He kissed her, long and hard and deep. 'I want you so much it hurts and it takes every ounce of my resolve to say we must wait until we are wed.'

'Then why *must* we wait?'

A smile hovered as he shook his head. 'You are as impetuous and as impatient as ever.' He dropped a kiss on her nose. 'Since we met, I have not always behaved as a gentleman should. As you said yourself, I thought nothing of stealing kisses from a maiden I thought I could never wed. It is important to me now to do the right thing.

'Allow me to be the gentleman now, Eleanor. I would have you walk down the aisle an innocent on our wedding day. You are worth waiting for, my sweetest desire.'

His sincerity shone through every word.

'Then let us wed quickly,' Eleanor said, leaning into him to capture his sensual mouth in a smouldering kiss.

'Never again,' he groaned, as he tore his lips from hers some time later, 'never again will I allow you to leave without a word. I know…' he placed his finger against her lips, which parted as she began to protest '…yes, I know very well it was my stupidity that made you leave. I know it, but it doesn't make it any easier to bear. I allowed my pride to become more important than our love.

'Never again.'

He lowered his head, caressing her lips with a tenderness that filled Eleanor with joy and wonder. She kissed him in return, and all the passion and the love she had hidden inside for so long poured out as she surrendered her heart.

* * * * *

1015_MB515

0915_ST19

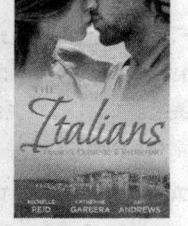

MILLS & BOON®

Why shop at millsandboon.co.uk?

Each year, thousands of romance readers find their perfect read at millsandboon.co.uk. That's because we're passionate about bringing you the very best romantic fiction. Here are some of the advantages of shopping at www.millsandboon.co.uk:

* **Get new books first**—you'll be able to buy your favourite books one month before they hit the shops

* **Get exclusive discounts**—you'll also be able to buy our specially created monthly collections, with up to 50% off the RRP

* **Find your favourite authors**—latest news, interviews and new releases for all your favourite authors and series on our website, plus ideas for what to try next

* **Join in**—once you've bought your favourite books, don't forget to register with us to rate, review and join in the discussions

Visit **www.millsandboon.co.uk**
for all this and more today!